Praise for *Corrupted Tides*

"Campbell's world building is positively exquisite. The world he creates is intricate and unlike anything I've read before. 'Corrupted Tides' will make you laugh, may make you tear up a bit, and will definitely have you yearning for more by the time you finish."
Alexus Mayo - ARC Reader @amayo.author on TikTok

I never felt like I was sitting in a scene too long, with one character or another. The world building and descriptions of the people made the world feel real.
Thomas Eads - ARC Reader @teadsreads on TikTok

"With unique and robust characters, high stakes adventures, and an impeccably detailed world and magic system, 'Corrupted Tides' leaves you wanting nothing more than to have the next book in your hands to continue the story."
Lindsey Harvey - ARC Reader @_the_endless_tbr_
on Instagram

"From page 1, 'Corrupted Tides' is an exciting adventure you will want to sink your teeth into. The crafted world and characters are as artfully ingenious as the kelp wine."
R. Lynn Hanks - ARC reader @r.lynn.hanks on TikTok

Also by S.M. Campbell

Eldritch Depths

Forthcoming
Tainted Seas

CORRUPTED TIDES

Eldritch Depths
Book 1 of 7

S.M. CAMPBELL

To my beautiful, wonderful wife. Thank you for pushing me back into writing, and I'm sorry I've been up so late working on this.
To my kids. This is going to be awkward if you ever read these books.
To my ARC readers. Thank you for your dedication and interest in my world. Let's hope this works.

CONTENT WARNING

This book contains content that is not suitable for younger audiences and may be considered triggering to some individuals.

- *Numerous and graphic violent acts*

- *Explicit, consensual sexual acts*

- *Harsh/crude and graphic language/insults*

- *Implied acts of prostitution*

- *Heavy drinking and substance abuse*

- *Religious deconstruction*

AUTHOR'S NOTE

Hello reader. What you are about to witness is the final stage of evolution in a crazy idea I had. While becoming deeply immersed in the video game *Bloodborne*, I was inspired by some fan art that depicted a fictitious sequel set on the high seas. I thought I could take it further (as I'm wont to do) and started writing down crazy ideas like: what if someone had a hammer made from an anchor and battled massive sea monsters called Deep Ones down in the depths?

That idea took hold in my brain with an all consuming grasp (I believe we call that an obsession), and I started drawing out what these heroic individuals would look like. I penned them *Deep Wardens*, and had every intention of turning these wild, ocean dwelling, sea monster slaying individuals into a cosplay. I drew up more weapons and started developing a logical reasoning behind every decision, which led to me deciding that a board game would be much more practical for this weird world that had been born.

It wasn't.

After two drafts of the game, a pile of cardstock pieces, and a notebook full of world-building, I realized that what I had created was much larger than a game or costume could handle. It needed to be a book. It needed to be a lot of books. Thus, *Corrupted Tides* and the world of *Eldritch Depths* was truly born into the monstrosity that you now hold in your hands.

I hope you get sucked into this insane story as much as I have. Grab your kelp wine, hold onto your sea glass, and I'll see you on the other side.

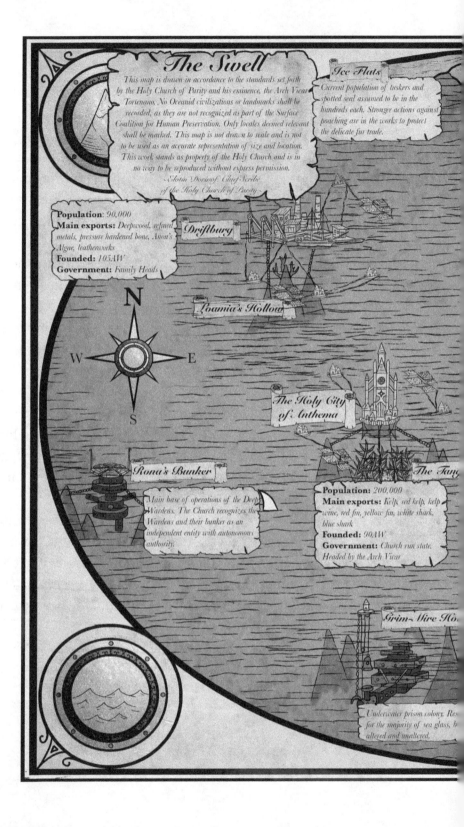

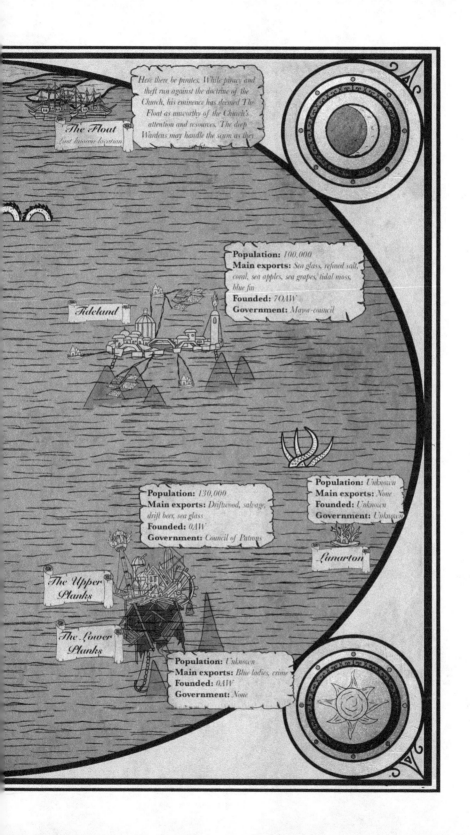

The Float
Last known location

Here there be pirates. While piracy and theft run against the doctrine of the Church, his eminence has deemed The Float as unworthy of the Church's attention and resources. The deep Wardens may handle the scum as they

Tideland

Population: *100,000*
Main exports: *Sea glass, refined salt, coral, sea apples, sea grapes, tidal moss, blue fin*
Founded: *70AW*
Government: *Mayor-council*

Population: *130,000*
Main exports: *Driftwood, salvage, drift beer, sea glass*
Founded: *0AW*
Government: *Council of Patrons*

Population: *Unknown*
Main exports: *None*
Founded: *Unknown*
Government: *Unknown*

Lanarton

The Upper Planks

The Lower Planks

Population: *Unknown*
Main exports: *Blue ladies, crime*
Founded: *0AW*
Government: *None*

CORRUPTED TIDES

S.M. CAMPBELL

PROLOGUE

The woman screams.

Water.

Lovers lost.

Anguish and betrayal.

Waters rise.

The woman screams.

A cut and fusion.

Sight beyond.

Madness, mayhem.

The waters rise.

Corruption.

It happens; it happens again.

It is here, it is then.

It is all at once.

The woman screams.

The waters have risen.

Ü lhülté spreads himself out, the immense wings of hardened flesh and protruding bone causing great surges in the deep waters around him. His mind is screaming with a thousand images and voices; but that always was and always will be. He places a large hand, mottled green and scaled against his skull, the millennia of throbbing pain taking its toll. He is tired, but he stands steadfast, the tendrils from his chin grown long with time.

This is not his world but is his now. Has been, will be. And the threat that has been coming is here. It pains him, for he knows why it happens. He knows what must be done.

Somewhere, down here in the dark waters is a woman. He knows her, but he cannot help her. It is not his job to help her. Time has caught up, the circles are complete, but he pushes his mind further and sees what he must do. His task will come but is not yet here. He is the 'Visitor', a guardian from another world. He bears his burden on shoulders the size of mountains, but it is still a heavy burden.

He sees himself stepping up to the task, his great sword spanning the lengths of cities as he approaches. Burning eyes stinging with sadness at what must be done. He raises the sword, but his sight ends. He can push no further, can see no further.

The outcome is unknown, but the path there is certain. He will wait as he has waited all this time. When the time comes, he will be ready.

He is a Deep One. He is not born of this world, but it is his now. He must protect it; he must kill for it. He must be willing to forfeit anything for it. A burden his fellows do not know. This is their world, but they do not know what comes.

He bears the heavy burden alone as he always has.

Only one knows, one beside him. His friend, his confidant. He reaches out to speak with his friend.

Architol, my silent friend. You have felt what I have felt.

I have.

Then you know what is coming.

I do.

I do not want to do this. I do not want this burden.

None do, but we are Deep Ones. We are ancients. We must persevere where others cannot.

Will I have the strength when the time comes?

I cannot say. But the time will come.

What can be done? Is everything written? Is all the way it will be?

Not all. There are paths, but we cannot make them. We can only be there when the streams of time align.

Can I not act now? Prevent this all?

Do you see yourself now?

No, I see myself then.

Then you cannot.

Do you see more? Your sight is not as mine, not shackled.

I do.

What do you see?

I see much death and pain. I see a hero born of time. I see two reunited and balance restored. I see the earth destroyed and the earth made whole. I see sins paid for and sins committed.

You see all this clearly?

I see the ideas that are these things.

You see the end?

I do.

And you shall not tell me?

It will be told in time. I must rest now.

Goodbye, my friend.

The Deep One waits, his wings folded in around his curled-up frame. He waits as he has waited, wishing he didn't have to—wishing he was not alone. Architol, Donto, The Sisters: all his fellows of the deep do not share his burden—but neither do they share his lineage. He is a Deep One in name, but not in blood and so this task must be his.

His blade is sharpened and ready. He waits for the end.

I

"The reasons for Loamia's madness remain a mystery to all who study such things. Once a great goddess of all green land and earthen fertility, she now is as broken and shattered as her mountains that lay scattered under the oceans. We may never know what drove her mad or why her ire was directed at our great Lord Fathus, but we give him thanks and praise for his intervention and for this new world that he gave us. May he always watch over us and may the Swell forever share its bounties with the lost children of the land."
~Excerpt from Arch Titritus' "Musings and Contemplations of the Four and their Divine Realms"~

"**I** can't pull you up fast enough if anything were to happen, Mistress. It ain't safe!" Rance said to the woman in front of him as she tied the kelp fiber rope about her waist and prepared to dive into the deep waters below her. The aging fisherman at the stern of the small coracle hated giving her as much rope as she always requested. His protests were the same every time, and every time she would smile, tell him she could take care of herself—and to stop calling her Mistress.

"I've been helping you get your fish traps up the better part of a year Rance. And you're ages older than me. When are you going to start acting like we're friends and use my name?"

"Sorry Miss Vila. It's just, you know, I'm just tryin to be respectful is all. With you being a lady of status and all."

"You're sweet, Rance. You also know that you would never be able to pull me up. That's why I get your traps for you. Now hang on to that rope just in case and I'll be back in a bit."

She patted his knee and dove headfirst into the deep, relishing the sting of the water as it hit her skin. Vila found his respect amusing and charming. Only in the floating city of the Planks could one be praised for being a prostitute, even by poor or respectable folk; people who either couldn't afford a Blue Lady or would never seek out her services for moral reasons. Rance was both poor and had no need of her services; just a good-natured old man who shared some fish with her when she would help bring his traps up.

She could never get the same respect in any of the other floating cities. There was no prostitutes guild to elevate her kind to status in cities like Driftburg or Tideland. And in Anthema, the church city, it was illegal, immoral, and punishable by death. Blue Ladies only existed in the Planks, respected and holding protected positions in the Upper Planks. The Lower Planks were a different story, but even in that crime ridden underworld, she didn't worry too much. Enough people had seen her fight and Madame Molena was very protective of her girls.

Blue Ladies were just another thing that made her city unique, and everyone was happy with that. The Planks prided itself on being one of a kind. It was the only city to pull anchor and let the currents take it where they would. Every other known floating civilization of mankind was permanently chained down and tethered.

The water was a frigid bath of murk and darkness, the gloominess swallowing up all light and warmth. The only illumination came from the faint glow of the sight stones tied around Vila's wrists and waist as she plunged deeper into the abyss. The vermillion light from the sea glass sight stones danced about her bare skin yet lacked the warmth of the sun's rays. Above her, the silhouette of the little coracle became smaller and smaller until it too was devoured by the near impenetrable darkness of the Swell. She wore nothing but her kelp wraps around her athletic form, preferring speed and flexibility over warmth and comfort.

Breathing deep through the blue air stone imbedded in her diving shell mask, Vila could feel the divinely and chemically enhanced stones work their magic and give her body the ability to thrive down here, if only for a while. The glowing stones in her mask also helped her survive the other elements of the deep like the cold and pressures, each one of the four having a different purpose. All shell diving masks came equipped with the same four types of enhanced sea glass stones: pressure, air, brine, and sight.

Vila enjoyed the sensation of plunging into the icy depths and feeling the freezing water push against her skin as the brine stone worked against the chill. It made her feel as alive as fighting in the pits did and just as dangerous. Neither arena was entered unless you had absolute certainty that you would come out alive, which she always did. Of course, that wasn't the case for everyone.

She floated for a while, staring into the darkness around and below her. A school of whitefin brushed past, looking for a meal around the once healthy ecosystem that surrounded the giant wooden structure behind her. The thin kelp fiber rope tied around her waist was run long, the slack giving her plenty of room to dive deep and explore, if not much help in case of trouble.

Below her, she could make out the faint outline of the chains that held the city in place. It had been a few months now since the anchors had been dropped and the city stopped floating wherever the currents decided. An underwater mountain range had been found, peppered with the ruins of structures from the Dry Age, marking a good stop for salvage and fishing. It would have been an actual mountain range, before the Swell rose and devoured the world. It probably even had a name once, a grand sight hosting magnificent cities of trade and prosperity. Now it was another set of nameless rocks full of soaked timbers, treasures, and sea life. Whatever name or culture it had was washed away when the waters rose, taking most of mankind with it and forcing the rest to adapt.

Vila turned herself downwards and pushed herself as deep as she could go, feeling the rope finally reach its end. She longed to go further down, to see what else the seas had to offer, but Rance would never hear of going down without a rope. He was a 'floater' through and through.

She felt the rope tug two times, Rance's signal asking if she was okay. She tugged back two times answering in the affirmative and looked around. She was below the bottom of the city now, its vast shape a dark mass silhouetted in the dancing sunlight.

The sight stone in her mask allowed one eye to see a little further in the dark than the other. Peering through the stone that covered her left eye, she could make out the underside of the city filtered in red from the stone's vermillion hue.

It looked just as ramshackle and treacherous on the outside as it did from within, but it held all the same. Broken hulls, whole sides of buildings; all pieced together in a giant mess of wood and fused tight with pitch; a rickety wonder of the world.

The Planks was the first floating city ever made, cobbled together even as the waters were in their first infant rise. Over the years, the city grew upwards, adding more wreckage and newer construction of coralcrete and imported deepwood. The original city structure became known as the Lower Planks and now was its own thriving environment of poverty, crime, and free will that existed underneath the very feet of the Upper Planks and its more relatively well-off citizens.

She felt the rope tug three times in quick succession, warning her of something. Vila looked around then looked up, sensing movement, and caught sight of a dark shape descending quickly. Through the red glow of her sight stone, she could make out one of the city's many giant diving bells barreling down towards her.

She kicked quickly to the side as the large structure of wood and rusted metal sank past, the pressure stones in its side keeping the whole unit from being crushed inward and snuffing out the salvage workers and miners who sat inside.

There would be several of them in there, heading down to the underwater mountain top to mine what they could from the ruins of the city below. Stone, wood, gold, bones; anything they could get their hands on and fit inside the bell or strap to the outside. Larger bells could fit whole portions of shipwrecks in them while bells from smaller operations could only afford to send a few workers in a small bell to carry back whatever they could fit. This was one of the larger ones that was probably looking for wood materials, sail cloth, and other objects to be recycled into new infrastructure for the Planks. It was a treacherous job with the innate dangers of the water itself being only one factor. Where there were fish, there were bound to be predators. Vila had seen some gruesome deaths in the fighting pits, but some of the mangled corpses that had come back up from the salvage yards made even her stomach curl.

She gave the bell a wave as it went past even though there were no windows for them to see a lone woman floating in the dark. Salvage was one of the main industries of the Planks, as the whole city could traverse the open ocean and find new salvage yards. And a whole floating city of industry meant more salvaging power than a simple reclamation ship could handle. She didn't envy the job, but she envied the depths they were able to explore.

Large cranes loomed out over the water all over the dock edges of the city, holding diving bells of various sizes that would be used to drop workers to the bottom. There were even a few illegal operations out of the Lower Planks that sent single person bells down, though the government was constantly working to shut those down. An uncontrolled breach in the Lower Planks could mean a death sentence to everyone, at least to the unwashed masses of the underworld. The Upper Planks would live on, patch some holes, and keep drifting across the seas as it always did.

She felt the rope tug twice then twice again in rapid succession, telling her it was time to return to the surface. It was probably a storm rolling in and Rance was getting nervous. Vila gave what could equate to a sigh through her air stone and spared one last look down at the disappearing purple glow from the stones on the bell as it sank out of her sight. It terrified her and excited her at the same time to think about delving into the deepest parts of the Swell. To explore the Tangle or visit the Oceanid city of Lensia; or even see a Deep One.

She had given up on those dreams, her life tethered to the Planks. Her mask wouldn't allow her to go down that far either. The further down you went, the less effective the stones in the masks were. Time limits became shorter unless you could afford larger glass and it still didn't stop all negative side effects on the body. Only the Deep Wardens, with their blessed glass infusions could thrive in the underwater world without fear of death by the elements. Vila had no interest in giving her life to the way of the Warden, even with the deep yearning to know what lay below. As much as she hated certain aspects of her life, giving up what control she had to be a servant of the ocean god didn't sound much better. She was as free as she could hope to be and fought hard to keep that little bit of control.

She gave a few hard kicks of her flippers and swam back up to the side of the city where Rance's cages floated in the drift, leaving the emptiness of the deep below her. She kept her body turned outward as she worked, constantly watching for predators that could swoop in from anywhere. Her fishing lance lay strapped against her back, ready at a moment's notice.

The cages were not as full as they were the last time she came down. Or the time before that. Vila hated that she had to go back up to the old man with less and less each time. She didn't know why that was, but it was happening to all the fishing operations in the city. She could even see it as she floated in the water. There were fewer schools of fish in the water around her and the amount of sea life that inhabited the sides of the city was dwindling.

No one knew why, at least no one that she talked to. Maybe someone up in a seat of real power had some answers to the recent drop in wildlife and food supply, but they weren't talking—not that anyone expected them to. The elected seats of the patrons existed only to line the pockets of the merchant lords with sea glass coin. They couldn't give a fuck about the rest of the inhabitants until there weren't any left to vote for them.

Sadly, she swept the meager catches into a single cage, strapped it to her back and began the swim back to the ocean surface and the sunny skies above.

"It's not your fault, Mistress Vila," Rance was saying as he eyed the small pile of fish at the bottom of his boat. She could hear the disappointment in his voice even as he tried to console her, and it broke her heart. She gazed out over the waters; her thoughts were distant as he counted his catch. There was a storm coming in fast on the horizon and they would need to dock soon before the waves kicked up.

"It doesn't really matter. It's not enough," she said.

"Eh, I'll be alright. I've had lean times before. 'Sides, this old body could afford to go without a couple ah meals." He accentuated his point by slapping his side, hands smacking against his gaunt ribs with a hollow crack.

"You know what I'm going to say."

"I do and I won't hear of it. I ain't takin your money. You work too hard for it."

She winced a bit at that. She did work hard in the pits. She fought her ass off not just for the money, but because she liked it. She liked the violent thrill every time she took down another egotistical asshole who thought he could shove her around because of her size and sex. She liked the small sense of control it seemed to give her in life.

But Rance was talking about her other work, the one that everyone really knew her for and the one she absolutely hated. Most people might respect the Blue Ladies (at least in public conversation), but for Vila it was a reminder that she was not truly free. Some chains ran too deep to break.

She gave him a sad smile and laid her hand on his. She couldn't remember exactly how she started helping the old fisherman, but he was one of the kindest souls she had met in an otherwise harsh environment. His pride be damned, she wasn't going to let him starve.

"Take the money, Rance," she said a little more forcefully than she meant to as she handed him a bag of sea glass coin. It wasn't much, enough for a few meals and some bait for his traps, but not enough for him to lose all his pride over. He let her place the bag in his hand, tears starting to sheen over his aging eyes.

"You're too kind, Mistress. I can't ever repay you."

"You never have to, and don't you ever fucking try," she said with a harsh smile. "We'll keep going. The ocean is abundant, this won't last."

"Aye," he said wearily. He wiped his eyes with wrinkled fingers and started rowing back towards the docks as a light mist began, harbingering the coming storm. "Are you fighting tonight?"

Vila tugged her kelp fiber cloak tighter over her shoulders and took a sip from the hot urchin tea he had brought. As much as she liked being down in the depths, the chill was unbearable once she was out of the water.

"Yes, there's a three-bracket match tonight. Some big names, and even bigger bets. Lots of rich lords looking to line their pockets."

"You be careful down there. You don't need me tellin you how to live your life, but just know I'm rootin for you. I hate seein yer scars and that pretty face gettin all beat up, but I know ya love it."

"Thanks, Rance."

They rode the rest of the way in silence.

2

*"You don't want that life, boy. Ain't no one with a right mind
ever choose to be a deep warden because they wanted to. You
do it cause ya had to. Worshippin the sea god is one thing:
servin him down in the depths? There's much better ways to
live yer life, I reckon."*

~A father to his son~

The little coracle bounced its way into one of the inset harbors
that bordered the city, rocking along until Vila snagged a
pier with the rope and pulled them safely to port. She opted to
take on the work herself and never tried waving down any help.
No one cared about the old man, but seeing if they could get
something free from a Blue Lady? Vila had been approached by
more dirty, disgusting men than she could count, and she didn't
want to advertise her station. She kept her blue pearl ringlet out of
sight whenever she could, tucked up under the leather bracer she
always kept on her arm.

As one of the elite members of the prostitute's guild, no one
could harm her without severe punishment in the upper city, but
they could hassle her to no end. In the Lower Planks, everyone
knew her as killer, but she kept the ringlet tucked away when

she could get away with it. Removing the bracelet that signified her status was a felony, which always seemed ridiculous to her. She supposed the law was put in place so that a bunch of rich men could easily identify a potential sexual encounter, but there was nothing in the laws about keeping it out of sight when able. Madame Molena would never approve, but she never approved of anything Vila did.

Placing her cloak over Rance's shoulders, Vila tossed the basket of fish up onto the dock and deftly hopped out of the small boat. Rance wasn't nearly as nimble and let her take his hand to pull him out. His hands were as boney as the rest of his body, and she felt another pang of guilt at the meager catch of the day. He deserved a better life, but so did most of the poor folk of the Planks, both Uppers and Lowers. She couldn't say the same about herself, though there were often times she dreamed about it.

Rance stretched his legs and leaned his head back, letting the now building rain pepper his wrinkled face and wash down his scraggly beard. Salt and grime drizzled onto the deck as the rains performed their work. Vila joined her friend in his basking, enjoying the sensation of the droplets as they stung her shoulders. The pendant of Parity around her neck glistened as drops of water ran down the patinated metal and translucent stones of sea and moon.

She garnered a few leering looks from the workers, scantily clad as she was in the meager kelp wraps. She had a full figure that the wrappings did little to contain, and she was fully aware of it. They could look, but there was nothing they could do about it, and she didn't much care. The scars that lined her body told of someone who wasn't to be touched without recourse.

"Let me walk you home," she said to the old fisherman, slinging the basket over her shoulder. He didn't protest and slipped his arm through hers for support as they started up the rain slicked dock.

"Let me make you dinner," the fisherman said, clutching her arm tight as they made their way down the slippery boards. "It's the least I can do."

"I'm not taking your food, Rance."

"Please! I don't get to cook for anyone no more, not since Hay-men passed. And you need to eat. You're too thin."

She stifled a laugh at the compliment but couldn't deny how good a hot meal sounded after the dive.

"Fish cakes and your famous urchin sauce?"

He smiled wide. "And a healthy mug of kelp wine. Got a bottle left, and I can't finish it on my own."

She gave his arm a squeeze, leaning her head against his shoulder. "Okay, you win."

There was a sudden yell behind them from one of the dock hands alerting the other workers to an incoming ship. Vila felt the wood beneath her bob as the waves rose and fell, signaling the vessel's entrance. If the waves were any indication the ship was big, the dark shadow that engulfed them confirmed it. Vila couldn't help a curious glance behind her to see the incoming boat. She expected to see a merchant vessel in for trade or a prison transport taking unlucky souls to Grim-Mire Hold. The large frigate that made its way slowly between the docks was neither, and it made Vila's arm hair stand on end.

The massive, black warship was an ugly mess of battle scars and dotted with more sea glass stones than Vila had ever seen in one place. Its double bows were lined with thick iron braces and painted with faded red markings that swirled around the pitch black deepwood structure. The figurehead was made entirely of sea glass and took the shape of a large, bearded man holding a scepter made of bone. Vila had never seen the sea god Fathus, but his likeness could be found all over St. Trillian's Chapel and in every home as a mantlepiece. Only three ships on the water boasted the likeness on their prow, however, and this was one of those legendary vessels. Everyone who knew anything knew of this ship and the crew that ran it. Vila wondered what the hell it was doing here.

"Shit!" Rance exclaimed to her left. "That's the *Hardor's Gaze!*" If the terrifying shape and the looming figurehead hadn't given it away, the large letters painted on the side in a deep red varnish confirmed the old man's observation.

Hardor's fucking Gaze. One of three vessels commanded by the Deep Wardens, dominating the high seas, and bringing swift justice down on anyone or anything that was deemed a threat to life in the Swell. Fathus' protectors and lackeys were the only humans that were blessed with the ability to thrive in the swell, putting them just below the Oceanids on the hierarchy of import to the ocean god. Vila always thought they sounded like a bunch of assholes, but she did envy the freedom they held. Near complete autonomy of will, unrivaled strength and stamina, and life on the open ocean—if one didn't mind the servitude to a divine entity who was known to swallow up the world with water.

"What are they doing here?" Rance asked, his voice cracking with awe and a little bit of fear. He kept saying what was in Vila's head and they were all valid points. The Wardens roamed the open seas killing poachers, pirates, and wayward sea beasts. If they were here on the Planks, then something wasn't right.

The looming vessel slowed to a stop as a crew of dock workers scurried about, tossing ropes back and forth in a desperate attempt to corral the black beast before it careened into the flimsy structures of the city docks. There was no sign of life aboard and Vila watched as the ship seemed to take on a life of its own. Sails furled up and masts folded down in an automatic fashion, sending shivers down Vila's spine. Enhanced sea glass could do many amazing things, but the sheer total and number of different types of glass that were at work made her tremble. She could only imagine what the inner mechanics looked like as the power from the glass pulsed through tubes and powered gears deep inside the bowels.

She and Rance watched in amazement as the ship seemed to transform in front of them. The rigging slowly retracted along the deck like the tendrils of some tentacled sea horror until they disappeared inside the vessel. The masts continued to fold down until they too sank into the ship. The final gaudy reveal came when the two bows split further apart and a large set of stairs as black as the ship's exterior unfolded from within the inky depths of the brig and landed with a heavy thud on the shuddering planks of the dock.

If Vila didn't know any better, she would have said that the storm had heralded the ship's coming—or the *Gaze* had brought the now raging weather with it. Either way, the giant vessel was made all the more ominous by the scattered lightning that silhouetted it against the darkening skies. As daunting as the ship was, the four Wardens who now trod slowly down the heavy wooden steps were equally as chilling. Barnacles battled for space on heavy iron boots, indicating a significant amount of time on the ocean floor. Thick armor and gruesome weapons adorned them, and heavy cloaks made from the skins of various ocean predators fluttered in the gusting winds. The looming black ship behind them (coupled with the clap of thunder and raging sea) made the four striking figures all the more ominous.

Each one was intimidating in their own right, adorned with their own unique outfit and weapons. Vila could name each of the Wardens by sight and she knew she wasn't the only one. There were currently twelve wardens in the service of Fathus and everyone who wasn't an idiot knew them by name. They were deeply revered by most, excluding Vila, and even worshipped to some extent. Three ships carrying the protectors of the deep roamed the waters, four Wardens per ship.

At the head of the group strode Agustan Tempé, captain of the *Gaze* and one half of the Tempé twins. He waltzed with a confidence that Vila found extremely annoying, his pressure-hardened bone saber casually flapping at his side underneath the heavy white-shark cloak that hung tightly to his imposingly tall frame. The stark ivory garment gave birth to the nickname 'White Warden', and he seemed to wear the moniker proudly, regardless of how gaudy he looked. A permanent sneer was plastered on his hawkish face, his imposing features standing out even under the crisp hood that covered his blonde locks. Vila hated him immediately.

Taking the steps behind him was Shaila O'Caan, who had doubled her legendary status when she slayed the wayward Beast of Northrock—with her bare hands if legends were to be believed. The giant horn, though many naturalists speculated it was actually a tooth, was crafted into an imposing lance that now lay strapped to her back. She looked extremely grim, her small eyes darting back and forth about the dock as if searching for hidden dangers around every corner. Though not a terribly large person, her oversized turtle armor gave her a berth that dared onlookers to try their hand at their own peril.

The third Warden looked entirely too happy to be with the grim group, dancing down the steps in his ridiculous looking armor of spider crab shell plates. Quinlan Lan stretched his arms as if he had just woken up from a restful slumber and stuck his tongue out, catching raindrops as they fell and lapping them up greedily. Vila knew he was more dangerous than he looked. His aim with the harpoon launcher that hung at his waist was the stuff of verified myths. Once Quinlan Lan had you in his sights, there was no escape.

It was the fourth Warden trailing behind the group that caught Vila's eye, or rather she caught his. Older than the rest by at least twenty years, Taragin Echilar stood at the top of the steps. His hammer-shark bracer was strapped tightly to his left arm while the right clenched a small handle made of bone decorated in unaltered glass. The chain attached to the handle was comprised of a spinal column strung together with metal links and sea glass rivulets. The bone chain disappeared up underneath his flowing cloak made from the flayed skin of the same spotted black-shark whose spine the aging warden clutched in his hand. Vila knew that underneath that cloak, somewhere, lay the skull of the same beast that gave up its life to make that cloak and now acted as the gruesome head of Taragin's deadly flail.

What she didn't know was why he was staring at her with such intensity.

His dark eyes bore into hers, and she felt the sudden desire to wrap her cloak around herself and disappear. She'd been leered at most of her life, weathering ogling looks and disgusting comments anywhere she went. There was no salacious intent behind the stare that he gave her though, and it chilled Vila more than the pouring rain that continued to fall. She wanted to dive back into the water and escape from that dark stare and sink to the inky depths.

"Vila?" The voice from her side snapped her back into herself. Rance was tugging on her arm, and she realized she'd been clenching her fists. Opening her hands, she saw tiny gouges in her palm from her nails. She barely felt it and watched the blood trickle away as the rain spattered her open palm.

"Thought I lost you there for a moment."

"I'm fine," she replied, though she certainly didn't feel it. Wardens stalking the city was a bad enough omen—a Warden with a strange fixation on her from the first moment he set foot on the docks? She shuddered, trying to break the feeling of dread that continued to wash over her. When she looked back up, the Warden had moved on, his back turned to her as he strode down the steps with heavy footfalls.

Augustan Tempé was talking with the dock master whose arms were flailing wildly. She couldn't hear what they were saying, but the man seemed to be unhappy with how much space the Wardens' vessel was taking up in his harbor. The captain of the *Gaze* laughed heartily and shoved the smaller man out of his way. His three compatriots closed up behind him, and Quinlan tossed a heavy bag of sea glass coin at the bewildered and frustrated man's feet. With a clap of thunder, the four protectors disappeared into the rain and the dark shadows of the city.

"What do you think they are here for?" Rance's quivering voice asked again. He seemed as shaken as Vila felt.

"I don't know," she replied, trying to quell the ominous feeling that was growing in her gut.

"Could it be about the fish?"

Vila would never insult her older friend but had to fight hard to suppress an eye roll.

"No, Rance, I don't think it's about the fish."

"Then what?"

Vila started walking again, ready to get away from the consuming shadow of the black vessel behind her. Rance was still gawking at the ship as she pulled him along the planks of the dock.

"I don't know, Rance," she said a little more harshly than she intended. She wasn't sure why their arrival had shaken her so much. The unsolicited stare from Taragin didn't help, but there was something deeper going on. If they were sent by Fathus on some mission, then it meant that something rotten was happening in the Planks and Vila wanted to stay the hell away from it.

"Best not worry about things we can't do anything about," she finally said.

"Aye, well I'm all for them protecting the waters and what not, but it gives me the willies seein 'em strut about. Maybe we'll find out eventually."

Vila hoped that wasn't true.

3

"Take your planks and your rotted boards,

Give me coral and shell and gold.

Your city may have whores and Blue Ladies,

But in mine I can die fat, happy, and old."
~A popular drinking song in Anthema~

Arch Vicar Tortenano gazed out the artistic glass window on the sprawling city below, trying not to focus on the comically enlarged breasts of Loamia distorted by the glass he was looking through. The representation of the long-gone earth goddess giving the world sustenance through her oversized tits was unseemly, but not uncommon in the artwork that could be found around the Grand Cathedral of St. Milios.

The church city of Anthema was spread out beneath the towering cathedral in a maze of gleaming coral rooftops and polished deepstone walkways. The spiraling structure of the cathedral was made with the sole purpose of being visible from every inch of the city. No matter where one went in the floating paradise, the twisting towers of coralcrete and shell were always in sight, reaching as high into the heavens as human ingenuity could allow.

The arch vicar gave a deep sigh and took another swig of sea grape wine from the shimmering gold and sea glass goblet clutched in his hands.

"Something wrong, your eminence?" The wiry acolyte at his side shuffled forward as the arch vicar placed the glass on the gilded tray beside him.

"I'm out of wine, for one," he said with a huff.

"Of course, your grace. I took the liberty of having another prepared for you."

The acolyte brought forth another glass and placed it in Tortenano's still outstretched hand with a gleaming smile. The arch vicar's face remained placid as he took the proffered glass and drained the contents.

"The skies disturb me," the older man said, a distant tone to his voice.

"How so, Lord?"

"Did you not see the great object that lit the night sky, not a week hence? Nor the ones that followed?"

"Can't say I did my Lord."

"You young never pay attention. The skies have not descended since the Great War. It can be nothing other than an omen. I feel a heavy burden as I seek to lead the flock."

"There is none more capable, your eminence."

"Humph." He held out his glass to the acolyte. "Another...what was your name again?"

The acolyte shifted nervously, watching the arch vicar's every movement. "Seeya, your grace."

"Strange name."

"I always thought so too, but my father was always quite unique. Never liked to follow the traditional paths."

"Was he of *the* Path?"

"Goodness no! A real heathen that one. I, however, learned the true value of the Church early on. It has brought me nothing but joy and prosperity."

"Prosperity is not why we are here, my son." The arch vicar drained his third glass and beckoned for another glass of wine with his hand, giving a large yawn as he did so. The sun was disappearing over the horizon of endless ocean and its last rays bounced lazily off the rooftops of the city far below. Blue, green, and purple light from the artistic glass danced across the old man's face as he closed his eyes. He yawned again, the rigors of work and drink taking their toll.

"I beg to differ, your holiness," the younger man continued to ramble. "Take yourself, for instance. Beautiful robes, glass chalices, a comfy gilded bed. It's quite nice up here."

The arch vicar turned away from the window, his face reddening.

"My boy...if that is...what you think...holiness is all-all-all..." His eyes widened as his words caught in a jumbled mouth and the aging priest stumbled into the arms of Seeya. The head of the Church of Parity let himself be set down into the plush chair by the windowsill, his eyes rolling backwards.

"Lord! Don't strain yourself. You've had a lot to drink."

"Not...that-that...what...is..."

The acolyte took the man's hands and folded them up neatly in the arch vicar's lap. The priest tried to sit up but found his head lolling back against the soft cushions as the younger man's smile turned to a mischievous grin.

"Like I said, your *holiness*. You've had *a lot* to drink. You don't know how hard it was to get all that coralweed juice into your wine and still have it taste halfway decent."

The old man's mouth moved as unintelligible sounds gurgled out from between his lips.

"Hush now, you'll be fine. Just a big headache and a few riches lighter when you wake up."

The young man discarded the stifling robes of his disguise and scurried about the room, packing as many valuables as he could into the hidden satchel strapped to his back. Goblets, coins, and more than a few busty statues of historical figures made of sea glass and coral. He took his time running his finger over the exaggerated features before he turned towards the real prize.

"Like I said, the church has brought me nothing but joy and prosperity. And continues to do so! Look at all this! All you fat fishes up here, wiping your ass with gold and glass. I'd be envious, but honestly? It's been quite uninteresting since I've been here. And those robes are itchy."

The arch vicar was completely asleep at this point, unaware of the ramblings from the thief that was now slipping the Grand Pendant of Parity off his plump neck. The gaudy pendant was as large as the thief's balled fist and adorned with all the symbols of the Four. The acolyte imposter gazed into the sea glass charms and moon rock rivulets, losing himself for a moment. It was no wonder he was hired to steal this particular piece. He placed the necklace into a separate pouch, tied it up and gave a sigh, no longer having a captive audience for his banter.

"You didn't even make it to my punchline. I was going to say my full name was Seeya. Seeya A—"

The joke was cut short as the doors to the arch vicar's chambers burst open and several heavily armed provosts crashed into the room, followed by a very angry and very naked actual acolyte.

"That's the man!" he screamed, pointing a finger at the thief while trying desperately to cover his manhood with the other hand.

A few thoughts crossed the thief's mind in the brief few seconds he had before the guards charged; the first was that the coralweed in the acolyte's drink must not have been as strong as he thought. The second was that he was now going to have to improvise, which he fortunately was quite good at. The third was why in the hell the man hadn't grabbed something else to wear before bursting in here.

All those thoughts quickly vanished as the provosts brandished their lances and ran towards the thief, yelling about virtue or some other such nonsense. The thief who called himself Seeya gave a wild hoot, his instincts kicking in. He ran towards the rushing guards, sliding under a pair of open legs and hopping deftly to his feet. Coral mail clattered as the guards reeled around, trying to lay hands on the manic thief. Seeya continued his wild yell as he leapt up onto the deepwood table in the center of the room and caught the arms of the chandelier that hung in the center.

The bewildered guards cursed and stumbled as the flailing legs of the spinning thief knocked aside shell helms and bone lances in a chaotic onslaught of luck and stupidity.

On the third spin, the thief released his grip and flew ungracefully onto the arch vicar's four poster bed, bouncing twice before flopping to the ground in a pile of sea silk sheets. He popped up, grasping the corners of the fabric in his hands, stretching it out behind him in dramatic fashion.

"Name yourself!" one of the guards shouted angrily, pulling a wicked looking dagger from his belt.

Finally. The thief grinned widely as he said "My name is Seeya. Seeya Aroun!"

There were no laughs, but Narrio Olitarth didn't expect any. He was amused enough for all of them. He kicked the legs out from under one of the guards who stood there with a dumbfounded look on his face and dashed towards the window. Clutching the silken sheet corners tight, he closed his eyes and dove headfirst through Loamia's beautiful, bouncing tits and soared through the air a thousand feet above the rooftops basking in the dusky glow of the setting sun.

For a brief shining moment, the theft artist formerly known as Seeya floated gracefully above the sweeping vista of the church city, his improvised parachute billowing and bustling in the wind above him. It was a beautiful evening he noticed as he took in deep breaths of the salty air and basked in the final moments of warmth before the sun went down. Until an arrow whizzed past his ear.

He didn't need to look up to know that he no longer had a functioning sail as the ground below him was now getting closer at an alarming rate. His panicked shriek bounced off the walls of the cathedral and disappeared into the gusting winds.

There was a shredding sound and Narrio stopped falling, his screams continuing as his brain caught up to the fact that he was no longer plummeting to his death. Hanging by the coattails of his shark leather cloak, he slowly turned around to see the stern face of Fathus looking down on him. The fabric had caught on the sea god's outstretched hand and Narrio wondered briefly if he *should* become religious.

The thought passed just as quickly as more arrows clinked off the hammered bronze statue, sending sparks flying. *Time to go* he thought, deftly pulling out his gaff blade and sawing through the thick leather as quickly as he could. He shrieked again as an arrow slammed into his shoulder, nearly causing him to lose his grip on the blade.

Now he was starting to panic as shouts could be heard from the windows below him and more shafts flew past from above. With one final slice, the leather came apart and he dropped again, realizing he forgot to look and see where he was falling to.

The answer came in the form of a crash and a feeling of immense pain through his legs and back as he collided with the sloped roof below. Clutching his gaff tightly so as not to stab himself, he tumbled and rolled down the roof top, taking up a healthy number of coral shingles as he went. He eventually reached the edge of the roof and felt himself drop yet again. His eyes bounced against the back of his skull as he crashed unceremoniously onto a flat roof.

Battered and not nearly as jovial as before, he stood up gingerly and looked over the edge, the sight lightening his mood. He was nearly down now! Just one more rooftop to go. He kissed the lucky ring on his finger and took a moment to examine the arrow wound in his shoulder. Most of the shaft was broken now, leaving just a small stick and the steel tip imbedded in his flesh. It didn't hurt as much as he thought it should, but his bloodstream was also flooded with adrenaline and some excellent, non-dosed wine. Safety first, then a bandage, hot meal, and another stiff drink. Not necessarily in that order.

He was aware of a number of scrapes and cuts all over his body and there was a sheen of blood coating his hands. Wiping them across his trousers, he holstered his knife and looked for a way down. The final gable roof below him was another thirty lengths down and his bruised form couldn't take another hard fall.

The sound of scuffling could be heard above him as more provosts joined the hunt and scrambled up onto the roof. Shouts were coming from all corners of the Grand Cathedral, and he knew they would get to him soon. He didn't like his prospects of survival at this point, seeing as the Church was not as forgiving as the religion they preached.

Down the deepstone street, quietly sitting in an alley was a rickshaw with a very bored looking young man in a dusty tunic. Narrio smiled. *Ah, Porto. Right where I left you.* At least some things could be counted on, and it seemed as if the young wanna-be thief that was hired to accompany him was one of those. Narrio thought he might have some work for the boy in the future, but now it was time to improvise again. He did a quick analysis of the surroundings: skylight, street, chum cart, alley, freedom.

Just as the first guard clambered up the side of his current roof top, Narrio gave one more wild yell and leapt through the skylight. Or he would have if the glass had broken. Instead it sent him bouncing backwards onto his ass with a jarring jolt through his legs.

Dazed, but not done, he leapt at the pane of glass again and began bashing it as hard as he could with the handle of his gaff. Small cracks began to appear, but not fast enough and he heard a yell behind him as the guard pointed his shaft launcher at the thief.

"You're dead, dog!" the man exclaimed as he fired off his shot. Narrio slid to his right as the arrow whizzed by and put the final necessary crack in the skylight pane.

"One of these days, yes," he said with a smile and dove backwards into the pane for one more try. This time, the glass gave, and he plunged down into the large room below him, hoping he had guessed the room's purpose correctly. He landed with a splash and sank to the bottom of the pool before pushing up hard to the surface. The waters of the bathhouse were warm and inviting and full of naked women; a delightful place if he wasn't desperately running for his life.

The female acolytes screamed at the bleeding man who was now splashing about in their pool. It was in this moment that Narrio remembered he hated water and started to panic as he thrashed his way to the edge, the pack on his back weighing him down. Arrows and heights he could do, but drowning? The thought lit a fire in his belly, and he desperately pulled at the water until he felt his fingertips touch the cool, coralcrete edges of the poolside.

Almost there.

Weighing much more than he had a few minutes ago, Narrio pulled himself up the edges of the wall of the bath house, using any crack and ornament he could find for purchase. His destination was a small, thief-sized transom twenty lengths up. The bath house now echoed with the shouts of guards as the lovely ladies covered themselves and ran from the room.

With no time to look, he hammered at the glass until it shattered and pulled himself through the opening. He was falling again and braced himself to land in the cart of bloody chum that lay below. The smacking sound of his impact was sickening, and the smell nearly made him vomit. The merchant who owned the cart screamed at the blood and gore covered man who emerged from the vile pile and ran off to call the authorities.

Narrio stood straight up and retched on the paving stones. Pulling himself together, he made one last mad dash down the street, around the corner, and threw himself into the rickshaw. Porto, to his credit, didn't look nearly as startled by the sight of the dripping thief that slammed into the seat of his vehicle as Narrio would have—nearly.

"Mister Olitarth!! You made it!"

"Fucking run!" the thief responded, throwing a blanket over his form, and trying not to vomit again. The boy did as he was told, and they set off down the road until the cart disappeared into the crowds of the market square.

Narrio gave a deep sigh of relief and vomited on the floor of the rickshaw.

The cart finally came to a stop and Narrio lifted the blanket off his head, taking in the sight. They were at the docks, there were no guards around, and the smell of the sea air was a welcome relief to the stifling stench inside his hovel. Porto wiped a towel across his brow, breathing deeply from the run and the adrenaline.

"I'll be honest, Mister Olitarth, I didn't think you could do it. Did you get...the thing?"

Narrio gave a sly smile and opened the small sack so the boy could see the gleaming necklace inside.

"The church always provides, my young friend."

Porto giggled as Narrio snapped the pouch closed.

"You didn't strut out the front door like you said you would," the boy commented.

"It was much grander though, wasn't it?"

"And gross."

"That's heists, my young compatriot. Always moving and flowing like the currents of the Swell. You can plan and prepare all you like, but sometimes you just have to jump into the flow and hope to the gods you end up in the right place."

The boy smiled back at him and Narrio finally allowed himself to relax as he sat against the cart. His body was racked with pain now, and he was sure that all the gore he had jumped into was not good for his open wounds. But the peacefulness of the evening took all that away for a few moments. Porto handed him some red kelp poultices as he pulled the arrow tip out with a wince. He applied the healing weed to his wounds, laying his head back against the rickshaw in exhaustion.

The sun had fully descended beyond the horizon and the stars were out in full force. The moon would be full in a few nights and was reflecting brightly on the gentle waters. He even saw a comet fly by, leaving a shimmering trail of green in its wake. He thought about what the arch vicar had been droning on about and realized he didn't care. He thought it looked pretty. Narrio closed his eyes, thinking about what a beautiful night this had turned out to be.

Until he heard the cracking sound of wood against his head and blackness closed in. His last thought before he fell into unconsciousness was that maybe he needed to work out some kinks in his process.

4

"Fourmonth, the Third Day, twentieth hour: Celestial object sighted in the night skies. Never before have we seen the sky or its lords give up their bounties, not since the dry age. One must ponder the meaning of it and if there shall be more. I estimate a great search to begin, a hunt for knowledge or power. For myself, it is knowledge. I deign to understand the deep mysteries of the skies and to what end they come to the seas."

~The personal record keeping of Malania Tortosfin, Head of the Astronomical Society for Celestial Learning and Comprehension~

Another comet flew overhead as Narrio blinked awake. His head felt like shit and his hand came away with clumps of bloody goo when he touched the spot where the hit had landed. He hoped more of it was from the chum cart he had leapt into than his head. He was going to kill that boy.

No, that wasn't quite right. He'd never killed anyone, that he knew of. But he was definitely going to give him a stern talking to.

His head still foggy, he tried to sit up and decided it wasn't time yet. Everything hurt and it felt better to just lay there and mope. He was quite sure that he had been robbed. It was the only thing that made sense—why else would the boy clobber him like that?

Gingerly, he lifted his head to look for the pack of valuables and was disturbed by what he saw—the sides of a boat, open sky above him with no sign of twinkling oil lantern lights or sight stones. With extreme reservation he sat up slowly and peered over the edge, his eyes greeted by an endless view of dark ocean below him and beyond. Panicking, he looked to his left and saw more of the same. The moon was looming large over the dark waters, casting its eerie blue-white glow across the gentle waves that lapped against the side of his vessel, knocking against the boards as if to get in.

He was in the middle of the fucking Swell. On a dinky little dinghy.

Narrio didn't like the water, although he was hesitant admitting being afraid of it. But a fear, or even an extreme dislike of it was an unfortunate thing, considering the entire world was covered in it. Apart from the floating cities and townships of humankind, there was no dry land anymore and hadn't been for centuries. Narrio always thanked whatever god might be listening that he wasn't born an Oceanid, the denizens of the deep world and children of Fathus.

Tonight was a night where he would have admitted the deep distain as fear, finding himself alone and sitting in an unknown craft in the middle of the ocean. He tried to tear his eyes away from the water but found himself staring deep into the inky blackness despite his inner voice telling him to get the hell back. Narrio had never been below the surface, but he had heard the deep world of the Swell was a terrifying and beautiful place of monsters and riches. Riches he liked, monsters he could deal with, it was the dark openness that sent his blood running cold.

Narrio Olitarth, master thief, knocked out by a child and left to drown in the black waters. He supposed it was a fitting end to his life's story, but he wished it didn't have to be. There were so many people left to rob, and he really, really, hated the thought of drowning.

Rolling back over, Narrio felt his gaff underneath his hip and felt elated that he hadn't been completely robbed. Looking at his feet, he saw the sack of treasures he'd taken from the chapel and his heart jumped a bit. Greedily, he tore open the sack and rummaged through the broken statues and other valuables.

The pendant was gone, the sole purpose of his venture into the church capitol. He'd been paid a lot of money up front to get the damned thing and was promised more upon safe delivery. The client had been very clear that the only thing they were interested in was that necklace and it seemed that was the only thing that Porto wanted too. If the sea didn't swallow him up, he knew he was going to be hunted down and given a gruesome death for deserting a job and running off with unearned money. Why the hell was he on this boat if the necklace was the only thing Porto was after?

A light rain started to fall as he contemplated his situation, giving him chills and plastering his raven hair to his face. Just when he was wondering if things could get worse, he realized he was not alone.

"Hello Narrio."

Narrio released the lever on his telescopic gaff, extending it to its full six lengths and spun around towards the voice. Sitting at the stern was a cloaked figure, their legs calmly crossed as they sipped something steaming from an antique pewter cup. A shining silver ring in the shape of plant life adorned their index finger. Covering the upper portion of the intruder's face was a silver mask molded into the shape of some extinct land predator; the glimmering fangs hung over their cheeks, capturing the figure's mouth in a gruesome smile.

What really set his spine tingling was the massive black ship that loomed over his rear port side. Narrio stared up at the menacing hull towering above him, uncomfortable with the fact that it and the person aboard seemed to have been here the whole time, watching him. All along the main deck of the looming vessel stood silent figures, garbed in black and wearing more silver masks in the shapes of creatures he didn't recognize. Narrio remained rooted to the spot as he held his gaff out, hoping he looked more threatening than he felt. Neither the still figure in his boat nor the people aboard the larger vessel moved, despite the drawn weapon.

"Hello..." he said cautiously, keeping the weapon pointed at the tea sipper.

The figure gestured to their left, indicating that Narrio should have a seat near them. Reluctantly, he did as requested, seating himself on a pile of rope with his back to the mysterious vessel. Narrio was bad at a lot of things, but he had developed a knack for knowing when to recognize danger and do as one was told. He could feel the watching eyes of the masked figures on him as he retracted his weapon to its shorter, yet still deadly form.

"Narrio Olitarth," the figure in front of him said after a long silence. "We were quite impressed with your escapade at the cathedral. A little sloppy at times but successful, and very little evidence left behind. No easy feat, snatching the Grand Pendant of Parity from the neck of the arch vicar himself."

Narrio swallowed deeply, hoping he was giving off a bravado that he did not feel. "I hate to disappoint you, but I seem to have lost track of it."

The figure gave a menacing smile as they brought the cup to their lips again. "Of course you have. The object has been returned and the buyer is no longer in the business of purchasing and selling religious items."

Narrio glanced about nervously, feeling a figurative noose tightening around his neck.

"That's...interesting?"

"Not very. We hired the man who hired you."

Narrio nearly pissed himself.

"Consider the stealing of the pendant your entry examination, though I know you never went to school a day in your life. Upon completion of the mission, you have now officially entered into a contract with us. Congratulations."

"Thank you..."

"You've had an interesting life. A street urchin in the slums of Driftburg with no known relatives. Forced to fight and scrape a living on the streets. You worked your way into the Bloody Streams, moving up through the ranks of the criminal underworld as their master pick purse until branching out on your own. Since then, you have made quite the name for yourself by never getting caught; thieving from the most highly guarded and protected establishments with a one hundred percent success rate."

Narrio smiled nervously. "A few missed details, but a more or less accurate retelling of my life's story."

The mystery person raised the glass one last time between the silver lips of their grotesque mask and placed the beverage down before leaning closer to the pick purse. "I say all this to outline two things: One, we know all about you and your dealings. We know that you are one of the best at what you do. Call it charm, wit, or blind luck, you've managed to complete some impossible heists. Two, we also know you owe thirty thousand to Chiafa Nolistrad, and she was very much waiting for your payment. We have bought your debt and will consider it paid once you complete your task. On top of another hundred thousand glass coin."

"That's kind of you." Narrio hadn't left on good terms with Chiafa, but he shuddered to think what kind of payment she had received in exchange for the debt.

"She was most appreciative."

"It's nice of you to offer another job, but I'm not really—"

"You don't have a choice," the figure snarled through the grinning teeth, causing Narrio to clutch his gaff a little tighter. "I'll make myself clearer. We have another job for you to do, and you are going to do it. That's all there really is to the matter. The point in giving you your life's story, Narrio, is to remind you how expendable you really are; even your own parents recognized that it seems. Refusal is not an option. You are a loose thread that can easily be snipped. No one will miss you; no one will care when we kill you. Which will happen if needed."

The figure tossed a bag of coin to Narrio, who didn't dare open the satchel. "But even loose threads still get paid. Fifty thousand now and another fifty upon completion."

Narrio shifted. "And if I fail?"

The thief could almost hear the glee in the voice behind the mask as they answered. "A very unpleasant situation would befall you."

This was not going well, thought Narrio. Dark cults were a little beyond his pay grade.

"What is the job?" he asked, his voice catching in his throat.

"Are you familiar with the goddess Loamia?"

"Not intimately, no," Narrio replied, preparing himself for a history lesson.

"When the great war began between earth and sea, Loamia, great goddess of the earth, crafted a weapon of mighty power to aid her in her battle against Fathus; the Terra Axe. With it, she could harness the power of earth and stone and rain terrible destruction upon the forces of the sea god. The war was great and terrible and the outcome of that battle you can see around you. Loamia lost and the earth was swallowed up by water in retribution for her betrayal and her attempt at taking Fathus' kingdom from him. The goddess was utterly destroyed by the sea god and her body cast down to the depths. The Terra Axe was shattered into thousands of pieces and lost forever."

"That's too bad."

"Despite your triteness, it is a shame. However, one piece remains. A single piece of stone unremarkable to any except those who are deeply familiar with the lore. This fragment rests in St. Trillian's Chapel in the Upper Planks, the birthplace of the Church of Parity and the Faith of the Four. You are to retrieve this artifact and bring it to our contact on the Planks. Further direction will be given for delivery to us."

Narrio reached out to pick up the cup from its resting place and took a sniff. He didn't recognize any of the smells and nonchalantly placed the cup back down. "Sounds simple enough. Why don't you do it? You've got the resources, clearly."

The figure cocked their head at him, answering slowly. "We cannot make our presence known at this point in time. There are others in our organization who do not approve of our...ideologies. I would think a man of your discretion would understand that. And as I said before, you are a loose end that would be easy to tie up should the need arise."

Narrio gave a small nod, gulping down the terror that was rising in him. Criminal underworlds and high-stake heists were his forte. Cults and secret organizations? He'd tried pretty hard to steer clear of those in his life. The gravity of the situation was setting in and he knew that success would be paramount. A little niggling at the back of his mind told him that even success might not deliver the promise of safety, and he had better have some contingencies in place.

"You want this kept secret. How do I know you won't kill me once I bring you what you want?"

"You are astute. We could and we may. But if you provide what we ask, we could have need of your services again. There are things under way that will shape the future as we know it, and faithful servants have their uses. Great rewards await those who are useful to our cause."

It was about as good of an answer as he was going to get. "Sounds like we have a deal then. I bring you your rock, you pay up, and I'll never say a word."

"Good."

"I'll need another ten thousand."

The cloaked figure sat back, the shadowed eyes of the animal mask staring into Narrio's. "For what?"

"Operating expenses," he replied. "I've never been to the Planks. I don't know the layout or the people. I'll need funds to make connections, grease some palms. Not to mention any necessary supplies."

"You have it there," they said, indicating the unopened bag of glass.

Narrio pocketed the heavy leather pouch and slouched back in a relaxed stance. Negotiating was all about confidence, even in the face of sheer terror. "That's my fun money. I have a promise of death on my head if I don't do this, so you need to pay the bills. My second fifty thousand on completion, ten thousand right now to actually help get the job done. Or you can kill me now."

The figure was silent for a moment, then looked upward to the black vessel and nodded their head. A moment later, another small bag landed in the boat with a heavy thud at Narrio's feet. He nearly jumped, struggling to maintain the cool calm that got him through most of his escapades. These people were certainly dramatic.

The cloaked one rose as a rope ladder was lowered down to the tiny boat. "Don't make me regret my decision. I can find others."

Narrio flashed his winning smile, wiping a strand of dripping hair from his face. "Not as good as me. You said it yourself. I'll get your stone."

Without a word, the mysterious patron ascended the ladder as the great ship unfurled its sails and pulled away, leaving the sailboat rocking in its wake and Narrio shaking in his boots.

"Damn," he said to no one. He realized that he had absolutely no idea where to find the Planks, or even where he currently was. The Planks were almost always in motion, and he couldn't spare the time to return to the Burg and use his sources to find the city. Narrio let out another curse, berating himself for his stupidity. There had to be some navigation charts or something useful in the boat.

He opened the the first bag and counted the coins, satisfied at the amount. In the last bag, on top of ten thousand in glass coin, was a star map and a rolled-up note made of dried kelp. Inside the note were coordinates and a detailed drawing of a rock with strange, swirled patterns. He assumed the coordinates were the current position of the Planks and the drawing was his quarry. Below the coordinates was a simple missive:

"Our contact will meet you at the Planks. Wear this so they recognize you. Best of luck. Snip, snip."

At the bottom of the bag, Narrio found a signet ring like the one on the finger of his patron. The organic shapes and patterns were dizzying and intricate, and the ring felt heavy in his hand. Slipping it on his middle finger, he stared at the ornate circlet in comparison to the green, sea glass ring on his index finger. He stroked the simple shape of his lucky ring as he closed the bag and stared out at the water. This was not how he saw his day going when he woke up this morning.

5

"There has always been a Del'Sor in the Planks for as long as the city has existed. Founded by Trillian Del'Sor and protected by his descendants, it was long believed that as long as one from that great line walked the streets of our great city, then the Planks would never succumb to the Swell and its dangers."
~From Yania Torino's "The Planks: A History"~

Vila struggled to keep her eyes open. She blamed many things; a full belly of wine and fish cakes or maybe the lack of sleep, but she couldn't blame a lack of charisma on the part of the priest who was leading the evening holy service.

He spoke with passion, she could give him that, she just wasn't interested in the subject matter. She wore the pendant of the faith because it was expected, not because of some gods who didn't seem to care much for mortal affairs. Fathus had never poked his head out of the water during her lifetime to shower the poor folk of the Planks with his blessings. Celenia and Lunas were too busy making the moon go round and round to give a damn about humans. Unless Solan was the literal sun, she had never seen any reason to believe he existed and Loamia was long dead if the texts were to be believed. If she hadn't counted wrong, that made five gods, not four. Religion was strange.

At any rate, Vila yawned her way through another evening service at St. Trillian's Chapel because, like it or not, she had feelings for the sweaty, red-cheeked cleric who so passionately believed in gods that she did not. He would be furiously frustrated if he saw her creeping in the back aisle, but she found him cuter when there was color in his cheeks; and she needed to use Hinaldo's door.

Hinaldo Del'Sor was the black stain that ruined the great legacy that built the Planks. Trillian Del'Sor, Hinaldo's great-great-great-grandfather, was a hero during the War of Earth and Sea, defending his small town and the local chapel from earth golems as the waters rose. Legends said he ultimately took down Loamia herself with the blessing of Fathus and rebuilt the small chapel stone by stone on the small floating structure that would become the Upper Planks. That chapel would become known as St. Trillian's Chapel, the birthplace of the Church of Parity.

The Del'Sors were an honored family in the early days of the city when the new life of landless living was at its most treacherous and delicate. Trillian and his descendants became the guardians of the chapel and defenders of the city, protecting the sacred relics within the church and providing support to the clerics who resided within the now towering structure. Even when Anthema was deemed the new center of the religious order, it was Marken Del'Sor, Trillian's only grandchild who fought hard battles in the council chambers to keep the building from being uprooted and the relics in their original home. He won, mostly, with a handful of artifacts being allowed to stay while the rest were shipped off to their new home in the massive cathedral in Anthema.

It was Marken's grandson, Hinaldo, who started the decline of the family name. He was known as a drunk who preferred fucking the clergy rather than kneeling at the altar. Vila thought she would have liked him, but naturally the stuffies in the Grand Cathedral didn't. If stories were to be believed, he had pleasured the current priestess on each of the four altars of the gods and had been found using several of the holy relics in rather crude ways on both her and himself. The thought made Vila snort out loud, earning her some disgruntled looks from those around her. She stifled the noise and slunk further into the shadows.

Evening services were usually filled with a hundred people in the relatively small chapel from all classes of the Upper Planks. Vila was very aware of the effect that living on a floating pile of rotten wood could have on one's mental state and didn't blame the people for seeking out some solace to the bleak reality they found themselves in. No one alive had any memories of the old times when dry land still existed and all the elements lived in harmony. Seeking out some peace and stability in the Church was common in all the floating cites. After all, Anthema was a state built entirely around the Church. The home of the Church of Parity wasn't on the top of Vila's places to visit should she ever decide to get on a boat and leave her home.

"Balance," Tem was saying, snapping Vila back to the present moment. "Balance is what we must strive for. It is what keeps us floating, keeps us alive. Just as this whole structure of timber and human ingenuity that we live on is built on the balance of beams and boards and the wreckage of ages past...so must we find balance in our lives. Harmony. Equilibrium. A perfect intertwining of all things both physical and intangible. Loamia could not find that, and she paid the ultimate price. But through her memory and lesson, we can do better. To be human is to learn...to assess...to balance."

He didn't know she was watching, but she sometimes felt like she provided a lot of inspiration for his weekly teachings. Balance this, purity that, reverence such and so. Why she put up with him and his self-righteous pondering was a mystery.

Is it though? she thought. Besides the fact that he was an extremely attractive male specimen with sharp features, muscular frame, and pull-able auburn hair, he was also the only person (male or female) that didn't ask anything from her, besides Rance. A life as a prostitute, even the highest order of Blue Lady, meant just about every encounter was a potential transaction. She could give Tem sex because he didn't ask for it. Sometimes, after a night of passion, they would share dreams of leaving the Planks together, even though they both knew it would never happen. She was a Blue Lady and the Planks were her home. He was chained to the Church through law and his own sense of devotion. It was part of what she admired most about him; his dedication and commitment to both the church and her, despite his disapproval of her activities.

Vila pulled herself from her reverie as the final prayers ended and the congregation began to file out of the church. Some wiped tears from their eyes, others kept their heads bowed in a penitence that would last a few hours before reverting back to whatever vices and shame led them there in the first place. Vila allowed herself an inner eye roll, but kept her head bowed and her blue pearl ringlet tucked beneath her bracer. She recognized a few faces from her profession whether personally or through other Blue Ladies, or even from the Green Girls below.

Part of being a Blue Lady was using the utmost discretion and protecting the identity of all clients, both hers and others. And considering the rates, most clients who hired a Blue Lady were very high profile or had a lot more to lose if they were found in a compromising situation. Any recognition on the part of either party would be ignored completely as it usually ended worse for the client than it did for the women.

Vila slowly made her way to the transept as the rest of the congregation shuffled out, keeping herself out of sight until the last patron had exited. No one noticed as she skirted the shadows and corners of the aisle, using the lack of window light to hide her amongst the tall columns of stone. Temson pulled on the chain that closed the massive stone doors, the only official entrance into the church, slowly dimming the sounds of the rain outside. Vila watched him take in the last bit of light as the creaking doors clicked into place, sealing off the sanctuary within. Candlelight from the altars provided the only source of light now. After Hinaldo's debauchery a hundred years ago, the elders decided it was best to enclose the church more fully, filling in all windows and leaving only the one door. Even the artistic glass on the outside was only decorative now.

She felt a little pity for Tem, knowing that by taking his oath he had condemned himself to a life in this holy prison. Food and provisions were delivered via a small slat in the wall by the provosts outside and he spent most of his time poring over scrolls in the sanctum. Clerics were not allowed outside the chapel walls except to visit prisoners and minister in the Lower Planks—and always under guard. No one was allowed in the inner sanctum either, and of course, no sexual relations. Two of those rules were broken on multiple occasions, but to the best of her knowledge Temson had never crossed the threshold to the outside world except on rare missions of ministry. The provosts always posted outside the door helped enforce the first rule, but she knew Temson would never break it. As to the second, Vila usually used the trapdoor into the sanctum, Hinaldo's special door that somehow got overlooked in the boarding up. The third rule was broken almost nightly.

Temson finally turned around and nearly dropped the censor of incense he was holding when he saw her leaning against one of the stone columns, a sly smile creeping across her full lips.

"Vila!" he exclaimed in what he probably meant to be more of a whisper than what came out. He rushed towards her, grabbed her arm, and started towards the sanctum door. "Do I even need to tell you how dangerous this is?" His question was punctuated by multiple glances back towards the main entrance as if anyone could enter at any moment.

"You know me well enough by now to know that danger doesn't scare me."

The flush faced priest fumbled with the set of keys manacled to his wrist, clumsily unlocking each of the five iron locks on the door.

"I wish I knew what did. You must use the other way, you MUST! What if the provosts saw you stay or counted heads?"

Vila strode into the hall to the sanctum and shut the door behind Tem, the locks clicking back into place simultaneously. Sight stones lit the small stone passage in a soft red light that complimented his skin color. She could see his muscular frame through the tight robes and wished she could stay longer.

"If only they could count," she chuckled. "You would think with all the Church's resources, they would hire smarter people. Present company excluded of course." She decided not to mention that Genario, one of the provosts, was a frequent visitor of Madame Molena's. She knew he had a fiancé and there was an unspoken agreement between the provost and herself; he would never acknowledge her presence in the church, and she would never acknowledge his presence in the brothels of the Lower Planks.

"If I was smarter, I would have thrown you out the first day you came up that ladder," he whispered, eyes closed as he let her run her hands under his cloak and over his torso.

"I believe you could do a lot of things, but that is an impossible task for you."

"Try me."

"I've made a life of beating men larger than you. And you've never seemed to mind being manhandled."

Temson blushed and relinquished the victory of the verbal sparring. He spun her around, so her body pressed against the cold stone, a small gasp escaping her lips. Their eyes closed as he brought his lips to hers, pressing in tightly.

"Neither have you."

"Only by you."

"I am glad you are here," he whispered.

They shared a long kiss as he traced her matted hair with his fingers, and she tried to ignore how awful she probably smelled. He didn't seem to care as he began pressing light touches on her neck with his lips.

"I can't stay long."

Temson stopped kissing her, his hot breath in her ear making her dangerously close to staying.

"You're going back down there, aren't you?"

"I have a match tonight."

"Again?"

"It's money, Tem. Unless you'd rather me lean more into my other job."

Temson sighed deeply. She knew how much he hated the fighting, but he hated her status as a Blue Lady more. They didn't talk about the latter much and he didn't press the issue, thankfully. But she couldn't hide the scars and wounds of the fights from him and often needed his help mending her injuries. He was involved in it whether he wanted to be or not and she had no intention of stopping.

They entered the dimly lit inner sanctum of St. Trillian's Chapel, the high-ceilinged room bathed in warm lantern light. Statues of the gods rested on the wooden mantles that lined the room and a desk littered with Temson's writings and sermons sat against the portside wall. Old scrolls lay piled in a corner and a plate of half-eaten food decorated his desk.

Temson moved over to the table, poured two glasses of kelp wine, and handed one to her.

"I'll need to get another order of this soon. My mother would never approve of how much I drink these days, but it keeps the boredom at bay."

"You're lucky they didn't make you sign that away too."

Temson laughed. "You wouldn't believe how much is consumed during training—good stuff too. It's the one vice they let you keep, although we all know the upper vicars are anything but chaste."

"You're not so chaste yourself."

He smiled slyly at her. "Some things are hard to give up. Celibacy was getting difficult before you climbed up that ladder."

"And here I was thinking you were a virgin."

"Ha, no. I did have a life before this, remember."

They sipped at their wine, sitting close together on the edge of the desk as they soaked up what time they had. "Do you miss it?" Vila asked. "Your old life?"

"I miss my family—sometimes. But this was the only thing that I could do, really. My siblings had already been hustled off to their chosen paths. Having a cleric was the last check mark to tick and there was only one of us left to do it."

"I understand not having a lot of choices." She swirled the contents of her wine as they sat in silence. The thick stone walls blocked out most sound from the outside world, but the gentle movement of the constantly bobbing city could be felt. Vila felt peaceful as they swayed calmly, hands clasped together; she could have fallen asleep right there if she let herself.

"Do you have to go soon?"

"After this glass," she said quietly.

He sighed. "Do you know who you're fighting tonight?"

"Moben Tarn."

"I don't know who that is."

"Me neither," she smiled, trying to lighten the mood. "I'll be okay."

Temson set his glass down and placed a hand on her leg.

"Are you sure you want to do it? You could stay up here..."

Vila threw back the contents of her glass. She didn't want to have this argument, not tonight. "I'm going down," she said forcefully, then transitioned to a mischievous smile. "Besides, we usually have a little more fun afterwards."

He smiled back weakly. "That's true."

Vila gave him a kiss and pulled back the rug in the center of the room. It was barely necessary as the stone facade of the door looked like any of the others. She slipped her finger into an ordinary looking crack and pulled the hidden switch. The locks clicked quietly as the door opened upward, revealing the dark tunnel below. The climb down the treacherous secret path would be long and Vila couldn't say she was looking forward to it.

She cracked her joints and stretched her fingers as Temson came behind her and wrapped his arms about her waist. He smelled like incense and sweat, a delicious combination that almost made her rethink the evening.

They stood there together for a few moments, soaking in each other's warmth. She knew she smelled like saltwater and fish, but he still didn't seem to care as he gripped her tightly and laid his lips on her neck.

"Come back," he whispered.

She leaned her head back and kissed him fully, staring into those shining blue eyes.

"I always do," she smiled.

Gently releasing herself from his grasp, she pulled her kelp fiber long-cloak tight and started the descent into the Lower Planks. She looked up, blew him one last kiss, and began the long climb down as the door shut. She was back in the darkness, the only light coming from the slightly glowing stones on her bracer.

6

"Blue Ladies might be the Lower Planks' gift to us Uppers, but the rest of the activities down there are a horrid drain on society—like the arenas. They represent the true nature of that cesspool, and personally I am glad of the separation between our upstanding civilization and our unfortunate parasite. If you ask me, the whole place should be flooded and rid of the filth. Murderous and vile, all of them. Not a good thing ever came out of the Lower Planks, except those magnificent women."
~Patron Silon Tartonus, High council meeting, One-hundred ninety-seventh Year AW, Second Month, twentieth day, eighteenth hour. Recorded by Lina Hamaren, scribe on duty~

T he hit came hard from the right, striking Vila in the ribs with immense force and taking her breath away in a sharp wince. She could feel the bone almost start to crack from the intensity of the blow. It wasn't the first one of the night, but if she was careful, it would be the last—or at least close to it.

The cheers from the onlookers as she took her beating did nothing to sway her. There was a mix of adoring fans who hoped their hero would make it out alive again and those who wanted to see her get pummeled to death by her much larger opponent, earning them back lost coin from previous nights' matches. Although much fewer, there were also those who had never seen her fight before and were watching in morbid fascination at the small, red-haired woman fighting desperately for survival. Oil lanterns lit the arena from every angle instead of the more expensive sight stone variety. Shadows stretched out in all directions as the constantly shifting structures of the arena caused the light to sway back and forth. Down here, everything moved in time with the never-ending motion of the Swell.

Moben Tarn drew back, rubbing his hand and watching her as she doubled over. He sneered as she wiped blood from her mouth, the outward sign that he was dealing significant damage. *Good, let him feel confident* she thought. She also knew she couldn't take another hit like that. He'd already laid a few strong punches in her chest and face, and she was feeling it while he barely had a scratch on him.

This fight had been a tough one and Vila figured out early on that she was going to have to weather some brutal punches to get the advantage she needed. Every fight she entered was different and her tactics had to change with each new opponent. Some nights she had the upper hand from the beginning and could clobber her rival into a bloody mess before they had the chance to react. Other times, like tonight, a different approach was needed. Tarn was huge with the endurance of a whale, but he was stupid and eventually she would be able to get the upper hand—if she survived that long. She needed to recede into herself, remove herself from her outside environment and focus on survival. She could do that, had done that. Every girl from the Lower Planks knew how to do that. The only way she was going to get through this was to take the beating and wait for the right moment.

The huge man took a step forward, cracking his knuckles in preparation for the final flurry of blows that every onlooker knew were coming. The final bets started to take place as the outcome of the night's fight seemingly became clear. She just needed him to get a little closer and let his guard down.

He took one more step, his stance indicating he was gearing up for a kick to the gut. This was it. She'd only have seconds to react, and it wouldn't be easy—or painless.

She struggled to keep her eyes open and tearless as his large, iron-clad boot came swinging upward and caught her in the stomach. She took the blow, arching her back and pushing upward off the ground to try and minimize the force of impact as much as possible. It still hurt like hell, and she felt the air rushing out of her as her insides struggled to remain in their usual place.

Using the momentum of the strike, she twisted her body away to remove her stomach as a point of impact and create imbalance for the much larger enemy. Her feet struck the ground, and she lashed out at the other leg still touching the bloody sand of the arena, her own iron-clad boot crashing into his ankle. Moben Tarn crumpled with a cry of pain as the bone cracked under the force and he crashed to his back side.

Vila let the shocked silence of the audience move her on, fighting through the pain to finish the battle. Many of them had watched her before, but Vila kept her strategies varied each time. Every opponent had a different weakness or tell, and Vila's skill was figuring out what that was and how to exploit it. This man's was his size. He was one of the largest opponents she had faced so far, standing three heads taller than herself with shoulders that rivaled the mythic bears that once roamed the dry lands; long before the oceans swelled.

No bears now, not in the Lower Planks. Just big, hairy, overconfident men who thought they could use sheer force to defeat a woman half their size. Not in here though. This was her arena and her fight to win. All trees fell with the right strikes, the old saying went. She had never seen a tree, but she knew how to place the right strikes.

Vila was on him before his head hit the ground, straddling his chest, and working quickly to end it before he could recover his senses. She crashed her elbow into his nose, feeling the satisfying crunch as bone and cartilage crushed inward. Now the panic would set in as the dying man would struggle to gain control over the situation. She batted his hands away as he tried to land blows, unable to see clearly through the blood that drenched his face and pooled over his eyes. One good grip on her neck and she would be finished, but Vila wasn't going to let that happen. Nor was she going to let him live—she'd made that mistake before. The last opponent she showed mercy to had cornered her in an alley, beating her bloody in a violent engagement to regain some lost pride.

She'd still won, but she never left another one alive after that.

Prize fights in the Lower Planks didn't have to end in death. The final call was always left to the victor, as the onlookers only cared about how much money entered or left their pockets and how much blood they could see spilled in one night. The crowds consisted of mostly Lowers and a few Uppers, with the Uppers usually financing the larger bets. Here, the usually respectable citizens could throw off the shackles of civilized life and let the un-bridled pleasures of human iniquity be free. That was the beauty of a lawless underground: the only rules that mattered were the ones set by consensus and agreement of the populace. And the agreement of the pits was that your life was forfeit the moment you signed on to sell your body for the enjoyment of others.

Vila brought her elbow down upon the man's bearded face again and again, each strike crushing his flesh and bone more and more. Eventually, the impacts hit a softer and squishier surface until the man was no longer twitching and lay still in a pool of blood and gore. Vila gingerly pulled herself to her feet and picked a tooth out of her arm, a sharp pain searing her side.

The sudden cheers from the onlookers were deafening, with even a few disgruntled yelps from those who'd decided to bet against her tonight. Everyone's blood was roaring and there were plenty more fights to go. Not for Vila, though. Her blood was hot and pumping, but it was also leaking out of multiple lesions and her ribs felt cracked. She would need to get her wounds looked at before the night was through, but the adrenaline would carry her for a while until she was back up in Temson's waiting arms. She also felt blood pumping between her legs, and she was anxious for release once she had her priest's body under hers.

Stepping over the lifeless body of Moben Tarn, her boots squelching in the blood and bits of flesh, she grabbed her thread-bare long-cloak off the wall of the fighting pit and slipped her pendant of Parity back over her neck. She was checking the straps on her bracer were still tight but she jumped back when she felt a hand gently rest upon her wrist.

The older man smiled at her, his pearly teeth glistening in the flickering light from the whale oil lanterns that continued to sway as he steadied himself. His teeth were just one clue that he was someone rich or important—maybe both. The other was his absolutely stainless and pristine outfit. A thick cloak of tusker fur was draped about his form, the hair stained a deep crimson and lined with un-charmed sea glass rivulets. The fat seagoing mammals were extremely rare now, being found only on some distant icebergs in the north, which meant he had a lot of money and some illegal connections. His expensive sea silk shirt hemmed with golden threads was also a far cry from the kelp wraps that made up her outfit.

"I didn't mean to startle you, my dear," he said, hands held up in a placating stance.

"What do you want?" Vila's guard was up. She wasn't in the mood for a proposition—not that she ever was, but he seemed like just the type to try to entice pretty young girls to his bed with a thick purse.

"I quite enjoyed watching you fight. You were exceptional."

"It wasn't easy."

"Of course not. I've always been impressed with those who can put themselves into such a dangerous and deadly situation. Never had the heart for it myself."

Vila tried to signal that she was done with the conversation, throwing her cloak over her shoulders, and turning her back to the still smiling man. She felt his hand tug on the arm of her cloak, and she whirled around, a warning of more violence flickering in her green eyes. He was leering at her bracer, studying the intricately cast form of the key—where, underneath, lay her blue ringlet.

"I was hoping we might talk a little more about further opportunities..."

Vila flinched, dreading where this was going. He couldn't have seen the ringlet during the fight—he must have been asking around about the Blue Lady with the fiery hair and multiple scars. She knew she stood out in most crowds so it wouldn't have been hard to track her down. The madame would be furious at her for refusing a job, especially if he was as rich as he looked.

"I want to sponsor you."

That surprised her and she narrowed her eyes at the man. "Sponsor me? For what?"

"Fighting of course! I've seen you move; seen the way you draw blood. You're vicious, and I want to help you take that further."

Vila pulled her cloak tighter around her shoulders.

"Who are you?"

"Ah, right. I'm so sorry." He held out his hand, waiting for her to return the favor. When it never came, he continued with his introduction through reddening cheeks. "My name is Vintar Maccio III. I own several merchant vessels and salvage operations on the Planks and—"

"I've heard of you." Everyone had heard of the Merchant Lord Maccio and the Maccio family. Half the ships in the ports were his, as were a good number of the larger diving bells. Of course he could afford a cloak from a nearly extinct animal; with money like his, you could buy almost anything your heart desired. Almost.

"I'm not interested," she said, turning her back on the man once again.

There was a shuffling of bodies and some oomphs as the man clambered through the crowd to get around the arena. She moved quickly through the open gate of the pit as some young boys rushed in to clean up the corpse and rake the sands smooth for another fight. Huffing his way in front of her, the merchant dusted his cloak with his hands and breathed deeply. Vila didn't care if she'd pissed him off; she had no interest in being owned by more people.

"You haven't heard my offer," he said, not trying to keep his voice low.

"I don't want to."

"You might when you know how your life could change with my money. I want you to be my personal fighter. You could still fight down here, for me of course, but I'm looking to expand the entertainment upwards and test out some new weapon varieties. You'd live in my estate and not want for anything. You can have riches, comfort, whatever you want. We'd work up a contract, you fight under my name, and we build an empire. You'll have the best medical attention and physical regimen that one can afford—and the best trainers. You are an animal in the arena; I could help you become a monster."

All those things sounded enticing, or at least would have if that was why Vila put herself through it. The fighting pit was the only place Vila felt she had complete control over her miserable life. The danger, blood, and pain all culminating in a freedom she couldn't achieve anywhere else. That was why she battered herself night after night; to lose that control would be worse than any death she could imagine. There was no way she was giving that to him.

"Take your fucking money somewhere else," she spat. "I don't want a benefactor. I don't need a benefactor." With that, she turned away one last time, pleased that she didn't feel another pull on her cloak.

People like Lord Maccio thought that with enough money they could own whoever they wanted, make them do whatever they wanted. She'd met men like him before under different circumstances. She was already owned, already chained to a life she couldn't leave; there was no way she was going to add another layer of servitude to that.

Vila went to the counter to cash out her earnings and glanced over her shoulder. The man was gone, presumably shuffling back up to his mansion. She hoped he got robbed on the way.

"Good fight tonight, Vila," Jarin said, handing over the small bag of sea glass coins.

It amounted to fifteen coin. Enough to stock her pantry for a day or two. She could make forty times that in a night, she thought as she felt the Blue Ringlet digging into her skin under the bracer. If she ran back through the crowd and found the merchant before he ascended topside, she'd never have to worry about stocking her pantry ever again. Would he take Rance in as part of the contract? Was the man so desperate to have her that he would let her have her life with Temson?

Vila pulled five glass out of the bag and slammed it back down on the counter: her entry fee. "Sign me up for another," she said, struggling to ignore the searing pain in her side and the blood that was caking on her face and arms. She placed two more coins on the counter. "And give me tincture."

7

"Not in all the of the Swell will you find a more wretched and lurid place than the First City."

~Unknown~

A fter a night and day of hard sailing with barely a rest, the floating monstrosity known as the Planks loomed up out of the mist. A large flame could be seen high above the city docks, even before the rest of the city emerged out of the haze. Cobbled together from old ship's masts and lit with whale oil, the giant beacon cut through the morning fog, signifying the city from afar to vessels and other floating townships. It was one of four towering structures that lay on the perimeter of the city and its light cast a permanent, orange glow across the Upper Planks. Narrio could hear whistling noises as the strong winds blew through the tangle of ropes and shrouds that hung about the city like enlarged cobwebs. Most were newer kelp fiber, but a few hemp ropes from the old days could be seen, their weathered fibers threatening to snap with age. The whole city seemed to take on a life of its own, the strange high-pitched sound creating an eerie atmosphere as the dilapidated structures loomed over him.

As much as he hated the water, Narrio had proved a competent sailor through sheer force of will and survival instinct. He was even a decent swimmer, though it wasn't like he really had a choice. He knew you either learned how to survive above the Swell or be consumed by it, and Narrio wasn't one to give in.

His boat came careening into port a little faster than he would have liked, causing some shouts to ring out from the early morning dock workers. With a few strategically placed ropes and well-timed pulls, they managed to keep the vessel from crashing into anything important or capsizing as it bumped along to a stop. Narrio grabbed his belongings, hopped onto the decks, and threw a generous tip of glass coin to the workers.

He had two thoughts as he exited the little boat: the first was that he was starving. He'd barely had anything to eat in the time it had taken to get to his destination besides some red-kelp jerky he'd thrown down to keep him awake. He'd been too shaken by the encounter with the mysterious figures and was desperate to be on dry wood to try and find anything else—they also hadn't supplied him with any food.

The second thought was that the large, black frigate docked to his left made him uncomfortable and it took a few minutes of dumbfounded staring until his eyes rested on the red lettering that flowed across its side.

Shit.

If anything could make his plans go up in flames, it was the presence of Wardens on the Planks. They normally wouldn't be a hinderance, seeing as they spent most of their time patrolling the waters. The fact that he was here to steal some ancient artifact and they were somewhere wandering the streets? Not a great start to the mission.

His stomach rumbled deeply, reminding him that thought number one was more important right now. He turned his back on the ominous vessel and started down the docks into the city, occasionally glancing behind him as if the ship might come alive at any moment.

The Planks stunk of fish, pitch, and human filth, although his hometown of Driftburg probably didn't smell much better. Anthema smelled okay, but he wouldn't expect the home of the Church of Parity to smell of anything other than incense and piety.

He risked a glance over the edge of the docks hoping to see the infamous Lower Planks but couldn't see more than a few feet in the dark, bobbing waters. All in good time, he thought. He had a feeling this venture would lead him to some dark corners of the Planks, including its famed and literal underworld. He definitely wasn't looking forward to that journey.

Narrio's first stop was a small shack at the end of the docks with a large sign advertising fried fish and cold kelp wine. His stomach rumbled an affirmative and he made his way inside, purchasing two helpings of fish, some urchin bites, and a mug of lukewarm kelp wine. He drained the first mug at the bar and ordered two more to take to the table with his meal.

Sitting down at one of the driftwood tables, Narrio allowed himself a brief moment to enjoy the hot meal before getting down to business. As he ate, he took in what little of the city he could see from his current vantage point. The aesthetic of the city could best be described as perilous. Every building that he could see looked like it had been smashed together from whatever had been dredged up from the depths and smeared over with coralcrete plaster—which the more he thought about it, was exactly right.

Over the rooftops he could make out some newer looking structures using more modern materials; they probably belonged to some of the wealthier folk. These stood out like a sore thumb against the eclectic collection of architectural styles and precariously balanced structures. If he wasn't afraid of the whole thing collapsing in on itself, he'd almost say it was interesting. As it were, the whole place seemed oppressive and lopsided, and he could only guess at what the Lower Planks felt like. The high-pitched whistle also hadn't let up since he'd landed, and it was starting to give him a headache.

Licking the last of the grease off his fingers, Narrio allowed himself a satisfied burp and kicked his feet up onto the table as he downed the last of his second cup, and took a big gulp of the third before pulling out his notebook. It was time to get to work.

He began making a list of all the things that would need to be done, starting with the three most important.

Retrieve the stone,
Escape the Planks,
Deliver the stone.

Satisfied, he moved on to the intermediate steps that would ultimately lead him to the completion of each goal.

Find the contact,
Scope the area,
Create a list of resources,
Explore the parish and learn its secrets,
Find out where the stone is kept,
Make a dumb plan to get it out of there,
Execute the plan,
Retrieve the stone,
Make a dumb plan to get back to the docks,
Execute the plan,
Escape the Planks,
Don't get lost at sea or eaten by monsters,
Deliver the stone,
Don't let the creepy mask people kill me,
Enjoy the spoils.

Narrio put down his quill and pad and leaned back. The details could be filled in later, if at all. He had a difficult time thinking through all the intricacies, his mind was much more comfortable with reactionary action. It got him into a lot of trouble, but it also got him out of a lot of trouble. It also made him difficult to work with, meaning he tended to perform best on his own. He didn't mind company to lend an ear to his ramblings but only if he was free to operate the way he saw fit.

He rubbed his eyes, unsure of where to start searching for his contact. The ring on his finger was the sign, he supposed, but he hadn't been given any other details about who he was meeting or what they would provide him with. He wasn't used to jobs like this, especially ones that ended up with him gutted and left as chum for the sharks. If he could be that lucky. Something about his mysterious benefactors told him that quick deaths weren't part of their modus operandi.

Alternatively, he could get caught by the Deep Wardens, Fathus' protectors of the deep and self-proclaimed guardians of all that is holy and pretentious. At best, they'd kill him on spot if it was convenient, but at least he knew they would do it quickly. At worst, he'd be taken to Grim-Mire Hold, the legendary sunken prison colony. Narrio shuddered at the thought.

Time to get started, I guess, he thought to himself as he knocked back the last of the wine. It burned his throat and left a warm, unpleasant feeling in his stomach. He packed his bag and was about to return his dishes to the bar when he realized he wasn't alone at the table.

Narrio nearly jumped out of his seat but thought that wouldn't be professional, so he opted for a shriek instead.

"Gods! How long have you been there?!"

The woman smiled at him, if not a little threateningly, and kicked her feet up on the table next to his. She had a patch over one eye that was a menacing contrast to the otherwise attractive face of high cheek bones, thick lashes, and full lips. Her hair was braided back against one side and pinned up with decorative coral pins. She produced a new pitcher of wine which she set down with a heavy thunk and took a sip from her own mug.

"Long enough to know that you don't have a plan yet."

She danced a blue coin through her fingers and Narrio noticed the large, silver ring on her index finger. The signet on the ring was an exact match to the one that graced his middle finger. This was definitely his contact.

"My first plan is to change my pants. Is this part of your group's test for you to get your masks and rings? Sneak up on enough people and you get to join the cult?"

"It's not a cult, and no. You're just remarkably unaware."

"Ouch."

The woman leaned forward and poured a heaping portion of wine into his empty cup. He could smell her perfume, a delicious mix of sea apples and sugar. He was keenly aware of how attractive she was, eye patch and all, his eyes wandering a little below her chin to rest on her ample figure that was pressing through the tight kelp-fiber tunic she wore. It didn't help that she wore a leather baldric between her breasts that accentuated her features.

Narrio gulped and averted his eyes into his newly filled cup. Getting sexually involved with a member of the death cult was definitely not on his list of to-dos.

"You can call me Renalia," the woman said, taking a long drink from her own cup.

"I can call you that or that's your name?"

"That's what I'll be known as to you."

"Fair enough."

"I don't know your name."

"They didn't tell you that?"

"No."

Narrio ran a few of his funnier pseudonyms through his head, but one look at her face told him she might not be the right audience. "Narrio. Narrio Olitarth."

"Pleasure, Narrio. My job is to help get you acquainted with the city and provide what support I can. Your job is to come up with a brilliant plan and acquire the stone."

"No pressure."

She grew suddenly serious and leaned in close. Narrio buried his nose in his cup so as not to become too infatuated as her perfume slipped its way into his nostrils again. He found himself time and time again falling for dangerous women, and it never ended well. Well, there were some happy endings, but they ultimately ended with him in a desperate flight for his life. Usually, naked.

"Don't fuck this up, for either of us," she whispered in his ear. "Let's go, I'll take you to the church."

"Can I finish my drink?"

"Quickly. I have places to be."

"Other than helping me?"

"Yes, so if you'd hurry along, I'd rather not spend all day with you if I don't have to."

Narrio took in the surroundings as they went, partly out of need for the mission and partly out of genuine amazement at the new city. The Planks was the oldest floating structure in the world and in his opinion, the ricketiest. How the thing was still traversing the oceans was a complete mystery. Driftburg made use of deepwood from the strange wateroaks that had sprung up in the ocean depths after the Great War, and coralcrete was a more common element in other establishments once the farming and manufacturing process had been refined. Both could be found here, but they were just two elements that made up the hodgepodge of building materials and methods. The Planks didn't have a deepwood farming operation, as it was the only city that would raise its anchor and free float across the Swell. Driftburg, Anthema, and Tideland were permanently chained to ancient mountain tops far below, giving them permanent access to the bounties below.

The Planks lived up to its name, as the whole city looked like it had been smashed together from various bits of sea-going vessels. Buildings were leaning at odd angles, lashed together with rope and sailcloth. Some even had ages old growths of broken coral and barnacles, indicating wreckage that had been dredged up from the deep. The streets were a series of mismatched boards, sunbaked and weather worn with new driftwood haphazardly nailed on top as pieces rotted out; and the infernal whistling continued as they made their way through the alleys.

"Does it always make that noise?"

"Whenever there's a strong wind, which is common. So, yes. You've never heard it called the *Whistling,* or *Singing* city before?"

"My knowledge of the Planks begins and ends with *Upper* and *Lower.*"

"You're gonna need to know a lot more than that soon."

"That's why you're here, right?"

"Right, so don't make my job any more difficult than it already is."

"Are you from here?" Narrio tried continuing light conversation as they walked briskly through the bustling streets. He liked the activity—he had found that, if he was careful and deliberate, more people meant less chance of being noticed. It was a lot easier to get caught if you were the only person snooping around at night. Make yourself completely uninteresting (which he could do begrudgingly) and find a dull activity to cover your real motives, then you were much more likely to succeed. It was incredible what people missed in broad daylight.

"Yes," came the short reply.

"Have you ever been to any of the other cities?"

"No."

"Do you want to?"

"No."

They walked in silence after that, weaving their way through the crowded streets. Narrio made a few stops at some stalls to snag a few more charge stones for his timepiece and various instruments, noting a price increase from his last restock.

Charge stones were another form of altered glass, unlike the neutral sea glass coins in his pocket. Divine magic from the war mixed with the extreme pressures of the deep had altered the plethora of glass on the ocean floor and given it special properties that could be bent to the will of man. It was one of the reasons sea glass was used as a currency; apply the right tinctures to it and you had new glass. Like charge stones with which you could power simple machinery like the star map.

Narrio replaced the stone in his timepiece as they continued walking, glancing over at Renalia every so often. She seemed nervous, so he tried breaking the tension again.

"You seem nervous." Great.

"You saw that ship in the harbor?"

He nodded.

"Then you should be nervous too."

"Why are they here?" He looked around as if expecting a Warden to jump out from behind a pile of fish. Even at midmorning, the streets of the Planks were awash with darkness from the piles of buildings and wreckage that blocked out the sun and created a plethora of dark corners.

"Just be extra careful. The last thing we need is you drawing their attention."

"I can be subtle."

She rolled her eye as they continued down the street. "We're here."

Sure enough, the chapel lay ahead of them, its stone facade lay in stark contrast to the wood and plaster of the rest of the city. It almost took his breath away to see the stone building amid all the driftwood and wreckage that comprised its brethren architecture. As they got closer, Narrio could see the building sat lower than the city streets, with the portion visible being only a quarter of the rest of the church.

Almost like a crater in the center of the square, the decks of the city center circled the building and long, winding switchbacks continued down to the bottom where the entrance to St. Trillian's chapel lay. The city really had been built up around it as it grew. He could see seams on the exterior, indicating where the false roofs had been added over time as the city grew higher and higher above the church. Narrio leaned over the rail and could see a full diameter of stone blocks that surrounded the church base, almost as if the whole building and its surrounding foundation were uprooted and set in the city center. It was a place set in two worlds; both Upper and Lower Planks yet belonging to none.

They made a pass around the entire exterior before beginning their descent down the switchbacks, Narrio taking mental notes as they went. The only entrance appeared to be the grand front doors, also stone, and guarded by church provosts in their signature turquoise frocks and polished yellow helms of hardened coral. They passed by a large and dramatic sculpture of St. Trillian himself holding a comically large sword and looking very serene.

"So that's the man."

"You don't seem impressed."

"The name Del'Sor doesn't carry as much weight in the other cities. He's good looking, but I'm not sure what all the fuss was about."

"Legend says he was the one to deliver the final blow to Loamia."

"Alright, I'm a little impressed."

The two set foot at the bottom and Narrio began his investigation of the exterior. Fastened above the arched door's keystone was a large sculpture of the Parity symbol. Narrio had never seen a moon crystal that large before and couldn't help but wonder at its worth. Aside from the door, there were a few artistic glass windows on the lower and upper levels. There were usually tell-tale signs of light and movement from the interior even with artistic glass, but he couldn't detect anything. Just the reflection from the outside. He guessed it was boarded or bricked up from the inside as if they were really trying to keep people out. Climbing the building was out of the question. The square structure left no angles or architecture to hide movements, and everything was visible from the city center above and the surrounding switchbacks. The roof was probably just as secure, its fragility likely just a facade.

Flummoxed but curious, Narrio ordered some fried squid bits from a nearby vendor and the two sat on a bench, watching passersby, and studying the church. The doors remained closed while a crowd gathered outside, waiting to be let in.

"Well...nothing's jumping out at me immediately."

"And here I was thinking you'd get it done before sunset."

"Not quite. Soon though. All shells can be cracked, you just have to find the right spot. Can we go in?"

"Morning service will be starting soon."

"Wonderful," he said through a gleaming smile, "Let's go to church."

8

"A remnant of the war and human civilizations, sea glass, as you all know, is the backbone of survival on the surface of the Swell. The ocean floor has it in abundance, though the retrieval and mining of it is extremely dangerous albeit lucrative. Over the past centuries, alchemists have figured out how to use the glass for all sorts of ingenious products with one of the most popular uses being in diving masks. Depending on the potency of the stones and the depths to which you descend, one could get several hours out of a mask before the stones are spent. And then there is blessed glass, the rarest of treasures. The process by which blessed glass is made is a tightly guarded secret of the Deep Wardens. Fused directly to their skin, Deep Wardens can take the unlimited energy straight into their bodies. A Warden need never surface if they didn't want to. They are masters of the Swell and deserve the utmost respect for their sacrifice."
~From a lecture on sea glass and its history by Arch Meister Nannia Polonov~

Rance threw the last of the cages back down into the waters as Vila sipped her hot urchin tea out of the animal's husk.

She savored the earthy flavor as the heat from the drink warmed her from the inside. The early morning sun was hiding behind a cluster of gray clouds, and a cool breeze tousled Vila's hair as she tried to stay warm. She shifted herself in the cloak, wincing at the pain in her ribs. Pulling the cages up today had been harder due to her injuries the night before, and her wounds screamed in protest—even with the red kelp poultices Temson had applied to soothe the wounds. Rance tried to ignore her grimace, knowing it was better to not call attention.

Sitting back in the small boat, he stretched his wrinkled arms, his joints cracking and popping loudly. He looked perplexed as he counted the morning's catch. It was meager again and Vila wished she could do better for him.

"I'm sorry Rance. I know it's not good," Vila said, feeling sympathy for the old fisherman. Even as an Upper, life on the planks wasn't easy for the working-class people like Rance. If you weren't part of the merchant upper-class, every lost catch meant one less meal on your plate.

"Huh? Oh, no, but I've had worse...look at this though." He reached down into the wriggling pile and pulled out a red and white spotted basker. At first glance, Vila couldn't identify what had caught his attention. The fish was already dead which meant it was no good, but other than that she didn't know what he was referencing.

"I'm not seeing it, Rance."

"Look at the eyes."

Vila leaned in and took a closer look. She saw it now—a spiral of tiny, crystalized formations starting at the socket and spreading out towards the gills. The crystals were dark black in color and as she stared, she could see swirls of purple moving through the inky black—almost as if the crystals were alive. The fish's eyes also had a glassy, ebony sheen to them that showed no reflection.

"What is that?" she asked.

"I really couldn't say. I've never seen anything like it, and it don't look natural."

Rance brushed his fingers over the crystals. He pulled his hand back quickly, leaving droplets of blood from the tiny cuts that now populated his fingertips. He let out a sharp cry of pain and sucked on his injured fingers.

"Rance! Are you okay?"

"Just some cuts, is all. Stung like somethin, but I'll live. Don't touch em, Mistress."

"I don't plan on it, and you shouldn't either."

They stared at the fish for a long while, neither of them sure of what to say. Vila had a growing suspicion that whatever was on that fish was part of the larger problem affecting the fishing around the Planks. Her concern at the lack of fish had turned into a deep unsettling feeling in her stomach as she eyed the creature, the crystals creeping out of its scales like a dark blight.

"I've never seen rocks like that," she finally said. She didn't have any new insights yet, but the silence was creating a sense of dread over the little boat.

"Neither have I. And not on any animal. Some sort of poison?"

Vila was silent for a moment, her eyes stuck on the creature.

"Rance...look..." She reached down and held up two more fish. They had the same patterns of crystal growing from around their eyes and crusting around their gills; but there were some differences. On one fish, the crystals were a deep azure, the blues moving around inside the crystalline shell. This one was still alive, as was the other one she held, although the rocks growing around it were a vibrant emerald green.

Crystals. Rocks. Iridescence. Colors. She realized she had seen these before. She'd seen their likeness everywhere around the neck of every religious person in the Planks.

"It's moon rock."

"What?"

She held up her pendant of Parity, the sign of the Four. Gold spirals wrapped around a stone disk. A piece of round, blue sea glass lay below the disk and a small shard of green moon crystal mirrored it above. Sun, Earth, Sea and Sky. The four (five) immortal gods and their realms represented in harmony and balance. But what she saw on the fish in front of her didn't look anything like harmony.

"Moon rock ain't black," Rance said, holding up his own pendant to show off his green shard. He gestured to one of the other fish. "Or blue."

"It can be. There are several different colors and types. The church decided green would be the standard color because it's what is most commonly available and that's the color of the Great Stone in the Grand Cathedral. Even the fake ones are green."

"How do you know that?"

Not wanting to reveal her closeness with Temson, she shrugged, trying to act nonchalant. "Read it in a book."

"Huh. I've never seen anything like that. Moon rock ain't got magical properties like sea glass, do it? And sea glass don't grow into your skin lest you fuse it there like them wardens do."

"No, at least not that I've ever seen. But I'd bet my hide that this is something celestial."

"Think it's got something to do with them meteors we've been seeing?"

"Maybe. I wouldn't know and I'm not about to make a guess. I'll take these and see what I can find. Check the others. If there is something infecting the waters and fish, we are going to need to be careful."

Rance nodded and began looking over the rest of the catch as Vila carefully wrapped up the tainted fish. When they had finished, Rance started navigating the small dinghy back toward the Planks. They sailed back in silence, the strangeness of the find sitting on them—a heavy burden of mystery that neither could fathom.

Vila bought Rance breakfast and he had argued vehemently, but she wouldn't hear it. Not with three of his seven fish covered in strange crystals from the skies. At least that was her best guess right now. She walked him to his house after the meal and set off towards St. Trillian's Chapel, running as fast as her battered body would allow. Temson would be finishing up morning services soon and she needed to talk to him about the fish to confirm her hunch and see if he had any insights. She ran through the streets with a sense of urgency pushing her that she couldn't explain.

Vila wouldn't admit it to the old man because she didn't want to scare him more, but she was deeply concerned. A lack of fish was one thing, but some sort of infection or corruption could be a disaster for her city.

She was so caught up in her thoughts as she darted through alleys to get to the chapel that she didn't see the Warden step out in front of her.

Shaila O'Caan didn't budge as Vila crashed into her breastplate of polished shell and the smaller woman bounced back hard on the driftwood street, her ribs shrieking at the sudden impact. Stunned, Vila tried to sit up and wiped a bit of blood from her lip where she'd bitten down upon falling. The imposing Warden lowered her lance at Vila's throat as she tried to back away.

"Don't move," a quiet voice came from behind her as Taragin Echilor stepped out of a dark corner, his heavy cloak shifting about and making him look like an ocean predator as he circled over to stand by Shaila. Augustan Tempé and Quinlan Lan stepped out from behind doorways on either side of her, completing the group and sending a sinking feeling through her gut. Augustan smiled, his disgustingly handsome grin making her sick.

"We'll take those fish off of you," he said, holding his gloved hand out to her. She could see the blessed glass that had fused itself into his right arm, clean holes cut into his bracer so that each of the four stones was visible.

"No," she replied, clutching them close to her, careful not to cut herself on the sharp rocks.

No one moved, but there was a tension that hung in the air like a tight thread, choking the air out of the shrouded alleyway. The tension was punctuated by the constant whistling through the ropes that wound above them and all around. The other Wardens looked to Augustan, waiting for their leader's rebuttal. To his credit, he didn't look flustered and responded with cool confidence.

"I wasn't asking, and I don't care where you were taking them. They are coming with us. If you don't hand them over, I'll cut your hands off and take those too." His saber was in his hand faster than Vila could react, and she pulled her chin up just in time as the bone blade flashed by her neck in a display of swiftness. The dull stains of blood lay in gruesome patterns around the intricate scrimshaw designs depicting epic battles with ancient beasts. Tempe's eye twitched briefly, the rest of his face remaining smug as he lifted her chin with the tip of his blade.

"Seems like an extreme reaction for a few fish," she said, muscles tightening in her neck as she tried to steady her breathing.

Quinlan stepped forward and knelt beside her, speaking in a gentler tone than his commanding officer.

"We know what you found on them. And by the way you were running, you know what it is too. But others can't know. Not yet."

"Why not?" Her throat felt dry, as if someone had poured a bag of sand down it.

Augustan pulled his saber back a small amount, but the danger never left his eyes as he answered. "Because whatever is causing it came from somewhere. We don't know where yet, but we have some theories. It wouldn't be beneficial to anyone if word got out and a panic started. This needs to be handled quietly and by us."

Vila fought the urge to hand over her quarry, her thoughts drifting to Rance's fragile frame. "I need to get answers too." She felt like she was pleading, and she hated it. Ignoring the tense stances of the Wardens, Vila carefully rose to her feet and tried to speak with more confidence than she felt as she pushed the blade away by the blunted side. "I can keep this a secret, trust me. Let me go, and I won't say a word."

Augustan sneered at her, and with an unparalleled speed his gloved hand shot out and gripped her by the throat. His breath was hot, spittle flying from his lips and landing on her cheeks.

"Listen, you little bitch," he said as he lifted her off the ground, a dark vein on his temple quivering. "I don't think you understood what I meant when I said I would cut off your hands. I meant I'd cut your hands off and let you bleed out in this alley. Right here. Right now. Then I'd take your pretty little stubs and use them to jerk off tonight, because I don't give a fuck what you what you need, or what you sa—"

His scream brought a deep satisfaction to Vila as she clubbed him in the face with one of the fish, the blue crystals leaving a string of deep cuts across his chiseled jaw and high cheek bones. His grip on her neck loosened a bit and then finally released all together when she slammed her iron studded boot into his manhood.

She dropped to the ground and was immediately restrained again as Shaila and Taragin latched their hands onto her wrists like a steel trap. The White Warden was back on his feet in an instant while Quinlan stood back, looking amused. Augustan's saber was at her throat again and Vila was sure he was about to follow up on his threat when a deep voice growled low from her side.

"Tempé. Enough."

Taragin's command stopped the younger man in his tracks, his jaw clenching tight as he stared at his inferior. The older Warden gripped Vila's right arm tight, his hand clutching her father's bracer. He stared at the cast symbol stitched into the leather; two metal mountains holding up four dull and unremarkable glass stones.

"If you give us the fish, we won't kill your friend." Taragin's voice was barely above a whisper, but Vila heard every word and the sincerity behind it.

Her eyes shone with an unbound fury, but she was helpless to struggle against the iron grips on her arms. She was going to have to give in, to relent at the threats even as every fiber of her being screamed with resentment. But she couldn't let them hurt Rance. The old man had never asked her for anything and always gave more than he took. Looking into each of the Warden's eyes, Vila believed every word they said. She dropped the fish.

Augustan got uncomfortably close to her face as she struggled against her restraints. His breath stank of a mineral smell, and it stung her nostrils as he glared at her.

"Not a word. We will be monitoring you, even when you think we aren't around. Watch yourself, girl. I don't make empty threats."

"Some hero," she sneered at him as her arms were released. She balled her fists, desperately trying to keep her rage from igniting.

"Not heroes, you little cunt. Wardens. Learn the difference."

With that, the four protectors of the deep disappeared back into the shadows of the alley. Taragin gave her one last glance laced with what looked like sympathy before he was obscured in darkness and Vila was left alone.

She waited for a while, her breathing heavy and her heart racing. Closing her eyes for a moment, Vila reached deep into herself and pulled out the calm that was receding further and further away. She found it and clutched onto it tightly as she limped the rest of the way to the St. Trillian's Chapel as fast she could, clutching a small handful of shards in her hand.

9

"It truly is a shame that St. Trillian's Chapel has become the sad husk that it is today. Already a withering remnant of fading memories, Hinaldo Del'Sor's escapades put the final nail in the coffin for the once great structure, and few mourned his passing. It has taken time for the church to recover some dignity and much effort has been made to assure the public that the priests of Parity are nothing but devout servants to the gods. As for the Del'Sors, I don't think that name will ever hold the same reverence as it once did."
~From Yania Torino's "The Planks: A History"~

T he sermon was not bad, Narrio had to admit, at least from a technical perspective. If he had been interested in the subject material, he would have found himself engaged. As it were, he spent most of the time glancing about the church, looking for clues and weak points. He'd been in barracks and prisons that felt less impenetrable than this lone stone structure. All the windows were covered in coralcrete plaster and painted over with murals of the gods and religious events. There was no evidence of his quarry anywhere in the sanctuary and only one door behind the raised pulpit that led anywhere. That door had, if he'd counted correctly from his vantage point, five iron keyholes that seemed to match the number of keys manacled to the cleric's wrist.

The priest was younger than Narrio would have thought, he would know after having just spent a significant amount of time in the capitol of the Church and surrounded by more clergyman than he was comfortable with. Nearly all the priests in the Grand Cathedral were men who looked near the end of their lifespans with an absurd number of acolytes and priests-in-training waiting on them and counting the days until they died off. Not including the plethora of young lady acolytes who seemed to get more than their fair share of attention from the elders.

He wondered how this young man got the position at his age—although, the more he looked around, the more obvious the answer became: this place was a jail. No light, guards at the door, and literal shackles on your arm. Thick clouds of incense hung in the air, making Narrio's nose itch as he tried to suppress a cough.

"Why is it locked up so tight?" he whispered to Renalia, cocking his head towards the plastered-over windows.

"Shhhh," she hissed.

Renalia looked extremely uncomfortable next to him, her leg tapping at irregular intervals throughout the entire sermon. She wore no pendant of Parity but seemed to know the words to the liturgy well enough, so it would seem she wasn't unfamiliar with the church environment. Narrio had learned them all as well for his latest heist and had promptly forgotten everything when he left.

"I want to talk to him after this is done," Narrio whispered again as the final rites were being performed. Their heads were bowed low, hands folded in penitence. Renalia's perfume battled for space against the incense in Narrio's nostrils.

"I don't think that's a good idea. Aren't you supposed to *not* be drawing attention to yourself?"

"Sometimes, the best way to not draw attention *is* to draw attention." He flashed her his winning smile.

"That doesn't make any fucking sense."

"Watch."

The service ended and the congregation slowly rose to leave and get to whatever the rest of their days looked like. Narrio smiled at her again, dug his fingers into his eyes until they watered, and ran a hand through his hair for good measure. He straightened his dirty jacket as he confidently strode up to the cleric who was blessing a few of the patrons before they were ushered out. Red faced, Renalia followed him from a safe distance looking like a cornered rat.

"Peace to you, Brother..." he said to the priest as he approached, his head bowed low, waiting to be blessed.

"Peace, my child." The cleric placed a hand on his head and said the words of blessing. With tears in his eyes Narrio raised his head and clasped his hands in thanks.

"Brother...?"

"Temson."

"Brother Temson...I was extremely moved by your words. I'm not sure the arch vicar himself could have painted a more beautiful portrait of divinity. Truly."

"Your words are kind. I only say what the gods give me to say." He smiled at Narrio, his gaze darting over the thief's shoulder at the door. "And I am sorry to cut this short, but they are ready to close the doors now."

"Yes, of course. I don't want to keep you. I only had one question."

"Of course." The man was starting to look nervous, but he maintained his smile as Narrio stepped a little closer, taking note of a shift in the shadows to his right.

"I've actually traveled a very long way to see this church. St. Trillian's Chapel is quite famous, as you are well aware, I'm sure. So much history and meaning here."

"Yes, it truly is a remarkable place."

"I have been visiting the holy sites of the world, studying the artifacts of the saints and the divine. I was wondering if there would be an opportunity to do the same here?"

"I'm sorry..."

"Professor Terous, Scholar of Divinity at the College of Deepwood in Driftburg. But please, call me Perpos."

The cleric seemed impressed, and his face took on a more sympathetic turn as he prepared to let the sad looking academic down. "I'm sorry, Perpos, I truly am. The inner sanctum is off limits to everyone except the clergy."

"Are there no artifacts or relics kept in the sanctuary to admire?"

"I'm afraid not. Only the instruments of the ceremonies and the art you see around you. I'd be happy to show you around the sanctuary on another day if it would please you. There is some wonderful art and history in this very room to appreciate."

Narrio plastered on his most gracious smile. "I would love that! You are too kind. I thank you for your time."

"Of course. Please do come back. I don't want you to feel your trip here was wasted, and I am always here to serve those faithful to the Four. Peace be with you brother. And you too, sister."

Renalia looked like she had choked on a fish as he addressed her and gave a curt nod. Narrio bowed his head again and took Renalia by the arm as they left the chapel.

"Sorry for the wait," he said jovially to one of the provosts as the heavy stone doors closed behind them. "I'd buy you a drink, but the sun just rose."

The guard's face remained impassive, but a brief chuckle escaped him as he straightened his back to resume his post. Narrio glanced back and forth, as if wary of anyone overhearing. "Let's say I was looking for the best the Planks had to offer; somewhere they know your name and treat you right. Where would I go? At a more appropriate time, of course."

The guard's eyes did their own quick back and forth, and then his mouth turned up on one side as he answered. "Jam Jam's is mah place. You won't find a better brew or a prettier owner."

"I appreciate your time," Narrio returned with a large smile, squeezing his companion's arm as they began their ascent up the switchbacks to the city square. When they were out of view of the provosts Renalia suddenly grabbed him by his collar and slammed him up against the side of the supporting structures. Narrio winced as his head smacked against the rotting timber and splinters showered down from the impact.

"Careful! You want to bring this whole place—"

"What the fuck was all that about?" she growled at him, not quite yelling but not anywhere near a whisper. "Professor of divinity? Cajoling the guards? Holy sites and artifacts? You might as well have just asked to walk in and steal the stone!"

Narrio tried to remove her hands, but her grip was iron, and she had pressed him harder against the beams. He knocked a dirty thought aside in his mind before choking out a reply.

"The best lies are often the ones that have an inkling of truth and a connection to the quarry. All he'll remember is a follower of the faith and lover of religious artifacts who was grateful to be in one of the most holy places on earth, and will feel bad that he couldn't help further. And now we know that the artifact must be somewhere in the inner sanctum."

"That wouldn't have been hard to figure out."

"Well, now we know for sure. And I was able to get a good look at those keys strapped to his wrist; unless you want to cut his hand off in broad daylight, we aren't getting in that way."

"And what about the nonsense with the guard?"

"We know he likes to drink, and that he will be at *Jam Jam's* tonight. And he's going to tell us who that red-haired woman was."

Renalia raised an eyebrow as her grip on his collar loosened a bit. Narrio had her interest now, letting the little clue dangle like a piece of bait. "Who?"

Narrio tried to contain his grin to no avail. "I'm sorry, you didn't see the beautiful woman hiding behind the columns in the aisle? I'm not surprised. She was probably sure that no one had noticed her."

"I can't say that I did, though I'm not surprised you noticed her," she smirked.

"Well, she was there, and I'll bet a thousand coin that at least one of those guards knows about her too. Probably the stupid looking one who likes to go to Jam Jam's. So, you have a job to do."

"Which is?"

"You need to find out everything you can about that provost. Family relations, place of residence, favorite drink; everything. And most important of all is what time his shift ends."

Narrio lightly gripped her wrists and guided them the rest of the way off his collar, noting that she didn't put up a fight or flinch.

"I'll admit, I'm a little impressed," she said as she crossed her arms and studied him. "But only a little."

"That's the nicest thing you've said to me so far."

"Don't get used to it. And what are you going to be doing while I do all this work?"

"Me?" His smile was slow and sly, as his eyes twinkled brightly. "I'll be preparing a new character."

IO

"The question of the moon and its twins has plagued theologians and astronomers alike since the beginning of mankind. When the gods first coalesced from the darkness and graced our world with their presence, the four major forces were represented in the divine form: sun, earth, water, moon. So, why then the moon twins? To find the answer, one must potentially look past the popular beliefs that all the gods were formed in the dark when the great energies of the universe exploded together and created the world we know. The answer might come from more recent history if radical theories are to be believed, yet there is no evidence to support such wild thoughts. For now."
~Excerpt from Arch Titritus' "Musings and Contemplations of the Four and their Divine Realms"~

The door slammed shut with severity as Temson thrust them both inside the inner sanctum, his cheeks reddened with anger. She had never seen him like this before, but she had also never been quite so brash in her entry. She didn't blame him, and she would have come up Hinaldo's door, but they needed to talk *now* and there was no way she was going to lead those Wardens to the back door while she was still flustered. Better to be spotted coming in the front.

"We talke—"

"Shut up," she cut him off. "I know we talked about this. This is more important."

She held out her hand and let the handful of black moon rock shards fall onto his desk in dramatic fashion, emphasizing her intensity.

"Where did that come from?" He stared at the rock intently, trying to make sense of what he was seeing.

"It was growing on fish that we caught in the Swell. There are blue and green shards too. Careful, it's extremely sharp." To illustrate, Vila held up her hand that had clutched the rocks as she ran, revealing the oozing slices that marred her skin. Now that the adrenaline was wearing off, she could feel the stinging pain from the cuts that she had ignored before.

"Vila! We need to get those bandaged!"

She waved off his concern. "I'm fine, they're minor."

Ignoring her stoicism, Temson pulled down jars of concentrated red kelp tincture and anemone toxins, and rubbed the foul mixture into a bandage of dried kelp fiber.

"Give me your hand."

He gently wrapped the bandage over her cuts, and she felt the cold sting as the poultice started to work. His fingers traced her own as he fastened it, the touch light and concerned.

"Tem, I'm fine. Please."

She took his chin in her hands and directed his attention back to the shards. He studied the rocks, carefully lifting them up and taking in the swirling colors inside. The flickering candlelight of the room seemed to soak into the rocks and bounce around the crystal interior in a fervent dance.

"I know you like history, so I'm going to reluctantly let you school me."

He raised his eyebrows. "On what exactly?"

"Everything related to these shards. They are moon rocks, aren't they? So why are they here? Where did they come from? And most importantly, what are they doing to the waters?"

Vila hated it, but she could feel the emotion rising in her voice and she choked it back. Temson noticed it too, but he kept quiet and rubbed his temples as he examined the object in his hand.

"That's a lot of questions."

"And I really need the answers."

"This is about Rance, isn't it? You're worried about what will happen to him if the fish are being poisoned."

"He doesn't have anything left, Tem. I have to help him and whoever else this if affecting."

Temson sighed and rubbed the bridge of his nose.

"Lunarology is a highly debated and controversial subject, but let's see what we can dig up."

For the next several hours, Temson and Vila pored through the priest's collection of scrolls, devouring anything related to moon crystals and the lunar gods. There was much that was already familiar to Vila from Temson's sermons and some of her own brief readings as a child, sneaking anything she could to read from merchants in the Lower Planks. They had mostly been children's stories, but she'd found that most stories almost always had some grain of truth to them.

Her favorite had been about the twin moon gods: Lunus and Celenia. While two of the five gods lived in the mortal realm of the earth, Lunus and Celenia occupied a celestial realm on the surface of the moon, while Solan the sun god stayed in his fiery kingdom.

When Loamia, the earth goddess sank into her madness, she was ultimately taken down thanks to the sea god, Fathus. But according to the writings, the other gods had a presence during the Great War of Earth and Sea too, albeit much underplayed when compared to the others. Great swaths of earth were scorched into oblivion by the sun god, while giant crystals of moon rock rained from the sky and brought destruction of unspeakable terror to Loamia's realms and her minions. Records of Celenia's involvement were brief to the point of negligibility.

Most of the giant moon rocks were washed away or buried under the mighty depths of the Swell as water took over the earth; at least one of the large rocks was recovered and placed in the grand cathedral of Anthema, and several smaller remnants had been found over the years. As the Faith of the Four took form and spread, small shards would be cut from the Great Shard and could be found in their rightful place in the pendants of Parity that adorned the necks of all the faithful. What Vila did not know before was the supposed psychic and transformative powers that some radical historians believed were inherent in the lunar crystals.

"That can't be true," she said, making sure she was reading the scroll correctly. "Moon rock has existed on earth for centuries. Why have we never seen anything like this before?"

Temson leaned back in his chair and stared at the ceiling. His wine sat unattended on the smoothed wooden desk, and he looked exhausted. Vila knew she should be grateful that he was taking the time to help her, but she couldn't help but feel annoyance. He didn't know Rance; he barely went outside the chapel. None of this was his concern.

"I really don't know, Vila. We have some samples of different shards like the ones you brought, but they aren't common. Any speculation about magical properties is just that, speculation. Nothing has ever been proven, though we know there must be some innate magic in the shards, or Lunus and Celenia wouldn't have sent them down during the Great War."

"So, moon rocks have power, but are dormant."

"Supposedly. This is all guess work."

"Why now? What's activating them?"

Temson stood up and finally picked up his drink. "That's if they are actually activating. We don't really know anything, other than that there are some fish with strange growths on them." He swirled the contents around before throwing the whole cup back and reaching for the bottle to fill it again. Vila's hand shot out and held the bottle firm to the table, her green flecked eyes staring deep into his bright blues.

"Tell that to the Wardens."

"What?"

"The Wardens that are stalking around the planks. I told you when they arri—"

"I know they're here, but what does any of this have to do with them?"

Vila removed her hand from the bottle and fought the urge to touch the place where Augustan's steely grip had choked her mere hours before. Temson noticed her reluctance and his demeanor grew more concerned as he sat back down and placed a hand on her leg. The encounter shouldn't have shaken her as much as it did, but something about the White Warden made her shiver. Moon shards were only one part in all of this.

"I don't know exactly, but whatever concerns we have about the rocks, they seem to share as well. They...cornered me on the way here."

Temson shot up, his face flush with concern.

"Did they hurt you?"

"Yes," she said as his eyes grew wide with worry. "And they made it very clear they would do more if I talked to anyone about this. They seemed pretty concerned about what was happening, and they don't want word getting out until they get to the bottom of it."

Temson was now stalking about the room, hands behind his head as he tried in vain to contain his rage. Vila calmly watched him as she continued looking through the scrolls on the table.

"I can't believe they attacked you. Did you fight back? How many were there? I'll—"

"You'll what, Tem?" she asked, her face placid. Temson was a scholar, a priest, and a pacifist. For all his muscle and strength, Vila didn't believe there was a violent bone in his body. He knew that she knew it too, yet he continued to try to act like he could or would defend her if it came down to it; a circumstance that she would never allow.

"What are you going to do? Hunt down four Deep Wardens in the streets and tell them to back off? Don't be silly."

With his back to her he let out a few heavy breaths before responding. She could tell she'd offended him, but she didn't care. It was all talk and bluster, and didn't matter.

"They wouldn't hurt you if they knew who you were."

"Stop it."

"Who you really are."

Now Vila was getting angry. She didn't want to have this argument again, yet somehow it kept coming up and she was fucking tired of it.

"Don't. I don't want to do this again."

"If you just owned up to your name and—"

Temson tried to dodge the chalice that flew towards him but only managed to move enough so that it bounced off the back of his head instead of crashing fully into his face.

"I said stop! I can't own a name that was never given to me, and one that I have no fucking interest in having! It might mean a lot to you, but it doesn't mean anything to me!"

"Why not? Why can't you just accept it and live up to it instead of..."

Now he'd done it.

"Go ahead. Finish that sentence."

"Instead of...instead..."

Vila rose from her chair, her fists curling and opening as she let the fury seethe its way through her body. She felt heat burn through her neck and up behind her eyes.

"Instead of being a *whore*?"

"I didn't say that."

"Don't fucking lie. I know that's how you really feel, even if you don't. You don't think I see it every time we're in bed? How you struggle to keep images of other men out of your head, even while you're the one inside of me? What else can I say Temson? That I hate it? That I wish I didn't have to do it? Because I do! I fucking hate everything about it, but I'm stuck in this just as much as you're stuck in this stupid building!"

She was on him now, pushing him against the wall in her rage. "Do you love me, or my name? I only have that name because my father got some *whore* pregnant." She watched him flinch every time the word left her lips and she reveled in it even as she felt a pang of guilt at the words.

Temson didn't respond and he didn't look her in the eyes. He kept his head down with his hands limp at his sides. They'd both taken it too far, farther than it had gone before. It was an unspoken contention between them, but always just under the surface. He could never understand what she'd been through or the delicate balance she walked every day, and she didn't have the energy to make him. Some things were just too painful and complicated.

"I'm sorry," he said finally, his head still hung low.

Vila knew he meant it. He wasn't a good liar and rarely said things he didn't mean. It just didn't matter right now.

"I need to find out what is happening. Thank you for your help."

Vila snatched her cloak from the chair, scattering shards and scrolls as she moved in haste towards Hinaldo's door.

"I'm not coming back for a while."

"Vila, please!"

She opened the trap door and stared into his eyes as glistening tears started to appear, his grief becoming physical in a trickle of emotion that would soon become a flood. She didn't want to be there for that.

"For a while," she repeated. It was the best she could do as she slowly closed the door and let the darkness of the shaft surround her. She descended the metal rungs in silence, her sights stones bathing the world in red. Only when the door above was no longer visible in the dark did she allow herself to cry.

II

"Sea glass gets a lot of credit for the survival of the human race, but I think a special nod should be given to seaweed. That glorious flowing plant of many colors may not provide all the technological benefits and survival aspects of Fathus' gift, but without it we'd all be naked and sober. Put all the sea glass you want in a mug, and it still won't get you drunk like a good glass of kelp wine."
-Partha Clerin, local drunk-

J am Jam's was packed like a barrel of fish with barely an empty seat to be seen and many elbows jostling for space. The kelp wine tasted like piss soaked in saltwater, but it got the deed done as evidenced by the crowd of laughing, stumbling Plankers populating the small pub. Narrio munched on some clam fritters as he worked on his third glass. His foot tapped in time to the raucous sailor's song that was reaching its final verses.

Set sail me boys, set sail me boys. Set sail right out to the sea.

*Neither Heaven nor Hell shall we call
our home, but somewhere just right in
between.*

*Set sail me boys, set sail me boys. Set
sail right out to the sea.*

*The wind it is strong, and the journey
is long. Slaves to the water we'll be.*

The jaunty tune ended with a roar of applause as the room erupted in laughter and cheers. Narrio couldn't help from smiling at the drunken energy and was decidedly happy to enjoy himself for a bit; the owner, who was currently running the bar, wasn't unpleasant to look at either. The woman was not what Narrio was expecting with a name like Jam Jam. He wasn't exactly sure what he had been expecting, but he found her to be plump in all the right places, her wares advertised in glorious gratuity. He was just wondering if he could use his teeth to rip off her kelp fiber wraps that barely contained her busty figure when a sharp tap on his shoulder brought him back to the present. Renalia stood over him, dour as ever with an eyebrow cocked above her eyepatch. Her pursed lips told him she knew what was on his mind.

"Are you done?" she asked, her arms folded so tightly he thought she'd never be able to pry them apart.

"Ogling? Never."

"You're a pig."

"Never said I wasn't. Are you ready?"

Jam Jam bounced over with two more mugs of the piss drink and Narrio handed one to Renalia who reluctantly slammed it back and gestured for another.

"I'm going to need a lot more of that if I have to deal with you for much longer."

"And here I was thinking we were just starting to become friends," he pouted, puffing his lips out as far as he could.

He was about to get excited as her fingers clasped his chin, when he suddenly realized there was a knife pressing gently against his neck. She leaned in close to his ear, her perfume winding up towards his nostrils like little tendrils. Now he was really excited.

"Am I in trouble?"

"Just checking to see if your reflexes are as quick as your wits. I'm not impressed."

"There's better ways to flirt you know."

"How drunk are you?"

"How drunk are you?" He pressed the point of his gaff into her stomach, just enough to let her feel the pressure of the steel against her navel.

"Point taken," she said, the knife disappearing as quickly as it had come. She looked him over, the corner of her mouth twitching. He gave her a wink and popped another fritter between his lips.

"He's over there." Narrio gestured over to a corner booth where the provost sat with his feet on a table, wildly gesticulating while his companions added more empty mugs to an ever-growing pile.

"Let's get started then. Something tells me it's going to be a long night."

Narrio grabbed two more mugs and danced his way through the room.

"Mind if we join ya gents?" he proclaimed loudly as he slammed the splashing drinks on the table and grinned widely. "Always a pleasure to buy a drink for the good servants of the city."

The provost's eyes moved a little too slowly, but he responded in the affirmative, a stupid grin plastered to his face.

"Aye...mates..." he slurred, the words pouring out like mud from a boot. "Mah pleasure to...serve the good people...do I know ya?"

"Perpos. Perpos Terous." He waited as the joke fell on deaf ears, imagining Renalia's eye rolling. Narrio chuckled to himself and continued. "We met earlier this morning and you so kindly steered me to this fine establishment!"

The man stared at him with a genial look that told him he didn't remember a thing. He introduced the pair to his friends, names and faces that Narrio wouldn't remember and that didn't matter in the current situation. The thief had a fish to fry, and fish were always better when soaked in ale. He beckoned for a few more rounds and jumped into the raucous conversation.

"An thet's wen ah shat mahself!"

The group roared with laughter as Genario sat there with a dumbfounded expression on his face, his brain not comprehending what he said that was so funny. The night had rolled on and the lively pub was beginning to bleed patrons as heads hit the table and more glasses started to break.

"Ah did! I shat mahself!"

Narrio pulled the man's drink away as he wrapped an arm around his shoulder. Tears streamed down his cheeks, not all of them fake. "My friend, you are disgusting. I think our good public servant has had enough for the night, gents. Let my companion buy you all one more round and pay your tab for the evening. It would be our pleasure for giving us such a pleasant night."

Renalia gave him a look he didn't understand as she and the others stumbled away from the table and back up to the bar. She deftly shoved prying hands away from her as they walked and slammed a bag of glass on the counter. Genario was still rambling even as Narrio slipped the coralweed tincture into his beverage.

"Ah did...shat mahself ret in the foot. Bolt whent clehn thru..."

"I'm sure you did. Time to go, friend."

Hoisting the much larger man was no easy feat, and Narrio cursed his lean frame as he dragged the provost away from the table and out the back door, Renalia close on their heels.

The slap stung Narrio's hand and he hoped it hurt the bewildered provost more than himself. It did the job though, as the waking drunk snapped into consciousness with alarm. The poor man pissed himself and Narrio struggled to hold back his bile at the awful smell. Kelp wine stunk even worse when it came back out; and mixed with the blood all over the floor of the butcher's shop they now occupied, it was horrendous.

It wasn't a place he really wanted to be, but it was close by, and the owner apparently owed Renalia a favor. It was also terrifying. Oil lamps flickered from the ceiling and the grotesque bodies of skinned sharks and dolphins hung from large iron hooks, their shadows elongated and swaying. Just the mood he needed to scare the information out of the bound guard in front of him.

Narrio stood as erect as he could, trying to make his figure look as intimidating as possible. The over-large cloak he now wore was padded around the shoulders to give a broader, more square appearance and he made sure the hilt of his bone saber was clearly visible to the crying man. This wasn't his favorite thing to do, but the job had to be done and Narrio did love a good character.

"You piece of shit," he growled, hoping that all his preparation helped give his voice a lower and more gruff resonance. Several minutes had been spent yelling in the alley behind the butcher's shop to achieve peak gravel. Renalia had hated the idea.

"What's going on? Who are you?" the man blubbered. The red kelp tincture seemed to have done the trick, as Genario was much more coherent now. The chemicals in the kelp acted fast to stimulate the brain and provide alertness to the consumer. It worked a little slower after the amount of alcohol the provost had consumed, but three large helpings had finally done it and the man was now fully sober—and he looked scared shitless.

Narrio cocked his head to the side, a black mask completed his costume and hopefully provided the final horrifying touch he needed to yield the results he was after. Only his mouth was visible, and he bared his teeth in a gesture of menace.

"Did you think we wouldn't find out? How much are you getting paid to turn a blind eye?"

"Please...let me go..."

"I'll make a few things very clear," Narrio said as he turned a chair around and plopped himself before the man. His hands hung off the back of his perch and he picked at his fingernails with a knife, dangerously close to the man's dripping nose. "First of all, you don't get to walk out of here unless you answer our questions. Second, you don't walk out of here with all your fingers unless you answer our questions without lying."

Narrio dug a little too deep and had to hold his tongue as the knife bit under his nail and a slow trickle of blood started to ooze out over the blade. He kept his cool as the man's eyes widened further than he thought humanly possible. Narrio gritted his teeth through the pain, using the oopsie to instill a little more fear.

"Third, and this is the most important, we'll kill your lover. What was her name again?"

Renalia, who had been stalking in the darker corners of the room answered, her voice like a smooth blade slicing through the air with an eerie intensity. "Hemela. Hemela Faan. She lives on Hardrow Street with her mother."

"That's right. We'll kill Hemela. Probably her mother too; haven't decided yet. So, you think you're ready to answer some questions?"

Narrio hated watching the man cry; not because he felt any empathy, but because it slowed things down and made him feel awkward. He didn't blame the provost; he just didn't want to have to sit through it. He hoped this would go quickly.

"Who was the woman in the church this morning?"

"What?"

Narrio slapped him again to keep the momentum going.

"The red-haired woman." Narrio conjured up the shadowed woman in his mind, trying to focus on details. "With...blue tattoos. Leather bracer."

"I-I-"

"You know who she is, don't lie to me."

The man was positively shivering, but he answered, nonetheless.

"I-I don't know her name! She comes in sometimes and stays. I think she's a Blue Lady, but she keeps her ringlet tucked away."

"What's a Blue Lady doing in St. Trillian's chapel?" Renalia chimed in from over his shoulder. Narrio cocked his head towards her and remembered she couldn't see his raised eyebrow. He had an idea of what she was doing there, and it almost certainly involved the manly, bearded priest and his religious instruments. But Narrio had a more important question.

"Does she come back out?"

"I...I don't know."

"Try again."

"I don't know! We seal the doors after service, and she stays in there. She doesn't come out the front, that's all I know. There are provosts posted all night and day. I think she only comes during my shifts and I'm the head counter, so I flub the numbers."

"Why? She paying you?"

"...I..."

"She fucking you?"

"No! She...she's seen me down...you-you-know...down in the Lower Planks."

The pieces apparently clicked into place for Renalia. "At the brothels."

"Yes..."

Narrio continued his questioning. "And you don't want Henala—"

"Hemala," Renalia corrected him.

"—to find out, so you keep little miss red hair's secret and everyone's happy. Did I get that right?"

"Please, we're supposed to get married soon. Please don't tell her!"

Narrio rubbed his temples. He could feel the ache of sleeplessness gnawing at the back of his eyes, but they were starting to get somewhere. He wasn't sure where yet, but these were pieces he could use.

"Let's recap. Red goes in, you flub the numbers because you couldn't keep your dick in your pants, and you don't know where she goes."

"No idea."

"Why the secrecy? What is she hiding?"

"You seen her? She ain't in there for the sermon, that much I can tell you. That cleric in there ain't allowed visitors, or relations with visitors."

"Why not?"

"I don't know, been that way a long time. Clerics of St. Trillian's Chapel ain't allowed to leave neither, cept on special business. That's why us provosts are there. The church elders keep that place locked up tight."

"Except it isn't if she's able to leave. Anything else?"

"Please don't hurt me or my fiancé!"

"I think we're done here."

There was a sickening smack as Renalia's fist collided with the back of the man's head and he slumped down in what Narrio hoped (for his sake) was a dreamless slumber.

"Did we learn anything?" Renalia asked, cracking her knuckles as she began untying the unconscious provost.

"Of course! We know there is another way in and out of the church. Weren't you listening?"

"Don't patronize me. He didn't say that, he just didn't know where she goes. She could stay in there and come back out the next day."

"Doubtful. You think he's paying her?"

"The priest? Because she's a Blue Lady? Not everyone pays for sex, not that you would know."

"I've had some free sex in my day."

Renalia ignored the comment. "Why? Does it matter?"

"It could. Payment means it's a transaction. Otherwise, there's an emotional entanglement to exploit."

Renalia stared at him, her expressions hidden behind the painted mask. He couldn't tell if he had impressed her or disgusted her.

"Are we going to talk about how lucky you are?"

"Hmmm?" Narrio's brain was somewhere else now, thinking about entrances and exits.

"You walk into that church one time, and you see the shadow of some woman, make a hunch, and prove it right. No one is that lucky."

Narrio removed his mask and wiped the sweat through his hair as he smiled widely. "It's my luck stone," he said, holding up his hand as the light bounced off the green ring on his finger.

"What?"

"You don't have a luck stone? Glass enhanced with the magical juices of a sea slug under the full moon's light?"

Renalia's mask flew over his head, but as he ducked he caught the briefest glimpse of an upturned lip. He also noticed her eyepatch wasn't on. Renalia's cheeks reddened as he stared at the large scar where her left eye used to be. Embarrassed, she quickly slipped the patch back on.

"May I ask about it?"

"Diving accident."

"Why do you cover it up?"

"Drop it."

He did.

"Now what?" she asked, grabbing Genario's limp legs as Narrio wrapped his arms under the heavy man's pits. They slowly made their way to the back entrance to deposit the provost who would wake the next morning with a terrible hangover and more secrets to keep.

"Are you tired?"

"I'm not coming to bed with you, if that's what you're asking."

Narrio smirked. "Alright, well now that we've settled that; we need to find a library."

Renalia raised her eyebrow again, a move that Narrio was beginning to become attached to. "You like to read?"

"I've been known to," he said with mock hurt and a hand over his heart. "Our mysterious chapel has some secrets about it, and we need to dredge them up; specifically, any secret entrances that may or may not exist. Surely there's some blueprints somewhere."

Now it was Renalia's turn to give a sly smile. "I know just the place."

12

"I have inspected the structure and can, with full authority, say that St. Trillian's Chapel is as tight a fortress as any. Please report to the elders that they need not worry about waywards and deviants as long as they imbue a stronger sense of chastity and discipline amongst their acolytes and younger vestry. A building can be boarded up tight, but if the heart within is rotten then it will do no good."
~Simius Pelar, Chief Building Inspector for the Upper Planks~

The Society for Upper and Lower History and Archival Preservation sounded a lot more high-class and cleaner than it looked. It was made from three different shipwrecks of various time periods and styles, and the hulls were fused together with large iron plates. Wooden masts acted as angle braces, holding the whole structure upright. Unaltered sea glass rivulets dotted the building, securing the boards and supports in place. With the hulls stacked on top of each at odd angles, the whole structure towered above its neighboring buildings. The final touch was a large piece of muslin sail cloth hanging from a mast at the top of the building, and its corners were tied down with actual hemp rope. SULHAP was clearly painted on the sail for all to see and marvel at.

Narrio did marvel at it as he silently cut a pane out of a second 'story' window, but mostly because he thought there were better ways to preserve history than this. He did have to admit the structure was eye-catching, which made the precarious climb up the side to the second hull more interesting. The rain was pouring down and making the oil and grime-soaked planks slick. But the combination of rain and structural nonsense also made for a relatively easy and unnoticeable entrance. Slipping his hand in through the cut pane, he fumbled around until he found the lock and pulled the circular window open with a loud groan from the iron hinges. After waiting a breath, he didn't hear anything or see any movement. The coast was clear for entry.

"We could have come during the day like normal people," Renalia said quietly as she squeezed through the window and landed gracefully on the carpeted floor.

"You said that already and I said, one: that's not nearly as much fun, two: I don't want to wait until morning, and three: we don't want to draw attention from the scribes."

"I thought you said—"

"That was then. This is now."

Renalia rolled her eye. "You're right. This makes complete sense."

"I'm glad we agree."

Narrio pulled out a sight stone from his purse and slid it into the pocket lantern that hung from his belt as Renalia did the same. The vermilion light bounced off the small mirrors inside and cast a red hue about the room. It glowed soft and rich, but most importantly wouldn't attract too much attention if seen from a window.

The room was stuffed to the brim with kelp paper scrolls and seal leather books, the rickety built-in shelves overflowing with history. There was a mold and dust smell in the air, and it made Narrio wrinkle his nose. Renalia however took a deep breath and gave a satisfied sigh.

"I love this place."

"You do?"

"I used to come here all the time. I volunteer sometimes too, organizing and cleaning mostly." She leaned in close to his ear, the heat of her breath sending a shiver down his spine. "So don't break anything."

"Huh. A woman of true mystery. I've been in a few archives myself, you know."

"Thieving?"

"Of course."

"How closely am I going to have to watch you?"

"I'll be on my best behavior. Lead the way, we're looking for anything labeled 'church' or 'secret entrance'."

Renalia led them down the long winding hall and up to a ship's ladder that led into the next hull. Around every corner were more shelves full of tomes, scrolls, artifacts in glass cases, and artwork. Narrio briefly wondered how much everything in here would be worth, but quickly pushed the thought from his brain. He felt like he and his companion were just starting to get on good terms, and she seemed to be in her element here. In a strange moment of graciousness, he decided not to be selfish.

The floors seemed to move and shift as they walked carefully through the maze of pitch-covered wood and dusty piles of papers. The swaying became even more intense as they reached the base of the third hull, which stood completely vertical on top of the others. Narrio felt like he was back on the Swell as the structure groaned and creaked in the wind. He could hear the heavy rain spattering against the sides of the building and the constant shrill whistle as the wind continued to batter the weatherworn ropes. He pulled his cloak tighter around him to block out the chill.

"I have a question," he asked as he heaved himself up onto a scaffold, careful not to disturb the busts of Lunus and Celenia by the window. Renalia was moving slowly, running her hands along the spines of the brittle books but she cocked her ear towards him. "How did you end up with the...you know...the cult people."

"You have no idea who they are, do you?"

"I didn't ask, no."

"I can't tell you much, except their name and basic beliefs. They call themselves the Shepherds of the Earth. Religious zealots."

"What do they want?"

"They believe Loamia was the true goddess of the humans, and her death was a crime. I'm pretty sure they'd like to see her worshipped above all others."

Narrio stopped for a breath. "But she's dead. Right?"

"That's what makes it strange."

He rubbed a hand through his rain-soaked hair as Renalia clambered up the long final ladder to the top of the last ship.

"I don't usually question the motives of my hirers, but should I be concerned that they're gathering ancient artifacts and weapons?"

"Weapon?"

"The Terra Axe? Didn't they tell you what it was?"

"No, they only told me there was a stone and that it was important."

"Huh," he said as he scratched his head. "So I should question."

"You should always question, Narrio. Always."

"You said they. So, you're not one of them?"

"No."

"But you work for them."

The woman looked down at him, an expression passing over her face and good eye. It was hard to tell in the soft red glow, but he detected some...was it sadness? Regret? It passed just as quickly, and then she hopped up the last rungs and was out of view. "So do you now," she called down. "I work for a lot of people, gathering information and leading secret ventures into dark buildings." Her head appeared over the ledge and she winked at him as he shambled up after her.

Narrio let her pull him up into the final room, and Renalia began combing through the scrolls, her eyes wandering over the age worn labels as she searched. There was a lettering system on each of the shelves, but Narrio couldn't make heads or tails of it, and was very grateful that he happened to be partnered with a volunteer librarian.

"Here," she said, pulling a few scrolls out of the shelves and stacking them in his arms. "Take those to that table over there and I'll bring some more. This could take a while."

Narrio slipped a hand behind his cloak and pulled out two small bottles of kelp spirits he had filched from Jam Jam's. "Good thing I brought these."

"You're terrible," she said as he handed her a pair of small glasses that came with the bottles.

She returned his genuine smile as she poured herself a glass and went back to searching the shelves. Narrio began unrolling scrolls across the old ship captain's desk and settled in for a long night.

"Well, I'm tapped."

Narrio leaned back in his chair and stretched his back. The pile of papers and opened scrolls littered the table in a mess of fruitless searches and useless information. The two had spent hours poring over histories and schematics of the church; the only drawings that existed were an unremarkable floorplan with limited information and elevations showing the false roof extensions over the years and the foundation plan. As he had surmised, the entire base of the church was stone and held up by four large beams that descended into the Lower Planks.

No secret entrances, no cross-sections showing tunnels, noth-ing. There were some strange symbols of mountains and circles drawn off to the side on the floorplan parchments, but they meant nothing to either of them. The histories were equally unhelpful; the church was moved stone by stone onto the floating structure of the Planks as the water rose until the original building had been recreated in all its simple glory. Over time as the city began to sink lower, new structures were piled on top of old and the Lower Planks were born. The church stayed the one constant as the inner walls of the Lower Planks were built up around it, growing higher and higher over time.

There were also some official letters of complaint passed from the Planks to Anthema concerning a one Hinaldo Del'Sor and his lewd exploits involving church staff and artifacts. Renalia was nose deep in a scroll outlining the history of the once great family when Narrio rubbed his burning eyeballs.

"Anything?"

"There has to be something here." Renalia was leaning over the scrolls with an intensity that Narrio wished he could emulate. "The Del'Sors were connected to the church before the Swell, and stayed active in its preservation. One of them had to have known if there was a secret entrance."

"If anyone had one installed, this Hinaldo character definitely seems like our man."

"I agree, I'm just not seeing any reference to it."

"Did he have any children or relatives?"

"Why?"

"If there are any relations to the Del'Sors around, maybe they'd have some insight to the church?"

"I'm only seeing a reference to an Iltar Del'Sor, his great-grand-son. He disappeared years ago." She rolled up the scroll, her nose wrinkling in frustration. "I think the Del'Sors are a dead end."

Renalia pulled back from the table and took a long pull from the bottle. Her cheeks were beginning to flush from the drink and

Narrio had the sudden realization that she looked lovely in the rain-streaked moonlight.

"So, we have to find this woman, the mysterious Blue Lady from the Lower Planks," she said, leaning back against the opposite table. "You should probably take a look underneath the chapel too."

Narrio hesitated. He knew he'd have to end up down there. He just didn't want to.

"Something wrong?"

"...No. Just thinking. I guess...yes...I'll start exploring the Lower Planks tomorrow and see what I can dig up."

Renalia eyed him curiously. "I almost forgot." She reached into her pocket and pulled out a large blue coin. She held it out for him to see and Narrio marveled at the work. It seemed to be cut from a single large blue pearl, and it had the image of Fathus carved into it, although in a rather compromising position with some busty Oceanids. "Bilger's fare. Can't get down into the Lower Planks without it; at least not through any of the official entrances."

Narrio raised his eyebrow and flashed a grin. "You've been holding out on me." He reached out to take the coin, surprised when she pulled her hand back.

"Are you going to give it to me?"

"You don't want to go down there." It wasn't a question.

Narrio hesitated. "It doesn't have the greatest reputation. It also sounds dark."

"You poor thing," she chuckled as she took another sip of her spirits. "You're not afraid of the dark, are you?"

"Hardly," he laughed as he reached for the coin again. She moved around the table, her eye watching him playfully as she kept the coin out of his reach.

"This is fun," she smiled, her cheeks red from the drink. "I think I've got the edge on you now. Was your drink a little too strong?"

Without a word, Narrio propelled himself over the desk, crashing ungracefully into Renalia as they tumbled to the floor. They rolled over and she held the coin in front of his nose, laughing while she taunted him.

"You're going to have to earn this," she said, pulling herself up and backing towards the desk. Her chest heaved as she tossed a strand of hair from her face, her eye flickering in the low red light. Her mischievous grin returned, and Narrio's brain finally caught up.

"I didn't think you liked me very much," he said, moving closer and hoping he wasn't misreading the signs.

"Stop talking before I regret this." Her hands were suddenly on his collar, pulling him in sharply as she bumped against the desk.

Narrio felt the redness burn its way up his neck and into his cheeks as he lifted her onto the desk and spread her legs wide. His lips crashed hard against hers, her hands grasping at his pants as he took her chin in his hand. He felt her teeth bite down on his lip and he released a pleasured groan.

His tongue continued to explore her mouth as his fingers worked quickly to undo the small buttons made of bone on her blouse. The final button wouldn't budge, and Renalia gave an excited gasp as he ripped the shirt open, sending the problematic button flying and allowing her full breasts to burst out of their hold. Narrio grasped them and squeezed hard as she leaned her head back, letting him trace her neck and chest with his tongue. She moaned as his lips found her erect nipples and latched on. He sucked greedily as his tongue caressed her smooth skin and her hand finally found its way into his trousers. Her hand was eager as she gripped him but when she found it soft, she backed off.

"What?" she asked, her breathing heavy and jagged.

"I...I don't know...I..."

She was flustered for a moment but regained her composure quickly. "Is there anything I can I do?" Her lips dripped with seduction and invitation.

"Hit me."

Her eye flared but she didn't question him. She slapped his face with a startling and satisfying sting. He growled in pained pleasure as another hit came from the left, leaving his senses scattered and adrenaline coursing through his body. She ripped at his trousers again and his erection rose to attention. Renalia spit in her hand and gripped him, her fingers soft and wet against him as she began to pump. Narrio leaned his head back, moaning as she moved faster.

He gripped her thighs, working quickly to pull her trousers down around her ankles before lifting her off the table. She didn't say a word as he slowly approached her and stared at the space between her legs bared before him. She was dripping and Narrio almost couldn't contain himself as he aligned himself with her entrance.

Savoring the moment, he took her by the chin again and slipped a finger inside of her, feeling a delicious warmth and wetness as he began to thrust. Renalia shivered as he pumped harder, his cock twitching, longing to sink into her soft flesh.

She slapped him again, her hand crashing against his face in a violent expression of lust. A growl ripped free from his throat as he removed his finger, her liquid dripping off. Grasping her shoulders, he pushed her down onto the table scattering books and papers onto the floor. She kicked her legs up to rest her feet on the antique table, knees up and spread wide. Gripping her by the thighs, he finally thrust into her and the feeling of his cock sinking into her sent ripples of pleasure down his spine. She writhed against the table as he pumped faster, her hands grasping at his jacket and pulling his face down to hers until their mouths connected in a violent embrace.

They moved in tandem, their speed increasing as he thrust harder. He pushed in deep and felt her muscles start to clench around him. Narrio ignored the creaking of the table that increased with each thrust, scrolls and books lying forgotten on the floor while he was inside of her. The whole building seemed to move with their passion, the lanterns swinging in delight.

Narrio pulled back, watching her pout in disappointment, wanting him to reenter. He pulled a dense tome from the table and, lifting her once more, slid it under her arched back. He gasped in pleasure as she suddenly gripped his throat and he thrust into the hilt, her legs wrapping around his body in a tight embrace. He pulled back slightly and started pumping again, his speed increasing as her cries became louder and dust shook from the rotted rafters above them. He joined her, knowing he was getting close to release.

"I'm going to cum," he said, her hand still holding his throat as he thrust harder.

"Cum on my tits." Her face was red and her voice breathy. She tightened her grip on his throat and repeated the command. Narrio didn't need to be told twice. He pushed in harder and faster, sweat dripping down his face as he stared at her flushed cheeks and bouncing tits until the last second. Pulling out quickly, he grasped his cock, feeling her wetness still on him as he stroked. She slid off the table and dropped to her knees, squeezing her breasts together with one hand while she stroked fast circles against her clit with the other. She leaned her head back in preparation, moaning as she stared at him. Her fingers moved in faster circles as he stroked himself harder.

"I'm cumming," she said, her eye closing, lips parted as she moaned.

He let out a groan of pleasure as he climaxed, his cum bursting out in a hot spray and covering her bare chest in milky white. Renalia echoed his sounds, her body shaking as she finished. Narrio's own body shuddered as he continued stroking and Renalia groaned as she rubbed him into her tits, her eye closed in ecstatic letdown. Narrio continued to stroke himself as the hardness dissipated and he was completely spent. He bent down and gently gripped her chin again, pressing his tongue inside her mouth as she moaned.

"Don't get used to this," she gasped as he released her and pulled a rag from his pocket to wipe her clean. He gently pressed the towel against her skin and wiped her down until there wasn't a trace of their activities.

"Might be too late," he said with a smile and pulled her up from the ground. They locked lips again, her breasts pressing against his shirt as the rain continued to fall outside.

"I've always wanted to do it in here," she said as she pulled away and buttoned her top back up, letting it hang open from the missing button. She leaned back against the table and took a long swig of the spirits, trousers still off as Narrio stared at her.

"It's going to be light soon," she said, working to pull her outfit back together. Turning to him slowly, she let out a sly grin as she tossed him the coin. "At least if you die down there, you will have this to think about."

Narrio didn't laugh.

13

*"Upon closer inspection of the shards, it is my firm belief
that we should be studying them for their scientific uses and
properties. If divinely blessed sea glass can be altered for
varying purposes using alchemical science, then it would
stand to reason that these gifts from the moon could be used
in a similar fashion. I propose further studying of these celestial objects take place so we may better understand their
fundamentals and what the source behind their innate power
is that I believe exists."*
~A letter to the Patrons of the Upper Planks from
Malania Tortosfin, Head of the Astronomical Society
for Celestial Learning and Comprehension~

V ila pounded her fist against the flimsy driftwood door again,
worried about the silence inside. Rance hadn't met her at
the docks that morning and that wasn't like him. She had immediately run to his small hovel in the Rotwood district, an aptly
and insensitively named neighborhood, where his little abode was
suspended four levels up on the complicated scaffold structure of
the district. Rotwood and similar districts were full of the working-class citizens of the Upper Planks. While relatively better off

than those who lived in the Lower Planks, fisherman like Rance and the other hardworking people who kept this city alive would never experience the luxury of their betters. The dilapidated and rickety structures echoed this and served as a reminder of where Rotwood's denizens stood in the pecking order.

She knocked one more time, about to kick the door in when she heard a faint cough from inside and a shuffling of feet. After a long period of hacking and scraping, the latch finally clicked, and Vila pressed the door open to see her friend.

Rance hadn't ever had very much, and he had always struggled to keep his little shack clean, but Vila was taken aback by the state of his abode after just a few days. Rotted food lay on the table, and unwashed garments thick with salt and grime lay on the floor. And the smell. It smelled of all the worst things humans could excrete from their bodies, mixed with a strange mineral smell that Vila couldn't identify.

Rance had his back to her and was shuffling back towards his dirty bed, coughing loudly as she stepped into the room. He struggled to get back into his bed and Vila moved over to help him up, the smell getting worse as she neared him.

"Rance..."

"I ain't...feeling so good, Mistress."

"Fuck, Rance, I can see that! You should have sent for me. What is going on?"

She laid his head back on the pillow as he held his hand up for her to see. The hand that had been cut by the mysterious shards. The skin around the cuts had started to blacken and flake, and tiny shards of black crystals had begun to form in spreading circles just like the fish. The veins in both arms were protruding from his thin skin, and the blood looked dark. Vila had to choke back a cry when she looked into his face; his eyes were beginning to film over and more shards were beginning to gather around his tear ducts, poking through pores and growing around the veins in his neck.

They were extremely small, for now, and difficult to see if not looked for, but Vila knew what to look for—even if she didn't know exactly what she was looking at. She knew one thing for sure and it was that her friend was not well. Perhaps deathly ill, perhaps too far gone. A tear finally battled its way out of her eye and rolled down her cheek as she listened to his ragged breathing.

"Rance..." she said again, her words choking, "You're dying."

"I'm sick, I'm not dying," he coughed into his hand. It came back speckled with blood and black flecks. Vila grabbed his hand and stared at it. More shards, tiny shards. Vila ran outside with a pail she found by the bed and threw the stale, moldy contents over the rails of the scaffold, ignoring the startled cries from the people below. She filled it up at the common rain basin and brought it back inside.

"Have you seen a healer?" she asked him as she returned. Sitting him up, she forced a glass of water between his lips, and his mouth moved slowly as he tried to swallow.

"Can't...can't afford it."

"That's not an excuse. I'm going to get a healer and I'm paying for it. I want you to drink this and lay still."

"It really hurts..." There were pained tears in his eyes as well now and his voice croaked from the strain.

She squeezed his hand, careful to avoid the sharp crystals and unhealed cuts. "I know. I'm going to help."

First, she picked up some of the litter strewn about the house and emptied the waste pails down the sewage chute. Setting a pot of water to boil on his last smolder stone, she searched his pantry for food. She found some dried sea slugs and mashed them into a paste with boiling water before searching his single room for anything else that could help with the pain. Finding a small amount of red kelp, Vila crushed it up with the sea slugs into a gross looking mush. The stimulating toxins in the kelp would at least help him stay more alert, but only in small amounts. She brought the bowl of gruel over to him and forced a few spoonsful through his cracked lips, gently caressing his head and encouraging him as he swallowed.

"I'll be back, I'm going to go get you some help," she whispered as he finished the last bite.

"Thank you, Mistress..." Rance closed his eyes and Vila checked to make sure he was still breathing before she quietly got off the bed and left the old man to a fitful sleep. The floorboards creaked as she made her way to the door, but he didn't stir.

Waiting outside the door was Taragin Echilar.

He didn't move a muscle, but Vila felt a panic rise quickly in her chest and spread through her body in a violent storm. Her fists moved without being told and she was suddenly crashing into the Deep Warden, striking at vital points wherever she could. The armored and heavily armed Warden grunted in surprise, his arms working quickly to swat off the onslaught of fists and fury. Vila didn't give him time to pull out the deadly flail that lay strapped behind his gruesome cloak, her hits coming hard and fast from every angle.

"Stop! I'm not here to—"

He was cut off by a rough hit to the jaw and Vila saw blood spray from his mouth even as she continued to strike. Taragin whipped around quickly and grasped her incoming left hook, twisting hard to bring her to her knees. Before she could raise her other arm up to block, his meaty, leather-armored fist came crashing down, connecting with her temple. Her vision swam as he let her arm go and pushed her back roughly with his heavy ironclad boot. Vila convulsed on the ground as the black cloaked Warden took heavy steps towards her, the rickety scaffold vibrating with every step.

"Don't hit me again. I just want to talk." He spat on the ground, blood and drool mixing across his chin. With a breath his stance relaxed back to the pose of a silent predator ready to strike at any moment, calm and deadly.

Vila's head was still reeling from the punch, and she pulled herself backwards, trying to put some distance between them. She thought she could take him if she tried again, she just needed to learn his moves. He stood there silently, and she realized the best option was to hear him out. She lifted herself to her knees and waved a hand in gesture for him to continue.

"I'll get to the point quickly because I need you to listen and trust me. And I don't want to get hit again. I know your friend is dying, I know why he is dying, and I know who you are. I'm here to help."

Vila stared at the older man, his graying hair was tangled with dried seaweed and his face covered in scars of past battles. Despite his terrifying appearance and the deadliness that Vila knew lurked within him, his face was not unkind as he spoke. She could see the truth in his eyes as he pleaded with her. She got to her feet with caution and maintained a safe distance. Onlookers above and below moved on, trying not to act interested in the strange and violent meeting that had just occurred.

"Let's go through those one at a time, shall we? How do you know he's dying?"

"It doesn't take much to know. I've also been keeping an eye on him—and you. He's getting worse."

"It's some sort of moon rock. Why is it spreading like that?"

"It is, and I don't know. Moon shards are not new, but...what I'm about to tell you must stay between us. Please."

"I'm not promising anything because I don't trust you."

"Understood. So, I'll ask again and maybe after this conversation is over, you'll believe me."

When Vila didn't respond, he sighed and continued.

"Moon shards of varying colors and styles have been pulled up from the depths ever since the Great War. We know Lunus and Celenia used them to aid Fathus in his war. But the magic in them had gone inert, so as far as anyone knew they were harmless. Until recently."

"Why would they be inert for so long? Why now?"

"Did you see the great comet in the sky?"

"Yes."

"Ever since that first comet fell, smaller moon shards found across the waters have started acting strange. Glowing, emitting strange energies, growing. But only when near a larger source of celestial energy."

"But that was nowhere near here."

"We think the smaller shards draw their energy from bigger rocks and that those were activated when the great comet entered the atmosphere. That's why we are here; we believe there is a large rock, shard, whatever you want to call it, somewhere in this city. And we think someone has it and plans to use it."

Vila joined her hands behind her head as she paced. The on-slaught of information was doing nothing to help her still ringing ears.

"Who has it? What are they going to do with it?" She hated having to ask so many questions, to feel like she had no grasp on the situation.

"I don't know that yet. But whatever it is, it won't be good. Those shards are dangerous, and anyone who is harvesting them either doesn't know about it or doesn't care. We have to find out who has the shard and what their plan with it is. Something big is happening. The skies are not well and it's affecting the waters—and all of us who live in them."

He stared at her, his slate eyes glistening with sincerity. She believed him, and it scared her to her core as she thought about Rance lying there, infected. She turned her head towards the door.

"What can we do for him?"

Taragin looked genuinely sad. "I don't know yet. But finding the source of the power is a start." He pulled a hand through his curly hair and gave a deep sigh. "But we can't tell anyone."

Vila's head whipped back around, anger flashing across her face. "You said that last time—"

"And we meant it. We will help him, but if word of his predica-ment gets out, it's going to cause a panic that we can't contain. We have to work quietly to help him and any others who are being affected."

"I don't trust you and I especially don't trust your captain."

"Tempé doesn't represent all the Wardens. He was wrong, but he was also right that this needs to be handled delicately and quietly." He took a cautious step forward. "Please. Vila..."

Vila flinched at the use of her first name, a name he shouldn't know. She knew what was coming. She didn't know how, but a hollow feeling deep inside her told her what the next words out of his mouth were going to be; she wanted to run. She wanted to hit him, smash his mouth in before the words could come out.

"I know who you are, I know your true name."

Vila was shaking.

"And I know you've probably run from it your entire life. But you're a Del'Sor and there's power behind that name..."

Vila wanted to scream at him. She wanted to throw herself off the balcony and be done with this. "You don't know me..."

"No, I don't. But I knew your father. I see him in you."

Vila clenched her fists so tight she could feel the blood well up from the unhealed cuts on her palms. Her father. Iltar. A man she'd never known yet yearned to know more about. And now here was Taragin Echilar, Warden of the Deep, claiming to have the missing pieces of her life; claiming to know her.

"Don't you dare try to emotionally manipulate me."

"I'm not. I promise. Iltar Del'Sor was my friend, a true friend. I knew him better than almost anyone else and his death pained me to no end. I was there when you were born, I knew your mother..."

Now Vila was very angry. Her lost relationship with her father was a source of hurt; her existing relationship with her mother was one of fury.

"Get out."

"Please..."

"Get the fuck out. I'll do this on my own. I don't need your help; I don't want your help."

Taragin was silent for a few moments, and it looked like he might leave. But just as he started to turn, he looked her in the eyes again. "I know you don't want to face this, but your friend still needs saving. I know where the moon shards are—the ones that are causing this."

He turned and began to walk away. As he did, he called back over his shoulder. "Meet me down below tonight, by the Pillars. Tenth hour. If you want to help him, I'll be there waiting for you."

Then Taragin Echilar launched himself over the railing and down four stories of scaffolding before landing with a heavy thud and disappearing into the shadows.

Vila wanted to scream, but she settled for a loud curse as she slammed her fist into the supports of the old, rickety scaffold; dust and debris showered over her, and the structure shook with her rage.

14

"Rest assured, the filth and vermin that call that cesspool their home would love nothing more than to rid the good Upper citizens of their jobs, wives, and all good things that come with civilization. That's why it is imperative that all undocumented passages to the Lower Planks be found and secured. The good people of the Upper Planks shouldn't suffer because the dredge below them was allowed to seep up to the surface.

Thus, I am proposing the "Lower Lockdown Initiative" to finally solve the problem. Using a method known as Bilger's Fare, we can assure that those who live below stay below and our upstanding citizens may still access the few benefits that exist within the god-forsaken hole."

~Upper Patron, Lanatar Ganas to the Council of Patrons~

N arrio had made up his mind about the Lower Planks mere moments into his venture; he hated it.

It was difficult to tell exactly how far he had gone down as the levels, ladders, and makeshift platforms all wove on top of each other in a chaotic fashion. One moment he thought he was going down, the next he was higher than he had been before. And then a steep ramp would take him back down three levels. The path was at least marked, so Narrio felt like he could find his way back up to the Crusted Whale when he was ready, if he paid attention.

What was really bothering him was the ever-present sound of the ocean droning outside the walls. Even nowhere near the exterior shell, he felt he could hear it groaning, like some great sea beast ready to attack. It could have been a sea beast for all he knew. It seemed as if every cross brace and floorboard was creaking at different tempos, a constant chorus of stress as the under structure shifted in the water. He already longed for the incessant whistling of the ropes in the Upper Planks; anything would be better than the deep sense of dread and claustrophobia that was threatening to crush his spirits as he continued his descent.

The whole structure was in constant motion, a nearby gap between boards providing frightening evidence of the fact as it shrunk and grew right before his eyes, and creating the sickening feeling of being inside the bowels of some living creature.

If there had been any other option, he would have avoided the Lower Planks altogether. But after the (mostly) fruitless night in the archives, he felt like they had come up with very little information other than hunches. The church was a sealed tomb, locked up tight from the inside with only one cleric who held the key. All of that left Narrio with no choice but to suck down as many drinks as needed to bolster his confidence and head into Hell.

He'd showed the blue coin in his pocket to Mathanar, the proprietor of the Crusted Whale, who'd supplied him with a signalman's lamp, some food, and a skin of drift beer. He told the thief he had twelve hours down there before he needed to check back in (and the man charged his customary and weighty hundred glass keeper's fee for the service). Mathanar marked down the number that was inscribed on the back of the coin in a notebook. If Narrio wasn't back in time, then the coin would be considered retired and the owner most likely dead. If the coin showed back up in circulation, it wouldn't be accepted.

He'd explained that it would then be sent off to get retooled and given a new number that would be distributed to all proprietors of passage to the Lower Planks. Only if he came back with the coin, could it be sold to someone else, and then they would be allowed to use it. He also had to come back up the same entrance.

It seemed Bilger's Fare was a fairly tight system that allowed for tracking of who came and went and for keeping tabs on forgeries. Of course, there were most likely other ways down into the Lower Planks, but Renalia warned him that if you weren't a permanent resident or didn't have Bilger's Fare, the way down was much more dangerous, and you were more likely to disappear than anything else.

Also, anyone who came out of an official exit without Bilger's Fare was immediately arrested, questioned, and given a hefty fine—at the minimum. Most people were deported back down below. It seemed to Narrio that the city, and a few fortunate business owners, had found some decent monetary value to the Lower Planks, and it explained a little more as to why it was allowed to exist.

The coin also provided a small chance of safety while exploring below. Showing the blue coin down in the lower levels usually kept people alive, seeing as how killing the bearer or stealing the fare wouldn't give anyone any benefit. Show your coin, and you may get kidnapped instead of killed. Hostage situations and ransoms to rich families were apparently common and that information only made Narrio feel slightly better; Renalia had not confirmed if she would pay his ransom.

So he had descended into the bowels of the oldest city on the water to continue what he hoped wasn't a fruitless quest to find a way into the church. When he had left the safety of the Upper Planks, the sun had been high, probably a little after midday. But as soon as he'd gone below, it became impossible to tell time by anything other than his timepiece. Passageways would shift from dim to dark to pitch black depending on where the lamps had been placed. There was no sign of any sunlight leaking through, due to the thick layers of pitch and coralcrete plaster that lined the substructure of the city above. And it didn't take long for the supports and beams of the city planks to completely disappear as the architecture of the Lower Planks, which somehow had even less order than above, swallowed up everything in sight.

Narrio checked to make sure he had enough life in his timepiece from the charge stone inside. Based on experience, he would need to replace it every eight hours, meaning he only had four hours left on this stone and only two spares. Charge stones ran at a high price that was seemingly increasing, and he hoped he wouldn't need many more as it could start to impact his fun money.

It was the tenth hour of the morning and he had to be topside by the ninth hour that night. He was hopeful he wouldn't be spending a whole day down here searching for that entrance, but Narrio had come to learn that whatever the worst outcomes you could possibly expect were, would mostly likely be the ones to come true. Renalia had graciously left this task to him, mumbling about some other important thing she had to do. Probably sleep, seeing as neither had gotten very much of it the night before.

He wanted to sleep too, but her job was to give him assistance and his job was to get the stone; clearly, she didn't feel like he needed her assistance in this. She might have been right, but he could have used the company; every step he took that led him lower into the bowels made his skin crawl and his stomach do somersaults as he thought about the threatening presence of the Swell that pressed in all around him. He needed to get this done as quickly as he could for his own sanity, and so he really hoped his hunch about a secret entrance was correct.

The fact that a whole second society existed right under the feet of the Upper Planks gave him that hope. There was a half dozen entrances to the lower planks via establishments that used the Bilger's Fare method and he had heard that there were plenty more unofficial entrances. How could there not be, as sprawling and maze-like as this place was? If he was a priest at that chapel, he most certainly would have found himself an alternative route to escape for some fun.

He was hesitant to stray from the marked path, but even if he had wanted to it was nearly impossible to tell where you were or where you were going as it was. Scaffolds ended in sharp drop-offs, ladders stopped at the boards above, or veered off in wild directions over open pits. He was constantly finding paths blocked by massive pieces of wreckage or patched over with hardened sailcloth and coralcrete. It was truly a nightmare of construction and until he could get a sense of where he was, it wasn't feasible to go wandering just yet.

He encountered very few others on the way down, although there were some tell-tale signs of life. A few broken hulls had makeshift doors on them with oil lanterns outside in some bizarre replication of a townhouse and he could hear noises coming from the inside as he passed. He even caught one couple engaging in lewd activities behind an old sailcloth, their moans mixing in with the oppressive drone of the ocean outside. Neither one stopped what they were doing when he stumbled upon them, so he let them be and moved on.

There was also an abundance of other life down here in the form of crabs and rats; the biggest rats Narrio had ever seen in his life. About halfway down, or at least what he could guess was halfway, a rat the size of a small bluefin ran across his feet and gave him such a start that he nearly fell off the open-sided platform he was climbing. He watched it scurry away before being leapt upon by some vagrant hiding in the shadows who skewered the creature with a rusty lance. The man looked over at him, almost daring him to take his meal. Narrio just tipped his tricorn as the revolting person snatched up the still wriggling rat and scurried back off into the darkness. The thief could hear squeals and the ripping of flesh, so apparently cooking the animal or even killing it first wasn't a priority. Disgusted, he picked up the pace.

He continued through the dark passages of ship's hulls and collapsed floorboards, traveling lower and lower until he saw something that caught his eye off to the left above him.

Stone.

Looming down from above was the foundation of the church, floating in the air and covered in mold and rot. Holding the foundation up, were four massive posts made from intertwined ships masts, one on each corner of the foundation. The middle of the structure was braced by large joists of rotted wood, resting on the rickety scaffold structure all around him. There was no other part of the path that touched the church foundation. He must have wandered into the center of the Planks, but it didn't offer him any other clues.

His path veered off in all directions with ladders, scaffolds, and shipwrecks colliding into each other and creating numerous ways around the foundation. Carefully marking where he was, he ventured off the trail and began clambering around the wreckage, looking for any signs of an entrance.

Every stone was a massive piece of green granite, carved up from some ancient quarry before the wet days. Smoothed from age and the slow drip of water that found its way down from leaky rain basins. Try as he might, he couldn't find anywhere that got him close enough to touch the church and examine the stones with his hands.

Even the giant support beams were out of reach; the only access were the rotting joists, and Narrio didn't want to test their strength. If there was a way in, it wasn't from up here, which really boggled his mind. He circled and circled, looking for anything he could: symbols, markings, hinges. He came up short every time until he couldn't stare at the green rock anymore. Giving up, he wandered back to the path that led ever down and continued his trek to the bottom, hoping he could think of something on the way.

After what felt like an eternity, Narrio finally reached the bottom of the Lower Planks. Well, at least, he was pretty sure he had because the boards had finally leveled out, somewhat, and there were no more ramps to descend. It was still claustrophobic, and the droning of the ocean was now emanating from below his feet which was petrifying. He closed his eyes to quell the sickening feeling in his gut, taking deep breaths to calm the nerves.

There were more lamps now and he had to wonder who in the hell lit all these, and how they managed to keep the place from burning to the ground. Did some poor soul have the job of lighting and maintaining all the lanterns in this place, or did some random passerby take it upon themselves? He found himself more confounded with every moment he stood still and started to move, desperate to spend as little time down here as he could.

After another a few minutes' walk, the air finally grew less stale and Narrio passed through several layers of sailcloth to find a delightful sight. The imposing structures and cramped spaces had given way to an enormous chamber that was ringed with makeshift buildings, bright lighting, and bustling with activity. This was clearly the epicenter of the Lower Planks; the hub of business and livelihood and it was the most beautiful thing he had ever seen when compared to the dismal trek he had just taken. Narrio almost cried but held himself together.

His timepiece indicated that it was almost the thirteenth hour. He had spent three hours wandering down here. At least he now knew the path and was confident he could make the next trip quicker if it came to it. He was already exhausted both physically and mentally, so he decided the best thing he could do was get more drunk, and a lovely nearby establishment named the Pissing Squid looked like it would do the job. He ordered three mugs of drift beer, sat himself down to rest and settled in to people watch.

He was quite amazed at how lively it was which almost helped him forget that he was ten fathoms below the surface. Almost. There was a constant, not-so-subtle motion to the entire structure that kept him from getting too comfortable. Even with all the noise, he could still hear the boards creaking and shifting as the water outside looked for a way in.

There were a plethora of restaurants, pubs and other business that seemed to be thriving in this hidden world. He noticed a few individuals wearing Bilger's Fare around their neck, advertising that they had bought their way down here. To Narrio, it just seemed like a good way to get robbed. Sure, they might leave the coin alone, but generally those coins and the passing fee were pricey so all it really did was tell people you had expendable cash to throw around. He kept his tucked away in his pocket and only intended to take it out if necessary.

There were also plenty of black-market goods to go around, with several merchants offering illegal wares, or at least illegally obtained wares. More dangerous varieties of altered glass, trick weapons like his telescopic gaff and even one merchant hawking what they claimed to be the blood of a Deep One. The merchant said it could cure all illness, miraculously heal all wounds, and provide the temporary ability to live underwater. He had his doubts as to the stuff's legitimacy, and he definitely didn't want to know how it had been acquired. At a high price of one thousand glass per vial, he wasn't about to find out.

Every structure in the square seemed to be made from some ruined hull of a shipwreck or the crushed remains of buildings that had sunk from the Upper Planks, doomed to live a new life below. Old sail cloths created passageways while endless alleys could be found through the winding openings between wreckage. Everything was wet too, either from the condensation coming from the freezing seawater beyond or the constant drips from leaky rain basins above.

Bordering the square of activity were the four massive columns made from ship masts tied together with hemp rope and held in place with large sea glass bolts. Narrio pulled out the sketch he'd made of the Lower Planks in the archives, referencing the columns in his drawing. The Pillars of the World: the huge beams that acted as support for the church foundation far above. And for the rest of the planks apparently, if the myriad supports and joists that spread off each beam were anything to go by.

So, the church was directly above him. Narrio casually drained his first beer and looked around above his head. Even in this larger space, he couldn't see past all the wreckage and scaffolding. Wherever the stone foundation of the church was, he couldn't see it from here.

How does one enter a stone foundation you can't get to? The only structures in direct contact with the church foundation were the columns. No one was climbing up the pillars from down here and it was nearly impossible to get to them from up at the base of the church. Narrio stared at the drawing, his mind working to find some sort of clue or answer to the riddle.

Columns.
Stone foundation.
Secret entrance.
Symbols.
Del'Sor.

Narrio continued to stare at the columns while he drained his second cup. Four columns, made up of ruined ship's masts. Tied together. Supporting the church foundation. Cut into the joists. All the same size.

No, not all the same size. One of them was bigger. It also didn't land visibly in the square. He stared at the column, his thoughts working against the mind-numbing effects of the alcohol and then they stopped all together when a stupendously stupid idea occurred to him. Most people would ignore them, but Narrio had found that the dumbest things were usually true and often correct. The thief slammed back his final drink and casually rushed towards the port-most column, unsure if he was wobbling from the stiff beer or the soft boards.

The base of the column disappeared far past the bustling hub of the square and into an unlit mass of ships hulls and wreckage. The looming heaps of rotted wood and jagged metal looking like skeletons of colossal sea-faring monsters. Narrio trailed it into the darkness, pulling out his sight stone and checking to make sure he wasn't being followed. The ground became spongier as he went, ruining all the alcohol's work on making him forget where he was. He had no idea if he could fall straight through and into the never-ending depths of the swell, but he sure as hell didn't want to find out. He had to duck more often than not and at one point found himself crawling through muck and under rotted sail cloths to find a path. Until he finally reached the base of the column.

He carefully examined the structure in front of him, working to recreate the image of the others in his mind. This one was bigger. Not by much, the difference had been invisible up at the foundation, but down here it was noticeably so, signifying...what?

Then he saw it; a small symbol carved into the base of the mast. Two triangle peaks, holding up four circles. Narrio thought they looked like breasts, and he stifled a giggle. He also stifled a yell of success as he held the old parchment up to the symbol; the two were identical. He'd bet all his earnings it had something to do with the Del'Sors, and he'd bet a lot more that this was old Hinaldo's secret way into some parish promiscuity.

Imagining he was sliding his hands around Renalia's tight undergarments looking for clasps and strings, Narrio gently caressed the wood and let his fingers travel around the soft grains and rotted ropes tying the bundle together. Again, he found no signs of hinges or latches or pivots. Nothing to signify a door of any kind. He let out a curse. This was it, it had to be, but he couldn't see a way in. He stepped back for a better view, wondering if one really could climb all the way u—

His leg dropped sharply beneath him, and he found himself scrambling for purchase on the rotting planks as his lower body was suddenly immersed in freezing, black water. He started to panic and would have succumbed to hysteria if not for the sudden red glow of vermilion light peeking through a crack in the column. It was hollow.

Kicking and pulling, he managed to wrench his body out of the unexpected hole he was in and dashed towards the column, his boots squelching and his body shivering from the sudden cold. The light was gone, but he was certain he had seen it. Something was in there. Something had been casting a red light. He looked around, desperate to find the source.

The answer made his heart sink as he slowly turned towards the gap in the wood below him, and the pitch black, filthy water staring at him like the dead eye of some ocean hell beast. Narrio had never believed in ghosts or spirits, but if he did, he was sure that Hinaldo the Iniquitous was laughing at the irony of the situation.

As cautiously as he could, Narrio removed his sight stone lantern from his belt, gripped it tight, and slowly dipped his hand into the water, turning the light down and towards the column. The faint glow of the sight stone appeared in the cracks again and he was both elated and mortified.

He'd found the way up, of that much, he was sure. It just happened to be through a twenty-span swim in the darkest and coldest water Narrio had ever encountered in his life. It wasn't the Swell, which made him feel a little better. It had to be some sort of ponor or understructure lake before the actual bottom of the Lower Planks. Maybe even a sewage line, judging from the smell.

Fuck. Me.

15

"I'd like to be an Oceanid. I think it would be neat."
~A little girl~

V ila stood on the edge of the dock staring down into the depths below her as ships came and went from the city. She watched the dark waters churn and smash against the barnacle crusted supports and cross braces below, feeling each impact of the waves in her bones. She imagined herself as those rotted pieces of wood; feeling the cold fist of water hit again and again, weathering and deteriorating over time with no recourse. She thought of Rance and how helpless he looked on that bed, his body slowly dying. She felt equally as helpless as him, as the wood below her being slowly stripped by the waves.

Taragin's words had shaken her to her core, and she tried to shake the feeling of insecurity that was quickly rising. Only two other people knew who she really was; one of them worshipped her for it, loved her for it. For the other, it meant nothing; just the name belonging to a distant memory and a night that ended with an unwanted child.

Now, Taragin made three, and his presence brought up all the pain and questions that she had lived with her entire life and had worked desperately to quell each day. Questions about her father; what he was like, and why he wasn't here anymore. Questions her mother would never answer. She rubbed her hand along the metal cast on her bracer, her fingers gently touching the smooth alloy mountains and the four sea glass stones above. She could almost feel the power in the stones, the energy thrumming through the leather and into her veins as they seemed to glow brighter with her touch. In the dusky light, they gave off their own ethereal light, more so than the stones in her mask, and somehow both cool to the touch but hot at the same time.

She could almost hear the water calling to her as she brushed the stones, listening to the crashing waves whisper her name. The seas were darkening in the dying light and another storm was moving fast on the horizon. Vila pulled her diving mask from her belt and shook the kelp fiber long-cloak from her shoulders. Things were moving out of her grasp, swirling around her in a riotous movement of inescapable chaos and she needed to gain control; regain the sense of self that came with freedom of choice. That's what the water offered her, the ability to live or die by her own skills and tenacity. Control in the chaos.

She stretched her muscled and scarred arms, the sting of rain beginning its dance upon her skin. Her blue tattoos shone in the purple light of the coming storm, and she closed her eyes, catching some of the nourishing water on her tongue.

"Miss! Miss!" she heard someone yell behind her, the voice distant in the growing downpour. She looked back and saw a dock worker waving his arms at her, gesturing wildly at the lightning in the clouds.

"Storm's coming! You need to get off the docks!"

Vila smiled at him as she slipped the mask over her face. "I am," she said quietly to herself. Ignoring his shocked look and cries of anguish, she picked up her fishing lance and took a running leap off the docks, diving headfirst into the icy depths below.

She had never braved the Swell in the dark hours, during a storm, or without a rope around her waist, for that matter; but the feeling of complete freedom and recklessness sent a surge of exhilaration through her body as she breathed in the warmed air through her mask. She went lower and lower, feeling the pressure stone perform its magic with violent pops that swept through her like a shockwave. She pushed hard, moving faster than she ever had before and the pressure stone was struggling to work fast enough against the immense grip of the ocean around her. She hadn't checked a timepiece before diving in, so she had no one to tell her when her air would be running out; and she didn't care. She needed to be down here, alone, and untethered. No one could touch her down here, no one could direct her life or pull her into tangled webs. Just her and the deep.

She could choose what path she took, what she would be; the hunter or the hunted, and tonight she chose the hunter.

She finally slowed her descent and twisted herself upright to look at where she had come from. Far above, she could see the dark shape of the Planks. The tiny glow of the stones that helped keep it afloat were distant and faint, flickering every now and then as the ocean currents swept debris and darkness through her vision. Lightning flashes crackled far above and silhouetted the beastly city in an eerie, electric glow. From this distance it looked less like her city and more like a behemoth of the deep. A Deep One made of wood and coral and sin. She could see the harsh movement in the water as the storm went about its task, sending waves crashing against the bulwarks.

Down here the waves couldn't touch her or move her, not like above. She floated in the dark, feeling gentle currents move past her, trying to pull her further in. She pushed back against them, forcing herself into a stasis. There were no merchant lords or Deep Wardens down here trying to drag her into their schemes. No transactions or payments. No moon rocks or the slow creep of death. Not here—down here she was death, the bringer of pain.

Vila pulled the bandage off her hand and looked at the tiny cuts that marred her skin in the red glow of her sight stone. Unlike Rance, there were no crystals growing, no signs of the sickness that was taking him. She didn't know why, and it brought a surge of anger to her. Why him? Why not her? She'd give anything to trade places with him, to make it go away.

She couldn't do anything about it, but she could hunt.

Flexing her hand, she worked to reopen the scabbing wounds, letting the blood flow. It leaked out slowly, but it wasn't enough. She needed more, enough to tempt her prey. She brought the blade of her lance close, bracing herself and gripping the blade tightly. With a quick jerk and a muffled grunt, the deed was done, and her red life source flowed out into the inky ocean. The ver-million glow from her sight stone reflected against the deep red of her spreading blood, the suspended scene almost eerie.

Now she waited.

Every nerve in her body tingled with tension as she floated in the dark, but she willed her body into stillness as she searched for signs of movement with her eyes and felt for them with her body. Her injuries and bruises reveled in the chill of the water, grateful for relief. Blood continued to leak from her hand, and Vila knew that she would need to reapply the bandage soon if she wanted to be strong enough. The blue light of her air stone was dimming, and she could feel the air getting thinner. All the stones were losing their charge and would need to be replaced. Soon, she would be forced back up to the safety of the city, but she stayed still, pushing it as far as she could. She wasn't done, not yet. She needed this, needed to have this moment of danger to herself.

She felt the movement in the water right before the terror that she had sought materialized out of the dark, just barely illuminated by the dying light of her sight stone. She released a silent scream into the deep as a mouth full of razor-sharp teeth emerged from the deep and sped towards her, muscles rippling and ready for a violent embrace of blood and flesh.

Vila jerked wildly as the massive shape of the white-shark sped past her, its fin smacking against her legs and sending her careening out of control. She spun in a panicked fervor of adrenaline, and for a terrifying moment she couldn't tell which way was up or down. The waters moved past her, pushing her, and spinning her until she felt them change again and knew the beast was coming back around. She wrenched her body, feeling a pop in her back from the violent effort and winced as pain shot through her spine. She ignored it and swept her lance through the water as the maw opened before her again and the predator surged towards her, hungry and deranged with the smell of blood.

Her lance connected briefly, and she kicked herself up, her muscles screaming from the effort of movement and the drag of the lance on hardened skin. The water warmed with blood, the lance having made a mark, but it wasn't enough. She felt teeth graze her leg and her own blood mixed with the shark's, worsening the already limited visibility. A dank taste of iron coursed through her air stone.

The monster disappeared into the blackness again and Vila became aware of just how thin the air in her stone had become and she felt a growing pressure in her ears. Her limbs were moving slower from the cold, and she could no longer see anything—her stones were nearly completely dead. The panic set in now, punching her in the gut like an iron fist and forcing her into a terrifying sprint for the surface. She ignored the pulsing pain in her leg and back and ribs and everywhere, kicking and thrashing wildly towards the surface. The surface wasn't visible, and she had no way of knowing how far down she was.

Vila tried to hold her breath longer and longer as she pushed herself to the breaking point, desperately trying to conserve whatever air was left. Her head was pounding and the endless dark in front of her gave no sign of relief.

The beast was below her, somewhere, speeding towards its wounded prey; the stupid, foolish prey that thought it could tame the wilds of the deep and become its master. Vila cursed herself as she pulled at the water, her muscles screaming in protest.

She saw a distant flash above her from the far away surface, and in it she glimpsed a brief silhouette of a black cloaked figure careening towards her through the water.

Before she could process it, the flash was gone and a massive jaw crashed against her body, ripping her flesh as everything went completely black.

"You are unbelievably stupid."

Vila blinked, her vision was blurry as she opened her eyes to reveal the haggard and bloody face of Taragin Echilar kneeling over her. She thrashed in panic, her mind trying to catch up and assure her she was safe. Taragin's strong but gentle hand gripped her shoulder, holding her still.

"You're safe. Unfathomably stupid, but safe. Drink this."

Without waiting for her to agree, he forced the opening of a container between her lips and made her choke down some vile mixture that felt thick in her mouth and burned its way down her throat. Pain racked her body, but she could feel it dissipating, even as she choked down whatever substance he had given her. She coughed violently and pulled herself up, feeling tightness in her back and a screaming pain in her legs and arm.

The panic threatened to take hold again as she looked at the ruined mess that was her leg. Monstrous gashes riddled her calf and exposed the muscle beneath the flesh. The dock was slick with gore and Taragin was ripping pieces of cloth with a fervor, working quickly to stop the blood.

"Am...am I going to lose it?" she asked, her voice coming out in a breathless gasp.

"No."

Vila laid her head back down and looked up at the sky, the terror still rushing through every fiber of her being and making her feel violently ill. The lightning was still crackling in the sky, and she closed her eyes as the rain spattered over her. Compared to the icy water she had just escaped from, the rain felt warm and soothing, giving her a needed sense of calm.

She was laying on the docks, the storm sweeping in, yet Taragin didn't seem to care as the winds rustled his graying hair and lightning flashed through the clouds. She most certainly didn't care either, taking in deep breaths of the salty air to calm her nerves.

"What did you give me?"

Taragin finished his work and wiped a gore covered hand across his brow, streaking his hair in crimson and making his grim face all the more threatening.

"The only thing that's going to save your life and let you return to whatever stupidity drove you down there in the first place."

"I needed...I needed to."

The older man sat back and let out an exasperated sigh.

"I'm not going to try to understand, because I won't. You'll live and, in a few hours, you'll be walking with very little pain. You need to take more doses over the next few hours, and the scars won't be pretty. But you seem to be no stranger to those."

Vila sat herself up again, the pain already beginning to feel less intense; still there but diminished.

"How?"

When he didn't answer, Vila leaned in closer and asked again. She wasn't taking anything again until she knew what it was. "What. Did. You. Give. Me?"

Taragin's eye twitched, as if considering whether giving up Deep Warden secrets would be acceptable.

"Blood of a Deep One," he finally said, the words hushed.

Vila stared at him, waiting for him to smile and say he was joking, which he didn't.

"You're lying. That stuff is all just squid ink and ocean goo thrown in a bottle to pull some extra coin out of everyone's pockets."

Now he smiled, a small lift on one side of the mouth that didn't quite meet his eyes.

"All falsities have a source of truth. There's a lot of benefits to being a Warden; access to the deeper powers of the ocean is just one of them."

"Whose was it?" Vila ran through the names of Deep Ones in her head, wondering which one of the twelve ancient beings would willingly give up their blood for the Wardens.

Taragin chuckled darkly. "That's all I'm telling you about it, so drink it and be grateful. I only have a few to spare. Now, enough about Deep Ones and their blood. What were you doing out there?"

Vila didn't really know how to answer that in a way that anyone other than herself would understand. And she didn't want to; he didn't need to know any more about her or her inner thoughts.

"I needed food for Rance."

Taragin squinted, studying her face for the truth. She could see all the thoughts turning in his head as he cycled through various responses. He ultimately sighed and dropped the line of questioning.

"I'm glad I found you."

He paused as if waiting for some acknowledgement of the grand favor he had done for her. He could keep waiting because Vila had no intention of thanking him. She was grateful to be alive and healing, but that's where the gratitude began and ended; Taragin Echilar wasn't getting anything from her.

"You mean you're glad you followed me."

He let out another dark chuckle and stretched his shoulders. Next to him, his vicious bone flail lay on the boards of the dock, the teeth of the skull covered in gore, both old and new.

"What happened to the shark?" she asked, gingerly pulling herself up and testing her leg. She couldn't walk without a limp and the pain was intense, but she could feel the strange substance working to repair damage and heal the otherwise life-threatening wounds.

The older man didn't answer, instead pointing behind her to a bloody and unmoving heap of mangled flesh. The predator's skull had been obliterated by the Warden's own skull flail, with little of it recognizable as the great hunter it had once been. Brain matter and bone littered the docks, and viscous red liquid was still oozing out slowly, being washed away in the heavy rain.

Vila felt simultaneously relieved and angry; thankful to be alive and furious the kill had been stolen from her. That she had needed his help. She had been stupid—not for going down there, but for being unprepared. She slowly hobbled over to the carcass and began carving out large chunks of flesh with her sea glass knife. Each stab made a rending sound as her knife dug through the sinew and released more gore onto the soaked boards. Taragin watched her go about her grim work, his eyes boring into her back.

"What are you doing?" he finally questioned.

"I need food for Rance."

He didn't answer and instead wandered off down the planks as she continued to carve up the meat. The stench of blood mixed with the salty air and tangy electric smell of the storm. There was too much here for one trip, and she knew the dock workers would scavenge the rest before she could return, but she kept carving and stacking, working to get as much from the shark as she could to bring to her friend. She felt the boards around her creak as Taragin returned and knelt next to her. He held piles of kelp wrap, probably taken from the curious workers huddled under their shelters, and began silently wrapping up the steaks.

"You don't have to help me with this."

"This is important to you," was his only reply as he quietly continued folding the wraps around the fresh meat.

"You're going to help me take it to him then," she said as she examined the offerings. It would be enough to last Rance days if she could get him to eat it. It would need to be cleaned and preserved, but she would do that for him. Vila stood, her leg faltering as she used her lance to stabilize herself while Taragin gathered up the bundles of meat in his large arms.

"You're going to help me take it to him," she repeated. "Then we are going to clean it, preserve it, prepare it, and feed him." It was a command and yet he nodded slowly in acknowledgement, his dark eyes showing no emotion. She decided to push her luck while he was still being accommodating.

"And then you're taking me to the moon shards."

16

"Perhaps after many more centuries, the Lower Planks will have emptied itself of its denizens in one form or another and truly embrace its inner nature as the lifeless, dark catacomb it was always meant to be."
~Myal Norena, Professor of Swellian Architectural History~

Deep breath.
Hold it.
Swim like hell.

Narrio repeated the mantra to himself over and over as he stripped off his cloak and other belongings that would only slow him down through the swim. Unlacing his knee-high boots, he placed them with his cloak, discarding as much weight off his body as he could. He wore his lightweight shirt and kelp fiber trousers and kept only his sight stone lantern and gaff. He replaced the fading stone with a fresh one and slipped his feet into the frigid water. The cold shot up his feet and sent an icy chill up his spine causing him to immediately begin shivering. He lowered himself in further, his breaths becoming shorter and quicker as the water reached his midsection and the submerged lantern clipped to his belt.

It wouldn't be considered a long swim to anyone else, but to Narrio it couldn't have looked further away. He was a capable enough swimmer, meaning he could flail about until he eventually got to his destination. Slowly letting his stomach go below, he moved his feet about in search of the bottom. When he was finally submerged up to his chin, he gave up the fruitless search and prepared himself for the final plunge and desperate swim to the column. He knew that the pool he was about to drop into wasn't the actual depths of the Swell, but it was of little comfort. Water was water and he hated all of it. With a silent curse for being born in the wrong era, Narrio took as large a breath as he could manage and plunged into the dark drink.

He immediately re-emerged in a fit of sputters and gasps, panic rolling in his gut like a fish on the docks as he grasped the edge of the hole.

"Fuck!" He screamed the word in rage at his inadequacy; this was the biggest turning point of his mission so far and he was panicking over a short swim.

He couldn't help but replay memories in his head of the cackling man and only father figure he'd ever known, albeit a really shitty one. The fear as he was shoved into that barrel and left on the water, feeling the slow trickle of the Swell drip into his dark prison and the air grow thin. *Punishment for being an insolent little shit*, were the precise words said.

Narrio quelled the painful memories, the trauma, and focused instead on the present traumatic experience he was about to willingly put himself through. He wished Renalia was there to slap him—he wished she was just here. She'd probably call him a coward before she shoved his head in and pushed him through the tunnel.

Thinking about her naked form and how much he wanted to see it again helped, so he used the image as his anchor point and focused. There was nothing else for it, no other choice. With a curse and a breath, he dropped once again into the water and let go of the edge, twisting around to orient himself in the right direction.

The dark water was salty and full of thick grime that clouded his vision. He cursed himself for not carrying a diving mask on his person, or at the very least a pair of goggles. He took a moment to gather his surroundings, noting nothing as he couldn't see a damn thing. He kicked his feet out behind him and felt something hard to press against. Pushing off against the object, he thrust himself headfirst into an unseen beam and tried desperately to keep from sucking in water as the pain shot through his skull and down his neck.

Hurting and terrified, he grasped at the piece of wood in front him and pulled himself forward. The sight stone bounced off unknown objects and illuminated the filth in a faint red glow. He quickly realized he wasn't going to be able navigate by sight alone. He was going to have to make sure he kept moving straight towards the column, and he was going to have to do it quickly.

He could already feel his lungs beginning to burn as he pushed and pulled himself through the tight corridor of water towards his goal. The limits to which he could hold his breath had never been tested and it was quickly becoming apparent that the answer was not very long.

Narrio grasped and kicked, willing himself through narrow passages and jagged openings with the all the grace of a dying fish. His shirt caught on a piece of wood, and he struggled to move forward as the villainous timber held him back. He reached out in front of him, searching desperately for anything to grab onto. His lungs screamed at him, and he could feel the dizziness setting in as his body fought to maintain consciousness. He was running out of time. He was going to drown.

Narrio wanted to live more than his lungs wanted to give up and so, using inner strength that he didn't know he possessed, he wrenched his shirt free and kicked himself forward, bashing into beams and wreckage. His head hit the floorboards above him, and he clawed at the underside, propelling forward as quickly as he could.

With no way to tell how far he'd gone or how much further he had to go, the thief dragged himself along, scraping his body along every jagged protrusion in his path. Suddenly his fingers no longer had a hold on solid wood, and he felt the chilly tingle of air. With his mind going hazy, and his body exhausted, he flailed until he found purchase again and pulled himself up into the glorious blast of cold air that awaited him inside the hollow beam. His head exploded out of the water, and he choked down air in greedy swallows, his lungs and body wheezing after having been pushed to their absolute limits.

Narrio allowed himself several cries of exhalation and glee as he breathed in the musty air. Nothing had ever smelled so fetid and delicious all at the same time and he found himself nearly moved to tears. He'd made it through the second most terrifying experience of his life and wallowed in the feeling of victory. Unclipping the sight stone lantern, he held it above his head and peered up into the hollowness of the passage that stretched above him. Endless dark awaited him, but he couldn't have been more grateful for it. Within a hand's reach above his head was a metal ring hammered into the beam with a large iron nail. There were more rings beyond that, each placed at more or less even intervals and continuing beyond his vision up into the dark. Handholds. A way up. The secret entrance.

He was right and he had never been so happy to be correct in all his life. Not wanting to spend another moment in the filth below him, he grasped the iron ring and began pulling himself out of the water. He could feel the tiredness already setting in, his muscles burning and body haggard from the "swim". Clipping the lantern back onto his belt, Narrio pulled himself up further until he laid hands on the next rung. He continued to pull himself up, rung after rung, until his bare feet left the dark water below him and he was completely inside the column. He was freezing, bloody, and exhausted, but he willed some strength into his being and began to climb again.

There was nowhere to go but up now, and he had no idea what he would encounter at the top, but it didn't matter. He'd found the way, and nothing was going to get him back in that water.

The climb was horrendous.

He had no idea how many spans he had traveled at this point, and he wasn't sure how much longer he could continue to climb. He was freezing cold, and his toes and fingers were bleeding from the constant rub of rusty metal against soft flesh. The hollow passage was uneven throughout most of the climb and there were many points where he found himself squeezing through extremely small holes that left even more abrasions along his already battered body.

He cursed Hinaldo and his cock with every rung he climbed, taking frequent breaks the further along he went. He climbed with his eyes closed, weariness setting in and threatening to take complete control. Everything was slick and water constantly dripped in his face from some unknown source above. Losing his grip and falling back down into the black pool far below him was a constant fear and he clung desperately to every rung.

After an eternity, the light at the end of the tunnel finally appeared before him. Or rather an L-shaped bend that forced him into a horizontal crawl. He figured he must be inside one of the joists that spanned the church's foundation, and after a time, the passage ended, and he looked up into another hole above him. He was able to stand up here and was delighted to see a large stone block that signified an end to his ordeal. He was staring at the bottom of the church's foundation. Narrio let out a hushed cry of triumph and held up his lantern to inspect the stone above his head. The solid piece of moldy stone stretched beyond the walls of his hollow cell, but in the middle, he could see the thin outline of a rectangular shaped piece barely big enough for a person of reasonable size. He climbed the last few rungs and felt a sudden urge to kiss the dirty rock above him. Running his fingers along the outline, he could make out the knuckles of a rusty iron hinge, the patina on the metal giving it a similar hue to the green stone door that he was staring at.

A door! A way in.

Whatever elation he felt at the find was quickly absorbed as a few hard shoves told him that it was not going to budge. He pushed himself up on the rungs until his shoulders were pressed against the slick stone and shoved against the rock as hard as he could. The sharp metal fragments dug into his bare feet, and he ignored the pain as he pushed with all his might against the unyielding rock. Narrio heaved a sigh of frustration and relinquished himself to the fact that he wasn't getting in. He was so close, so fucking close.

He leaned his head back and closed his eyes again, careful not to fall into a slumber as his exhaustion warred within.

Doors could be opened. They had hinges. They had keys.

Narrio opened his eyes and looked at the stone again, studying it in the fading glow of his lantern. Instead of a keyhole, his eyes rested on a small circle outlined on the stone door. The lines were faint and covered with grime, but inside the circle was a familiar shape; two peaks holding up four small circles.

He gripped at the holes in the circles, working to move the shape in any direction he could, but just like the door it was completely immovable.

This was the mechanism, it had to be. Old Hinaldo wouldn't have been careless enough to rely on just the climb to ward off intruders into his sex haven. Whatever that symbol was, it had a counterpart, a counterpart that when slipped inside would give him passage into the sanctum above and deliver the fruits of a hard-won victory. He just had to find the key. His thoughts drifted to the mysterious woman, the red-haired vixen that could come and go as she pleased into a building with only one entrance. She had to have the key. But why?

Exasperated with the endless searching for answers, Narrio sighed heavily and prepared himself for the long climb down. He was going to have to find this mysterious key holder, but not tonight. He had no idea how long he'd climbed now and knew he would need to return to the surface before his Bilger's Fare became void. And he desperately needed a good night's sleep, a hot meal, and as many stiff drinks as he could manage before he passed out.

A soft companion to share his bed wouldn't go amiss either.

With those delightful thoughts dancing about in his brain, Narrio began the long journey back towards his greatest fear waiting for him at the bottom.

Narrio was back in the inky black pool of filth and terror with a renewed sense of bravery. The swim was a little easier on the way back having done it once, but he still found himself catching his shirt and scraping his legs along the sharp splinters. His lantern was nearly dead now and he relied solely on instinct to find his exit. With his lungs telling him that he needed to surface soon, he felt sure he was nearly there when something moved against him.

Before he had a chance to even wonder what it was, he felt a sharp pain in his leg and was thrust backwards, hitting his head on a wall.

A jolt went through his body as the creature sent out an electrical shock meant to stun its prey, which unfortunately seemed to be him. Narrio felt his lower half go numb and his heart skipped a few beats.

The water was growing warm around him and he couldn't tell if it was from blood or because he had pissed himself.

Grasping at anything within his reach in a panic, he flailed his legs behind him as he felt sharpened teeth digging into his calf.

He wanted to scream in pain but was equally as terrified of sucking in water.

The thing wouldn't budge and Narrio had no choice but to kick and pull madly forward, hoping to the gods he could find the opening.

The only thing worse than drowning was being eaten alive. And the only thing worse than that was being eaten alive while you were drowning.

Suddenly, his outstretched hand didn't feel like it was in water anymore.

He groped around until he found a handhold in the gaps of the floorboards.

Grasping with a strength that he didn't know was left in his body, he pulled himself upwards until his head burst out of the water. The creature on his leg was still thrashing around, unrelenting in its grip.

Narrio gasped for air, sucking it down like his life depended on it and gave a feral yell as he pulled himself up out of the hole, crawling on his stomach to get away from the black pit. With the last of his sight stone's light, he saw the creature still morbidly attached, though in the dimness he couldn't tell what it was and he didn't much care. The thing seemed to be trying to burrow into his leg.

"Fucker!" he yelled, desperately pawing around his person until his hands clasped around the shaft of his gaff. The mechanism sprung open with a satisfying click and then six lengths of hollow metal with a wickedly sharp blade were in his hands. He rolled over, the thing on his leg turning with him. It took two hard thrusts before it relinquished its grasp and a third straight through its eye before it stopped moving, its life leaving its body in a series of aggressive twitches. Gore clumped on his blade and splattered across his face. Narrio lay back, his heart beating faster than it ever had before and he was sure there was nothing left in his bladder.

His leg began to burn with a deep, throbbing pain as his adrenaline faded. He pulled up the lantern and shone it across the wound. It looked like a mess with his leather trousers shredded and blood seeping out onto the floor. The pain was excruciating even through the numbness. He tried to move his feet, but they still weren't responding.

He took a few more deep breaths, as panic fought to escape and take hold again. Closing his eyes, he ran through the mental regiments that usually helped in times of extreme stress.

You are breathing, which means you are alive.

You are thinking, which means you are aware.

You are going to be fucking fine.

He felt much better until his light passed over the creature that was trying to make a new home in his calf only moments ago. Something wasn't right.

The first clue was that it seemed to be an eel, but the last he had heard eels didn't burrow inside human bodies. The second was that it looked like a fucking mess. One eye was completely demolished by his gaff point, but where the second one should have been, there were green, crystalline formations protruding from the socket. Its skin also had a slightly translucent hue to it, and he could see its insides twitching as the final electrical pulses petered out.

Whatever it was, or used to be, it wasn't normal and Narrio now found himself very worried about the mangled flesh he called his leg. His blood was red, which was oddly comforting and there were no crystals growing so it was about as much as he could hope for. It was something he knew he was going to have to watch though;

if he was able to get out of here. That thing wasn't natural, and he wasn't going to sleep comfortably until he knew what it was.

Retracting his gaff back into its handheld form, he cut some strips of leather away from his leg and used them to bind the wound. His wrap job looked like shit, reminding Narrio that becoming a healer was never on the table. He'd need to get a poultice or tincture of red kelp when he returned topside.

Laying on the floor with his breaths coming out in ragged gasps, he continued to work out the panic and stress. He needed to get up, he needed to get out of here. The successful find of the door spurred him on and he slowly pushed himself upright, using a rotted cross-brace as support. The pain in his leg was intense, but not unbearable. He'd move slow, but he'd move, and that was the important part.

Narrio grabbed his cloak from the floor and gingerly slipped his boots over his freezing and bleeding appendages. He laced his boots carefully and wrapped the cloak around his shoulders. He was aware of how much he was shivering now, both from the cold and the pain. He wanted to leave the disgusting creature where it lay, but something inside him told him to take it. Whatever was wrong with it had him deeply unsettled and it was better to bring it back and show Renalia. She was smart.

He slung the monster over his shoulders, careful to avoid the glowing green shards that peppered its skin and with slow, heavy steps, he made his way towards the exit. Desperate to get out of the Lower Planks—for a while at least.

17

"It is the firm belief of the Industrial Coalition, that the survival of this city is in peril if we are to continue as we have been. Salvage and scavenging cannot be the main operation if the Planks is to not only survive but thrive. If we are to rival the other cities in the future, then we need to be looking at how our great city can evolve. That is the basis for our proposal to redevelop the Lower Planks into a place of industry. We cannot compete without a more constant and reliable source of resources, like the deepwood operations of Driftburg. Outlined in our plan, you will see our proposal for new methods of developing, manufacturing, and exporting that would take advantage of the substructure below our very feet."
~Vintar Maccio I, Head of the Maccio Family Salvage Yard~

R ance somehow looked even worse when they brought him the food. Whatever corruption was seeping through his veins was taking its toll quickly and without mercy. There was a bottomless pit in Vila that threatened to swallow her whole every time she thought about losing her friend. It was painful to look at him as she wiped darkened goo and tiny flecks of crystal from his eyes, the shards leaving more cuts along his cheeks as she cleaned.

They had left him to rest and now strode through the city with purpose and speed, Taragin leading the way. Vila followed the Warden through the dark streets of the Upper Planks, her hood pulled up over her head to ward off the rain. Her leg continued to burn from the nearly fatal wound, and she was still a little lightheaded from the blood loss, but the second vial of Deep One's blood was now working its way through her system, and she could practically feel her leg stitching itself back together in miraculous fashion. As vile as the stuff was, the feeling of power and healing that coursed through her body was a little addictive and she found herself thinking about her next dose as they walked.

Taragin didn't seem concerned with being seen and paid no attention to the worried glances from rain covered windows as they passed by in the night. She could see the shape of his enormous skull flail underneath his cloak, and she noticed that he always had a hand on the bone handle at his side. He came across as a man of violence—ready for a fight at any moment and it was something Vila could empathize with. She put a little more pressure on her leg and moved quickly to catch up to him, wincing as the healing ligament continued to throb.

"You said that this was happening in other places. Are the other Wardens investigating this elsewhere?"

Taragin didn't look at her as they continued to walk, his gaze focused on the alleys and corners, eyes darting as if searching for danger in every dark shadow.

"Yes. We were sent here, while my compatriots are doing what they can elsewhere."

"Like Anthema?"

He glanced at her, studying her with a shrewd gaze.

"What makes you think that?"

"It would make sense that if there is a large source of power here sending out energy, then the Grand Shard in the cathedral would be starting to emit as well."

"Astute. Yes, it's a fact we are very aware of and concerned about. Four from our group were headed there while the others were sent to find and investigate the perceived source. We have not heard from anyone yet."

"Have you found other instances of what's happening to Rance in the rest of the city?"

"Yes. And my companions here are handling it."

Vila grabbed his arm and pulled him to a halt.

"What does that mean?"

He stared at her, pausing for a long beat before slowly giving his explanation. "There have been other reports, both in people and wildlife. We have worked quickly to contain them, but word will get out soon and more cases will come up. We are only here to find the individual who delved up the rock and stop them before they can do more harm. Finding the ultimate source of power and putting a stop to it is the only real solution."

"What did you do with the people?"

"You won't like the answer."

"Tell me."

Taragin continued to stare at her and Vila knew the answer before he said it. "They were going to die anyways. It wasn't my command."

"That doesn't make it any better! You killed innocent people, because of you not wanting the word to spread? What kind of monsters are you people?"

"Your hands aren't clean either, Vila. I've seen you in the pits."

"That's not the same."

Taragin only shrugged and kept walking. Vila caught up with him and grabbed his shoulder again.

"Why haven't you killed Rance?"

"Because I need your help, whether Tempé agrees or not. If you help me, we might be able to save him."

"Your captain made it very clear how he felt about me and my involvement, yet you're taking me to the rock anyway. Why?" She hated having to ask so many questions, the feeling of confusion and helplessness rising with every moment. Taragin gently removed her hand and continued walking.

"I convinced him that you could be an asset to us."

"Because of my name."

"Yes. Because of your name. I was assigned to keep an eye on you. Involving you wasn't specifically forbidden. I deemed it necessary, so here we are."

"Don't try to seduce me with some grand talk of honor and legacy. You may have known my father, but you don't know me. We are going to save Rance and get rid of whatever is causing this and then I don't want any more involvement in your affairs."

Taragin stopped walking, his graying locks dripping in the downpour. They were behind one of the Planks' many refineries, the alley covered in black soot and refuse. The air was thick from the smokestacks that protruded from every rooftop, causing the rain to fall in ebony droplets that stained and smeared on their skin. The alley was a dead end and Taragin peered back out around the corner, checking for followers or intruders. Seemingly satisfied, he approached a slightly discolored plank at least two spans wide by the edge of one of the bordering buildings. Kneeling next to it, he started pulling at the nails holding it down, grunting as he worked.

"And what if this whole affair is bigger than that? Bigger than just Rance," he said between strained pulls.

She steeled herself, unwilling to yield, unwilling to let him have the answer he was looking for. She couldn't do anymore, and she didn't want to. Heroes were never really free, always the pawn of larger schemes and plots. And legends rarely cared for the people they were supposed to be fighting for; the Warden in front of her being a prime example. She didn't want any part of that world. If she was supposed have been one, then she would have known her father and not been born an illegitimate bastard.

"That's what the Deep Wardens are for. Not me."

He gave her a sad smile before setting to work on the nails again. After a few more strained grunts, the last of them came free and he removed the board from its resting place, the inscription *T.I.* barely visible as he moved it aside. A narrow hole lay in its place, barely wide enough for a human to fit through.

"Is this a secret Warden entrance?" Vila asked with more rye than she intended.

Taragin chortled. "Nothing nearly so grand. We used to use this when we were younger men—boys, really. I'll admit I'm a little surprised to find it still here. The patrons always tried to keep a tight handle on who was entering and leaving the Lower Planks so we had to get creative when we couldn't afford the fare."

"They still do. Can't go in or out without Bilger's Fare or special permission." She pulled her ringlet out from her bracer and gave it a dangle. "It has some benefits, I guess. Although I prefer my own entrances as well."

Taragin stared at the ringlet thoughtfully. "Huh. Do you mind if I ask how you came to be in the profession? It seems in conflict with your other interests and skills."

"You can ask all you want. It doesn't really matter how it happened; it happened."

"Fair enough. Are you ready?"

Vila looked down into the hole, seeing only a single ladder that stretched into the dark and disappeared. It clearly hadn't been used in ages and Vila didn't trust it to hold her weight, let alone the much larger Warden and his gear.

"You first," she said, gesturing to the ladder.

Taragin holstered the handle of his flail and squeezed himself through the small opening. Testing the rungs on the rickety ladder and, satisfied with the results, he began his descent. Vila waited

until she could only see the glow of his sea glass in the dark, then
shimmied through the hole to follow him down.

Hunkered down inside the ruined hull of an ancient frigate, Vila
and Taragin peered through the wide gaps into the alcove ahead
of them. Vila knew there were many areas of the Lower Planks that
she had never explored before, yet Taragin seemed to navigate the
maze he led her through with ease. She imagined him and her
father exploring the caverns of shipwrecks and ruins, getting into
trouble, and acting like kings of this underground world. That was
a luxury she'd never quite had and wouldn't dare to emulate. Even
as a Blue Lady and a deadly fighter, she was always cautious about
where she went down here; there were just places you didn't go by
yourself, especially as a woman; attractive or otherwise.

This was clearly a less trodden area, with centuries of mold and
growth covering every inch of the small openings and rotting ruins
they passed through. A good half of the trip was spent on her hands
and knees, crawling through layers of muck and filth that now
caked her body as they sat in the hidden spot. Moisture dripped
from the ceiling of their hole and splattered onto her hood as she
stared out into the large, cavernous opening in front of her.

Huge beams held up the ceiling of planks and hulls, and sight
stone lanterns were strung all around, marking it as a place of
gathering in an otherwise abandoned section of the Lower Planks.
The bustling activity also gave it away.

Vila studied the scene quietly, taking in the sight in front of her.
There was a large worktable that stretched thirty lengths in the
center of the room, made from the spine of some massive creature. Every inch of it was covered in tools and shards of varying
colored moon rock. Figures milled about, transporting large crates

back and forth throughout the room. Everyone was hooded and masked, their faces and bodies shrouded in mystery.

Beyond the table lay the point of their journey down here. Standing on end and supported by wooden jack braces were the largest pieces of moon rock that Vila had ever seen. There were four of them; black, blue, green, and red, glowing faintly and casting their light about the room. Each rock stood at least ten lengths high and were oddly shaped, with crystalline protrusions jutting out at every angle. Workers gathered around the behemoths, scraping and cutting at the rocks with care before handing the sheered pieces to another who would load it in a cart. Once the cart was full, it would be transported over to the large table in the center and unloaded for the workers there.

She watched as the hooded and masked figures labored, using chisels and saws to work at the crystals in front of them. She could see sparks of energy fly as they chipped and carved, making the heavy furs and leather they were all covered in a logical form of protection from the sharp rocks. One of the figures held up the item they were working on, and Vila had to suppress a gasp. In their hand, they held a sword of black shard, finely honed and soaking up the red light of the room. The figure waved it around with skill, testing its weight before swinging it widely at a nearby post.

The sword sliced cleanly through with nary a splinter scattering.

"Weapons," she gasped quietly. "They're making weapons out of them."

Knowing what to look for, she could start to see the instruments of death that would be made from the half-formed lumps of rock before her. There were more than just swords; she spotted daggers, lances, axes, and even a wicked looking club that was studded with razor sharp shards.

"You knew about this?" she asked Taragin, her eyes wide with shock and disbelief. She expected to find one, maybe two large rocks protected by a handful of sleepy guards. She was not expecting a bustling manufacturing center for divine weaponry.

"Now you know why I wanted you to come down here. You needed to see this, to see what is happening."

Vila felt the heat rising in her neck as she started to put the pieces together—she had been used again. "You can't help Rance, can you?" she asked slowly, the words rolling out with a dangerous flair.

"I don't know. We—"

"Don't fucking lie to me." She turned toward him, her face close. She made sure he could feel the heat of her breath, see the accusation and fury in her eyes. "You either don't know how or won't. Which is it?"

Taragin Echilar ground his teeth, formulating his answer carefully. "Both."

She hissed, spittle flying in his eyes. He didn't pull away as he wiped the saliva from his face and held up a hand.

"We don't know how to reverse his condition and we can't spend the time trying right now. Look," he pointed back out into the room, his voice growing stronger and more commanding. "Those are objects of unknown power, raw power that hasn't been seen on this earth in centuries and someone is harnessing it for war and profit."

He looked back out at the factory, his eye twitching as he spoke with a deep sense of dread. "This is bigger than your friend. It's bigger than the wardens or even you, but we are the only ones who can fight it or stop it. We've been monitoring it in shifts since we found it and none of the weapons seem to have left the planks yet or made their way to the surface, but it's only a matter of time."

Vila was caught between the need to find answers for Rance and the sinking feeling that she needed to do something about this new information. If those instruments started hitting the market, there would be even more cases like Rance, and they would be worse. This wasn't just a poisoned water system.

"Then let's burn it down. Why are we just sitting here? Why haven't you done anything about it?"

"We need to know who is running the operation. If we take out this factory and don't catch who's in charge, they'll just escape and rebuild. We need to find the actual head of the serpent and cut it off at the source."

"And you don't know who that is."

"No. Obviously someone with money and resources, but they've been very careful to cover their tracks."

Vila held up her hand to him, watching through the cracks as a new activity began in the corner of the room. Vila hadn't noticed it before, but there was some sort of metal shaft protruding through the floor, capped with a turn handle and vent pipes. Purple sea glass studded the large pipe and glowed with power as they performed whatever task they'd been altered to do. Several figures had gathered at the shaft and were now working to turn the rusted handle. With an explosion of sound, the hatch burst open, and a gush of water blasted into the room before dying off, the stones glowing furiously. They had to be larger versions of pressure stones, altered to keep the water from overflowing the room.

"That's a direct line to the Swell!" she exclaimed in a whisper. "It has to be. That's how they're getting the weapons out of here. Some idiot poked a hole in the bottom of the Planks."

"It would appear that way." Taragin studied the hatch, his face grim with concern. "We are too late."

As he spoke, a large figure emerged from the shaft, dripping with water, and landing on the deck with a heavy thud. They wore a massive diving helm on their head, the circular iron shape covered in survival stones. Heavy iron boots clad their feet and they stepped towards the crates of weapons that were being carted over. The iron-clad figure pointed a heavy gloved hand at the shaft and spoke in a deep and resonating voice from the grates in the helm. Vila couldn't understand what they said, but the command was clear; bundles of weapons started being lifted out of the crates and taken over to the shaft where another helmeted figure waited with open arms. The wares were leaving.

"We have to stop it," Vila said through gritted teeth.

"There's too many of them. And it won't do any good. They'll just make more. We have to find out who—"

Vila grabbed the Warden by the shoulder and spun him towards her. "We can't fucking wait! Those weapons are about to leave and once they're out there in the world it's going to be chaos. You brought me down here and said I need to help, so I'm getting involved. But not for you, or for some grand cause. My friend is dying because some asshole is trying to profit off those rocks and this is the only thing I can do. I'm not going to let more innocent people die because we just sat here."

She bore into his eyes, her chest heaving with emotion and fury. Taragin studied her face, taking in the passion and seriousness that poured out of her. Slowly, he unclasped his flail from his back and scooted back from the wall while he tightened the hammer-shark bracer on his left arm. He pulled his leg back, preparing a solid kick to the rotted boards they were looking through. Once he did, there would be no going back.

"Are you sure about this?"

She wasn't, but she nodded her head as he handed her a falchion made of pressure hardened bone, its edge wickedly sharp. Intricately etched pictures swirled around the blade depicting creatures Vila had never seen in battles of epic proportions. She gripped the hilt tightly, its weight satisfying in her hands.

"That was your father's," he said right before he smashed his foot through the rotted planks and the chaos began.

18

"To be a Deep Warden is a blessing and a curse. To count oneself as a servant of Fathus and traverse the Swell is a consecration of the highest degree, reserved only for his favored Oceanids and the Deep Wardens. Those few who choose the path, and are selected, are truly blessed and fortunate. The curse of the Warden's life should not be overlooked, however. We mere mortals would be lost without Fathus, and we should count ourselves lucky that he would deign to give us meager attention after the treachery of our god. Warden's carry that burden always, enacting justice and sometimes brutal love upon Fathus' world. It must be a heavy burden to carry, and one only the strongest of us could endure."
~Excerpt from Arch Titritus' "Musings and Contemplations of the Four and their Divine Realms"~

The rotted wood exploded into the room from the force of Taragin's iron boot and his enhanced strength as yells of alarm rang out amongst the masked group. Weapons were brandished and the desperate attempt to save the secret operation began as Vila and Taragin burst into the alcove.

"Leave one alive!" Taragin yelled as they split in opposite directions.

Vila had counted at least fifteen individuals in the room, including the two new arrivals from the shaft. She had no idea who was a capable fighter or not, so this was going to be a battle based on speed, surprise, and instinct. Taragin sped off towards the worktable which lay near the only perceivable exit from the room—besides the metal shaft that led down to the ocean below. His flail was out now, revealed in all its gruesome glory and swinging wildly about with a five-span reach. Vila had seen the scrimshaw markings on the jawbone that told of past battles with ancient horrors. Based on how the Deep Warden moved and fought now, she was sure those were true depictions and who the victor in those fights was. The jawbone head of the flail still had many of its teeth, honed to razor sharp edges and stained with blood. Where teeth were missing, sharpened sea glass blades had been set in place, the myriad colors creating a dizzying mix of death and joy as he swung the weapon through the room.

The flail caught one of the workers in the head and their skull exploded in a gruesome display of brain matter that flew around the room. The lifeless body of the worker was still stuck to the flail as Taragin continued his swing, smashing the corpse into another helpless laborer as they failed to put enough distance between themselves and the raging Warden. The two bodies were crushed together and smashed into the table, slicing both living and dead to shreds on the sharpened shards and weapons that lay about.

Taragin released the handle and brandished his bone saber, slicing the foot off an oncoming attacker at the ankle. Blood sprayed across the Warden's body, turning him into an even more terrifying harbinger of death. Before the man had hit the floor, the aging Warden's skull bracer came around and crushed the man's face in, producing another deluge of gore and blood. He used the sword to separate the corpses from the head of his flail and picked the handle back up as he switched the saber to his other hand. He set about continuing his butchery as Vila raced towards the shaft. If one single weapon left this room, she would feel the failure and she was determined not to let that happen. Most of the workers had mustered their courage and brandished various weapons of shard, rushing like fools at the raging Warden.

That left three for Vila; the masked one with the black sword, and the two armored and helmeted figures who were now running towards her, the ground shaking beneath their heavy iron boots meant for the ocean floor.

The figure with the sword was faster than their heavily clad companions, reaching the woman first but their attacks were wild. Vila ducked under their wide swing, easily avoiding the blade that sliced high above her head. Lashing out with her own saber, she sliced through the tendons in the attacker's leg that released a gush of hot blood across her arms and screams of anguish from the masked figure. They dropped the sword and fell to their knees, the fight bleeding out of them as they desperately tried to crawl away from her. She placed a heavy boot on the dying person's bleeding leg and their scream of pain was cut short as she shoved her blade through the base of their neck. The blade shot out underneath their jaw and Vila wrenched hard, ripping her father's falchion up and through the skull. The head split open with a sickening squelch as her sword came free, littering the floor with the tangled mess of brain, sinew, and bone.

The whole process had taken seconds, but it was too long, and Vila was caught off guard as one of the massive, armored hulks smashed into her side, the overlarge metal gloves smashing into her skull and ribs as they crashed into each other.

Her blade was wrenched from her hand and clattered across the ground, far out of reach as she hit the ground hard. She winced and rolled to avoid the smashing fists of her attacker as they pounded the ground where her head was, her vision reeling and blood oozing from her ear.

Her leg was not fully healed from her battle with the shark, and she could feel the flesh reopening as she wrenched herself off the ground and rushed for her sword. Everywhere was slick with blood and she lost her footing a few spans away, feeling heavy footsteps behind and in front of her as her attackers closed in.

The second armored figure had found the shard blade and was preparing to bring the deadly instrument down on her skull as she twisted away, using her size and speed to her advantage. She fell again in the blood but regained her footing as the blade swung near, its sharpened tip slicing through her cloak. She felt searing pain as the blade found flesh and a warm sensation poured out onto her leg.

There was a sudden sound of metal crunching and a terrible pop as Taragin's flail came down on the helm of her opponent. Gore splattered against the inside of the glass in a mess of red and pink and small sprays burst through fissures in the crushed helm. Taragin pulled hard and the corpse flew across the room, dislodging itself from the jaw and crashing against the metal shaft protruding from the floor.

He turned back to his final two opponents; the terrified workers desperate to get away from the killer in their midst. Vila felt a surge of irritation at the litter of bodies around Taragin, but she quelled the feeling, as her own desperate struggle was not yet over.

Vila used the violent intervention of her companion to her advantage and swept down upon her falchion, picking it up deftly and returning to the fight with the last helmed menace. The figure backed away, batting at her blows as fast as they could, but their diving suit slowed them down and Vila's blade was a blur of blood and bone.

A hit finally found purchase and sliced through the suit's thick leather exterior, and she could feel the satisfying impact of blade upon bone as she cut deep into their right arm. A spray of red shot out and a voice cried out in a deep resonance from inside the helm.

Vila pushed closer, pressing the advantage and swept her sword up again, slicing into the soft flesh of their upper arm.

The figure stumbled back and slipped on the gore slick ground as their feet gave out from under them and the rotted floor planks shook as the figure crashed. Vila ignored the debris that fell around her from above and leapt onto her kill, driving her sword straight through the viewport and into the waiting face inside. The glass shattered as the point drove through until it bumped against the back of the helm and the body lay still.

The violence released a cascading feeling of pleasure and heat as she straddled her kill. Her breaths were heavy as she grasped the blade firmly, the point still driven into the corpse's skull.

There was a roar in her ears that she attributed to adrenaline and blood rush. Even through the pain, her body felt good, felt hot. She let her groin press hard against the metal rivulets on the diving suit below her, feeling the hard metal against a growing wetness. She desperately wanted to finish, feel release and orgasm as she rubbed her clit against the hardened metal, her hands warm in the blood around her.

She was pulled from her pleasure by a muffled shout from Taragin and realized that the roar in her ears wasn't from the adrenaline but from water rising around her hands and feet. The sound was coming from inside the chamber, as was the water.

She looked up to see Taragin, his left arm hanging limply at his side and his right holding the throat of the last terrified weapons maker. The Warden was screaming inaudible words at her and she followed his gaze over to the metal opening in the floor.

A geyser of black ocean water was erupting from the shaft opening, flooding the room as the Swell found a toe hold into the city. Vila stared in horror at the tower of water, her eyes resting on the dented shaft and broken shards of purple sea glass hanging from their divots—rendered useless. Taragin, in his blood fury, had thrown his enemy right into the only thing keeping the ocean at bay; like a fucking idiot.

Vila was waist-deep in dark, salty water as colors danced across the tumultuous surface from the glowing pillars of moon shard. Leaving her sword imbedded in the now floating body, Vila waded as fast as she could over to the shaft, ignoring the searing pain in her side and the floating gore around her.

Taragin was hanging on desperately to the lone survivor; he would be useless anyways with only one working arm. Reaching the shaft, Vila pulled herself up on the handholds and tried to push the hinged cap back into place.

She screamed as she pressed against the tower of rushing water, her muscles burning in protest. The pressure was too intense, and she was unable to get it past a vertical position. Her strength finally gave out and the cap folded back into her, throwing her off her perch and into the deepening pool.

Vila flailed in the swirling pool, trying to get her head above water as moon shards and an eyeball swooshed past her. She emerged to an eerie silence; the deafening roar of the water blast now gone.

Shaila O'Caan stood on the shaft, fighting to hold the metal door down as Quinlan Lan spun the lock into place, sealing the ocean out. Shaila's eyes rested on hers and she gave Vila a nod. Vila didn't return it and instead lay her head back in the water and allowed herself to float, her body screaming with pain and tension. The brutal fight was done; they had kept the weapons from leaving and almost destroyed the entire city in the process.

"Well, my friend. That could have gone better."

Quinlan picked his way through the debris as the last of the water drained through the cracks in the walls and out into the rest of the Lower Planks where it would eventually find a new home. He and

Shaila fished moon shards and weapons out of the water as Vila helped Taragin tie up the last survivor of the massacre.

"Do your job, Quin," the older Warden growled and pulled the stopper on his last vial of Deep One blood, draining the contents in a single drag. He'd slipped one to Vila and taken the last two himself. Blood poured from inside his sleeve, coating his hand and splashing into the fetid pools of water at his feet as he waited for the magical liquid to do its work. Vila finished her own and reveled in the sickeningly good feeling as the black blood entered her system again. Taragin set himself down on the steps and pulled his arm onto his lap, his face showing concern.

"Let me look at it," Vila said, pulling the cloak off his shoulders to reveal the wound. A jagged line of ripped flesh ran from shoulder blade to forearm, the muscle shredded and mutilated. It wasn't a clean cut, and it would take time to heal even with the blood elixir. She began ripping shreds of fabric off one of the corpses to bandage the wound and wishing she had a poultice of some kind to stave off infection. She made a makeshift sling and wrapped it over his shoulder as he tenderly lifted his arm up into it.

"I'm not going to lie, it's bad Taragin. You'll need to keep that still."

"I'm afraid it's worse than that," he said quietly, holding up the offending weapon. It was a wicked looking blade, uneven and wavy in shape. The blade was clearly meant to shred flesh and had done just so to the Warden's arm. The blue blade of moon shard glowed faintly with an unearthly light, resonating with some deep unknown power.

"It's only a matter of time before I start looking like your friend. And not much, if his condition is any indicator."

Vila stared at the blade and the wound, unsure of what to think. Her mind was racing, puzzles spinning about as she tried to work out the inconsistencies.

"I don't know. I don't think it affects everyone the same," she said, holding up her hand to him. The cuts from the moon shards on Rance's fish had almost completely healed thanks to the blood elixir, but the scars were still visible in crisscross patterns across her hand.

"These were from those fish you took from me days ago. Don't you think I would have started showing signs of infection at this point?"

Taragin stared at her hand, his face puzzled as he clearly thought about the horrid fate that awaited him if what she said wasn't true.

"You haven't seen any signs? No shards?"

"None. I hit Tempé with the fish and cut his face. Has he not shown any symptoms?"

"No. I don't know what to make of it. Only time will tell, I suppose."

"For the both of us," she said as she pulled back her cloak, revealing the bleeding wound from the black blade.

Taragin's eyes widened. "Let's hope you're right. You need to get that bandaged up."

"I have magical Warden juice in me now," she winked. "Take care of yourself and I'll tend to me."

Quinlan skipped over as Vila began wrapping shreds of kelp fiber around her stomach, pulling them as tight as she could.

"What about them?" he said, pointing his harpoon launcher at the worker who stood tied to a rotted beam. The figure's mask was still in place, their features hidden. Vila moved towards them, wincing as she went. Her leg felt nearly normal, but the rest of her body was battered and aching from the fight. She approached the serene figure carefully and slid the mask off. The woman under the mask snarled at her, brown eyes flashing with fear and anger.

Taragin joined Vila, gently placing a hand behind her back in a supportive gesture. This was her mission now, her quest to complete.

"I want answers," Vila said as confidently as she could.

The woman spat in rebuttal, spraying thick globules of phlegm in Vila's face. She didn't dare wipe it off; she wouldn't give her the pleasure. Instead, she stepped back and swung her father's blade up in a sweeping arc, taking the woman's ear off at the base. Screams and blood erupted from the prisoner as Vila picked up the ruined hunk of flesh from the filthy water.

Something snapped inside her, a thread that tied her to a more human and compassionate reaction—a thin line snipped by moon shards. She shoved the ear into the prisoner's mouth and clamped it shut, the panicked woman's eyes growing wide as she began to retch and flail. Vila held her there, taking a sick pleasure in the struggle as the Wardens behind her just watched.

"I have a friend who's dying because of you. I get to watch him suffer as thousands of tiny black crystals grow from his skin and eat him from the inside out."

The woman continued to shake uncontrollably, bile dripping from her clamped mouth as her eyes began to roll backwards from shock.

"I'm going to take your ear out of your fucking mouth and if you don't tell me what I want to know, I'm going to shove my fist up your cunt and rip you apart from the inside out, do you fucking understand me?"

She screamed the words, her rage fully released in a storm of fury and hatred. Even if she found out who was ultimately funding this operation, Vila knew she might kill this woman. Not because it would solve anything or help Rance, but because it would feel good to watch her writhe as Vila twisted the life out of her in retribution. She removed her hand, and the woman vomited her own ear out onto the ground. Thick globs of putrid bile and unrecognizable chunks followed as the woman retched on Vila's feet. Keeping her face placid, Vila wiped her hand across the woman's shirt and continued her questioning.

"Who do you work for?"

"You're going to kill me, no matter what," the woman croaked.

"Tell me who hired you, or I will kill you slowly and painfully."

The woman shook her head, tears streaming from her eyes as she coughed up more chunks onto the ground.

"Go ahead and cut me up. Mutilate me. You're going to do it anyways."

Vila slammed her fist into the woman's gut, putting all her force behind the punch and sending another stream of vomit spewing out of the prisoner's mouth. The woman shook her head again even as she gasped in pain. Vila hit her again and again, the bile becoming less as the woman's stomach emptied. Every hit was met with the same silent reaction as blood began to leak from the corners of her mouth.

"See..." she whispered, her voice strained and fading. "You're enjoying this. You want to hurt me. Admit it."

Vila cracked her knuckles and prepared to smash the woman's teeth in when a loud crack resounded through the chamber and gore splattered across Vila's face. The woman's head snapped back as Quinlan's harpoon smashed through her skull, pinning her head to the beam, and practically splitting her in two. Her lifeless eyes rolled back, nearly tumbling out of the ruined sockets, her mouth hung open, tongue limp.

Vila spun around to see Agustan Tempé holding the harpoon launcher, a sheepish Quinlan standing behind him, hands clasped behind his back.

With a flick of a button, Agustan retracted the rope on the harpoon. There was a sickening sound of flesh rending as the harpoon whizzed past Vila's shoulder and back into the shaft of the launcher, leaving droplets of red on the White Warden's cloak. She could feel the gore that had smattered the back of her head upon the harpoon's retreat, the warm bits of flesh and blood dripping down her neck.

"You..." Vila didn't have words for how much she hated Agustan Tempé in that moment. Nothing could come close to describing the terrible things she wanted to do to him.

"She wasn't going to tell you anything," he smirked, tossing the launcher back to its owner. "And she was right. You were enjoying that too much. I just saved everyone some time."

"August," Taragin growled. "We needed her. Now we have no idea who is behind this."

Agustan stepped up to the older Warden, his eyes glistening dangerously in the flickering light of the sight stones and moon shards. His hood cast long shadows over his face from the dichotomy of light sources.

"Then maybe you should have listened to me before you ran in here and fucked everything up."

He turned towards Vila. "I'm guessing this was your idea. Trying to play hero? I thought I told you to stay out of this and now look what you've done. Nearly sank the entire city."

Vila seethed as the strong hand of Shaila O'Caan gripped her shoulder, squeezing in a placating gesture.

"Get her out of here," Agustan commanded to Shaila. "And Vila? Drop the Blade."

Vila's hand trembled, reluctant to give up her father's weapon. Tempé watched the struggle on her face, his sneer growing wider, cheek muscles twitching. She looked to Taragin who gave her a small nod, and she let the precious weapon fall from her hand. Tempé kicked her blade away with a grin and turned back towards Taragin.

Vila felt the larger woman strengthen her grip and she let herself be pulled away, hands clenching until her knuckles threatened to break. She shoved the Warden's hand away and strode towards the jagged exit back into the heart of the sub-city. Behind her, she heard a sickening thud and the pained grunt of Taragin Echilar as Agustan inflicted his version of leadership on the aging Warden. Vila didn't turn her head, afraid of what Tempé would do to him if she showed any concern.

Taragin would have to take care of himself, but Vila made a silent oath that she would kill Agustan Tempé for it.

19

"It has always been suspected that the divine realm of Lunus and Celenia hold sway over unseen forces in our world. The state of the water can be tracked to the ebbing and flowing of the moon kingdom, its size, and position in the night sky. What power is at play is unknown to all but Loamia, who incurred the divine wrath of the moon twins in her madness. What stories would she tell of the cold and terrible power of the full moon's light?"
~The personal record keeping of Malania Tortosfin, Head of the Astronomical Society for Celestial Learning and Comprehension~

R enalia jumped as Narrio slammed his cloak on the table, the weight of the strange creature inside slapping against the wood. The package landed with a heavy, squishing thud as moldy water splashed across the driftwood furniture and dripped onto the floor. Narrio hadn't cared who he startled as he stumbled out of the entrance to the Lower Planks and returned the Bilger's Fare to the proprietor of the Crusted Whale. He was sure he looked quite terrifying in a bedraggled and sad sort of way. His leg was throbbing and the journey back up had taken twice as long as the already tedious trip down.

Filthy, wet, and bleeding, Narrio flopped himself into the booth next to Renalia and let his head fall to the table. She slid a mug over to him and inspected the cuts on his neck and head. Her fingers were cool to the touch as she wiped some of the blood away and pulled his dripping hair over his ears.

"You look truly awful. What happened down there?"

"Look in the cloak."

He wanted to go to sleep so badly, his body finally giving out on him. He couldn't even bring himself to pick up the mug of kelp wine, which was disturbing. Renalia slowly lifted the folds of the soaked garment and peered inside. To her credit, she didn't scream or jump back at the sight of the monstrous creature that stared back at her with its crystalline gaze and butchered body. Her face did take on a seriousness, however, as she let the cloak back down. Her eye danced nervously about the room before she stood up and slipped her arm under Narrio's.

"What are you doing?" he exclaimed, desperate to lay there as long as he could. She pulled him away and grabbed the grotesque bundle, abandoning the mugs of wine which Narrio managed to grab as he was hurried away.

"We're going upstairs, you can tell me everything there."

"I'm too tired to do anything else, I'm sad to say."

"We're not doing anything until you've had a bath. Now go. We can't talk down here."

The scalding water felt incredible on Narrio's skin, soaking the grime and blood off his body with every tender scrub. His right leg hung out of the tub and Renalia had done a much better job of bandaging the wound with a red kelp poultice than he ever could have. He'd somehow found the energy to knock back the mug of kelp wine, which had helped the pain and he now regaled his companion with the harrowing tale of 'Narrio versus the Demon Eel'.

She listened with interest, although there were more than a few eye rolls at the flourishes that peppered the story. When he was done, she leaned back and sipped on her wine, eye thoughtfully trailing out the window. It was raining again and Narrio found himself wondering if the city was ever dry. The whistling noise through the ropes was also a delightful reprieve from the low drone of the Lower Planks.

"So, you think this mystery woman has the key to the door," she finally said, her eye still on the rain splattered windowpane.

"It's the only thing that makes sense. I think she's a Del'Sor."

Renalia cocked her eyebrow, her face showing no small amount of skepticism. "Really, Narrio, a Del'Sor?"

"She must be. Why else would she have a key to the secret door? If Hinaldo or one of his ancestors made that door, then his descendants could have had the key, right? If that woman is coming in and out that way, then we must assume she has a connection to them at the very least. And that symbol was all over the drawings we looked at. I'd bet it's some family crest."

"That's a lot of assumptions."

"It's all we have. Some of the greatest discoveries in the world were based off wild assumptions."

"You'll have to tell me exactly what those are some other time. Also, her being a Del'Sor doesn't really play a part in all of this, correct? Nobody cares about them anymore."

"I guess so."

"Wouldn't the priest have a key?"

"We could assume that, but getting to him is almost impossible, if he even has it. I think tracking her down is our best bet."

"How do you plan on doing that?"

"She's a Blue Lady, right? I figured we'd start at the brothels and work from there."

Renalia's face reddened a bit, an emotion passing over that his brain couldn't quite work out.

"Of course, and heading down to the brothels is all for the job, right?"

"Purely business." He held his hands up in defense. "I'll keep my hands clean. We just need to identify her so we can figure out the next steps. If she has the key on her, then we have to find a way to get close."

"Please tell me you're not going to pay a Blue Lady so you can steal from her. That seems low, even for you."

"I'm shocked you'd even think that. I'm a thief, but a thief with an ethical compass, regardless of what people think."

"Good to know."

"I'll poke around the brothels up here and see what I can turn up."

Renalia's arms folded tightly across her chest as her eyes narrowed at him. Narrio looked over his shoulder to see what she was looking at and realized he was the source of the ire in her stare.

"There are no brothels in the Upper Planks."

"There's not?"

"No, Narrio, there's not. It's illegal up here."

"Then what about Blue Ladies?"

Renalia's stance softened as she realized the depths of his ignorance. She placed her hands on his naked shoulders and he didn't like the way she stared at him as if he were a child.

"They're *Blue Ladies*, not prostitutes. Every other girl in the profession, the so-called Green Girls? They're not allowed up here. Ever."

Narrio tried to come to grips with what he was hearing. He knew Bilger's Fare locked down the Lower Planks to some degree, but he had assumed one could join the Upper citizenry if they went through the proper channels.

"Even if they quit?"

Renalia's laugh carried sad undertones as she slunk back to her chair. "The Lower Planks is not just a separate city, it's a prison. The patrons may *say* you can earn your way up, but it's mostly a lie. Green Girls, prize fighters, regular people; if you're born down there, there's no way up for you unless you earn your passage through unsavory means."

"Like a Blue Lady."

"Yes."

"That's...kind of fucked up."

"Welcome to the Planks."

Narrio sat in his bath in silence, a feeling of sadness welling up in him. He'd made some assumptions without understanding the nature of how things really were, and the truth was hard to deal with. He didn't like this new sympathetic side that was taking hold of him and he tried hard to shake its grip.

"Well, I guess that's a problem for another day."

"Right...someone else's problem."

Narrio emerged from the tub, his naked form steaming from the boiling water. When Renalia didn't immediately pounce upon him, he sullenly wrapped a towel about his waist with a pout and poured himself another glass of wine. They needed to get back to business.

"I'll go back down tomorrow and see what I can find out about our blue mystery. I'm exhausted, and you haven't filled me in on your day."

"What do you want to know?"

"What were you doing? Did you find out anything useful?"

Renalia scoffed. "I wasn't doing anything concerning your mission. Like I said before, your job is to find a way into the church and get the stone. I'm here to offer assistance when needed—and able. Helping you isn't my sole reason for existence, you know. I have a life here, and people to take care of."

Narrio raised his eyebrows as he pulled his trousers on, fastening the bone clasps in place. He hadn't really thought about what her life was like outside of the job. To him, this was his life right now, an all-consuming purpose ending in life or death and a fat paycheck. It hadn't occurred to him that for her, it was just a small piece of an unrelated life.

"You have family here?"

"No one romantic, if that's what you're asking."

"It wasn't, but that's good to know." He smiled at her, noting she didn't return it.

"My brother and his children; I help them out when I can with whatever I can bring in from various jobs. I doubt I was paid anything close to what you're getting to steal the stone."

That stung a bit, the guilt coating his insides.

"I don't know what it's like in the other cities," she continued, "But here? If you're not a merchant or a patron, life can be shitty. Even for Uppers."

Narrio sat down across from her, hoping he sounded as sincere as he was starting to feel.

"What does your brother do?"

"He works the salvage bells. It's extremely dangerous and salvagers don't get paid nearly as much as the ones who own the operations. He can be down there for days at a time, so someone has to be with the children. Their mother died last year, so I'm all he has left."

"I'm sorry."

"Thank you. And don't you dare try to give me any money."

"Agreed. Do I get to know about the eyepatch?"

Renalia drained her glass and stood, her gaze landing on the squishy package laying on the table.

"Not a chance. Now are we going to talk about the eel in the room?"

Narrio had almost forgotten about it, and he wished he had. Renalia uncovered the putrid beast, the stench filling the space and driving out the formerly pleasant smells of perfume and wine.

"It's really ugly," she said, staring at the skin which was still giving off an unearthly green hue. "What are those rocks growing out of it?"

"I don't know. Some sort of crystal and it's not natural. I'm not scared of much, besides water, but that thing scares the hell out of me."

Renalia stared at him like he had a crystal-crusted eel crawling out of his ears.

"What?"

"You're afraid of water?"

"Deathly." He was too tired to deny it.

She continued to stare at him for a moment before erupting in laughter as his face reddened. "Narrio! We live on the ocean. You can't be afraid of water."

"You're right. I'll just stop. Silly me. Can we talk about the eel-thing now?"

She wiped a tear from her eyes. "Don't be mad at me."

"I'm not mad."

"Yes, you are, your eye is twitching. I'm sorry, it was just surprising that's all."

"I would have done much better in the dry age, that is for sure. You should see how well I swim," he said, going for humor to bury the reasons for the phobia. He gave her a genial smile which she returned. "As I was saying that thing is not right."

"No." She grew thoughtful as she paced around the room, her eyes never leaving the grotesque corpse of the eel. "I'll take it to the archives tomorrow and see if the scholars can help me find something. But we can't let it distract from the main task, so wrap it back up."

"It has to stay here tonight? It smells awful."

"Put it in the bath, and then come to bed."

Narrio raised both eyebrows at her as she moved into the other
room.

"Unless you're too exhausted."

"Not at all."

Narrio jerked out of a fitful sleep, his skin sheened over with
sweat as the nightmare faded. Vivid images of being pulled into a
black abyss of dark water by a multi-headed monster with glowing
green eyes still flashed through his head as the fog of sleep slowly
dissipated. He worked to control his breathing as he came to his
senses, his eyes adjusting to the room faster than his brain could.
Steadily the dark shapes receded into the corners of the room,
no longer resembling horrendous creatures of the deep trying to
devour him; the wetness on his skin was no longer the icy grip of
the Swell, but his own sweat beading from fear.

He repeated his mantra over and over until he finally felt the
shaking in his arms and legs start to dwindle. Renalia snored lightly
next to him, undisturbed.

Staring through the open door at the tub in the other room,
the feral part of his brain waited for some monstrosity to come
sliding out and slither over to finish its meal. Narrio shook his head,
shaking off the last remnants of nightmare. Sleep wasn't going to
happen again, at least not for a while. He needed to get up and
move, maybe even get something to eat.

Quietly slipping on his trousers and lacing up his boots, he threw
his shirt over his head and exited the room, wincing at every creak
in the floorboards. Renalia rolled over, her snores growing a little
louder as she took up the now unoccupied warm spot of the bed.
Her naked shoulders glowed in the moonlight streaming through

the window and Narrio wanted to jump back in bed and bask in her warmth. Maybe when he got back.

Pulling his cloak off the hook, he slipped his arms through the sleeves and exited the room. He crept down the stairs into the tavern hall below where a few patrons hadn't made it up to their rooms. Narrio settled into a seat near the window and munched on a piece of leftover bread as he sniffed at the contents of an unfinished mug. Finding it not completely off-putting, he washed down the meager meal and laid his head back, feeling the cool night breeze hit his skin from a broken windowpane. He was about to drift off when a low voice in his ear nearly sent him leaping out of his seat.

"You have a lot of explaining to do."

Narrio gripped the edge of his seat, knuckles turning white as he realized the voice was coming from outside the window in the darkened alley. A figure was just out of his line of sight, unaware of any eavesdroppers but keeping their voice low regardless.

The mystery person's companion, however, was in full view as they pulled themself up out of a trapdoor in the planks. The extremely tall and attractive man stood up and basked in the light of the nearly full moon, their white cloak made of shark skin glowing in the light. His face was chiseled, and his eyes glinted with arrogance and violence underneath his hood. Narrio thought he looked unhinged.

The thief pressed himself against his booth and slowly scooted closer to the window jamb, hoping the two men remained unaware of his presence. Something about the interaction spoke of secrecy and deadliness and he was sure that he would be killed immediately if he was found out. Why they chose a back alley to have a moonlight meeting, he didn't know, and he didn't much care. All he hoped for was to survive for the next few minutes and if he learned anything useful, that would be a plus.

"I've taken care of it. Taragin won't step out of line again and none of them know about our arrangement. We just need to proceed as planned. The full moon is only two nights away."

The name Taragin sounded familiar to Narrio, but in his fear-addled state, he couldn't quite place where he'd heard it before. The mystery man was talking again, his voice straining to stay a whisper as he seethed in anger.

"Taken care of? I lost millions in profit on those weapons. Your people ruined the shaft, nearly sank the city and are still skulking around my rocks like rabid dogs. You said you would keep them away, that nothing would go wrong and now look at where we are!"

"You'll get your weapons and your rocks back. Soon, you'll have all the power you want."

"You better be right, Tempé. You fucked this up and you can't afford to do it again."

The tall man suddenly grinned, his perfect teeth flashing and sending chills down Narrio's spine.

"I'd think carefully before proceeding with that line of thought. I don't need you in this arrangement for it to work. You're just the easiest of the paths to getting what I want."

"And what is that exactly? My contact had already led me to the moon rocks before you showed up. You promised me your Wardens wouldn't find out about the operation, which they did. What do you gain from all of this?"

Another wave of fear and confusion shivered its way up Narrio's spine as a piece connected for him and his brain slowly realized where he'd heard those names; Taragin Echilar. Agustan Tempé. Wardens. Deep wardens. The man was Agustan Tempé. The terrifying White Warden was standing right outside the window as Narrio sat there like a dolt, holding his breath, and pissing himself.

Agustan rubbed the back of his head, that sinister smile never leaving his lips. "Just make sure Del'Sor is there when it happens. And remember; I want a big crowd."

The Warden turned away and strode off into the moonlight, leaping onto a nearby rooftop and disappearing into the night. A rickshaw sped past the window as the mystery party returned to wherever they came from. Narrio waited until he was certain everyone was gone and then bolted up the stairs, back into the room, and threw himself into the bed. Somehow, he'd managed to take his clothes back off in his terrified flight and now lay in the warm bed shivering as Renalia, still deep in slumber, rolled over and wrapped her arm around his waist.

His mind was reeling from what he'd heard, he pressed himself against her warmth as he lay awake and stared out the window at the nearly full moon. He wished he was smarter, because something told him that everything was connected in some way; the eel, the Wardens, the woman, the moon. Even the stone somehow. He just couldn't put it all together and he was scared to try.

Narrio clasped Renalia's hand against his chest, feeling his heart racing. He closed his eyes and tried to dream about being a farmer on some green crop of land in an age of sun and trees—far far away from the water.

20

"Of course, the Blue Ladies should be allowed to come and go as needed. Can you imagine the outrage if we banished them to the Lower Planks like their inferiors? Do you know how many letters I would get from my donors? Really, Hylean, I thought you were smarter than that."
~Patron Machaeus, long dead~

Vila sprang out of bed. Someone was in her room, and even half asleep, she swung her sea glass knife at the intruder. The girl reeled backwards as the blade came very close to cutting her throat.

"I'm so sorry Mistress!" the young girl screamed as she fell, cowering in the corner with tears starting to appear in her eyes. Vila thought she recalled her name was Lanya, but she couldn't be sure. She had always tried to remember all the names of the Green Girls, but they came and went so quickly through Madame Molena's that it was hard to keep track. Vila dropped the blade and touched her side. The pain from the previous night's wounds was subsiding, not yet gone, but better. She looked down to find her bandages soaked through and her bedding covered in a darkening red smear.

"What do you want?" she croaked, afraid of the answer. The madame only sent a girl to find her when she had a job that required her Blue Lady services.

"The madame wants you...."

Vila leaned her head back and sighed. The pain was dull, but she wanted more of that blood tincture; longed for it even. She wasn't sure if she would see Taragin for a while and there was no way she was getting any from the others.

"Tell her I'll be there as soon as I can."

"She-she was very insistent that you come with me."

"Now?"

"Yes Mistress."

Vila cursed loudly, sending the girl cowering again. She hung her head, stretching the tense muscles in her neck. She barely remembered falling into bed last night, her body and mind exhausted from the altercation in the workshop. She had so many questions about what would happen next; questions she was sure she wouldn't get the answer to. Tempe's iron fist had a lock on it and Shaila was very clear that Vila was to "stay the fuck away", as she so eloquently put it.

She didn't even have the energy to visit Rance and the raw emotion he brought up was draining to the point that she couldn't think, couldn't provide any sympathy or support to the dying man. She also didn't have answers for him, even after all the discoveries and that hurt most of all. She had bandaged her injuries and relented to the consuming and overwhelming need to sleep. She barely felt rested.

"What time is it?"

"Seventh hour, Mistress."

She'd slept for twenty hours, and yet she swore she felt worse. Every fiber in her being screamed at her in protest. She didn't want to look at a mirror, but a feeling of glee passed over as she thought about the look on Molena's face when she saw her. It gave her the energy to get up and follow the girl.

"Alright, let's go."

The girl hesitated, her eyes stuck on the bloody sheets and Vila's half naked and battered body.

"Shouldn't...shouldn't you see someone?"

Vila smirked. "She said now, didn't she?"

"Yes Mistress."

"Then let's go. We wouldn't want to keep the madame waiting."

The smell of incense and sex hit Vila harder than a punch from some of her larger opponents in the arena. She hadn't had to come here for some time, as Blue Ladies were allowed to operate independently unless called on commission. The whole place stunk, and she hated it. Madame Molena's was one of the more upstanding brothels in the Lower Planks, but it was still a brothel. Naked girls barely past their childhood years wandered past, fully exposed, and covered in makeup. She didn't know most of them, as new stock needed to be brought in on a continual basis. Rich men liked them young and fresh—it made her sick.

She could hear one sided sounds of pleasure coming from the curtained rooms along the hall of beams and lap siding. Mildew could be seen creeping along the edges, the entire place thick with body heat and moisture. She marched on, intent on making this interaction as quick as possible. With any luck, the madame would tell her she had an inquiry about hiring a Blue Lady for a night; Vila would make up some excuses about being too tired (which wasn't a lie tonight) and if she played her cards right, she could go on with her healing in peace. She also needed to see Rance, even though she dreaded how much he might have deteriorated.

Vila reached the madame's personal chambers, closed off by ship captain's doors taken from a wreckage and retrofitted to make a grander entrance. Red curtains hid the rotted beams in the hall and gold adornments laced the edges and trim. The whole thing was gaudy and obnoxious.

She didn't even bother knocking. If Molena wanted to see her so badly, then she could stop whatever she was doing. Vila pushed the door open and was surprised to see the older woman sitting casually on the couch, crystal glass of wine in hand, talking to a well-dressed gentleman with graying hair and a well-kempt mustache. His thick, crimson-dyed tusker skin cloak hanging off the lush couch as he cajoled the madame with some story he thought was hilarious.

Vila had never wanted to run from a room so badly as Vintar Maccio III's eyes met hers and he smiled. As a Blue Lady, Vila was usually able to be more choosey about how she conducted her business, but sometimes clients were pushed on her. It shocked her to see him waiting in the madame's chambers considering his previous offer had been about sponsoring her in the fights—an activity that the madame did not approve of. She was immediately wary of what trap she was walking into.

"Vila," Madame Molena said as she entered. "You came quickly, good girl. Come sit down and have a glass." Her tone was genial, but Vila could feel the older woman's emberassment at Vila's appearance.

"No thank you."

The woman's glare was deadly but gone sooner than it had appeared. The madame smiled, her mouth twitching in effort to hold back a scathing reprimand. Vila couldn't care less, and she wasn't going to sit down and relax either.

"As you wish," Molena continued. "This is Vintar Maccio III, he owns several salvage operations here and abroad and, I should add, brought this lovely bottle of Toren Reserve with him. It's a vintage brew, all the way from Anthema. You really must try it."

"No thank you," Vila said again. The madame's face was beginning to turn red, and Vila knew she would be in for it once the merchant left, but she didn't care. Not right now. The man stood gracefully and reached out to take Vila's hand to his lips. She pulled back, leaving him awkwardly holding his hand up in the air. He casually straightened and gave a slight wink, the charade of this meeting being their first became clear to Vila. Her stomach rolled as she wondered what he was playing at.

"Madame Molena has been a gracious host while we waited. She runs quite the charming business here."

"Charming is one word for it, I guess."

He cleared his throat. "Yes, well, I guess we can get down to the reason for my visit..."

"Please do," Vila replied, holding her palms wide, gesturing for him to continue. She stared daggers at him, daring him to go on. He looked at the madame, seeking permission that it was appropriate. When she nodded her head, he sat back down and continued speaking.

"I've come to hire your services for tomorrow evening. I'll be blunt and say that it is not for anything salacious or crude. I'm sure you've heard that before, but the word of a Maccio is never broken. Rather, I'm hosting a party, in honor of the coming full moon. Second one of the month, so it's quite the big deal. I consider myself something of an amateur astronomer and am hosting the event to view the skies; maybe catch a glimpse of the Lunar Kingdom. And I might or might not be looking to scrounge up some charitable donations to the astronomical society's chapter here in the planks in the process."

Vila hated parties and social gatherings. It brought too much unwanted attention and prying. She also didn't want anything to do with the rich lord. His touch left a slimy feeling on her skin that she couldn't shake, and he seemed entirely too interested in her for some reason; a reason that she did not want to encourage or explore. But one look at the madame told her that she wasn't going to be able to refuse the ask.

"I feel like my guests would be much more charmed and generous if I had some accompaniment, especially one of such a stunning nature."

Vila almost snorted as she watched the madame redden further. First, he wanted to sponsor her in the fights, and now he wanted to parade her around to his rich friends. Vila didn't want any part of it.

"You flatter me," she replied, fully aware of the lack of gratefulness in her tone. "But I'm sure the madame could find you someone more suitable. As you can see, I've had a few rough days and I don't think you would find me good company for your distinguished guests. I'm sorry to have wasted your time."

The smile that was returned was much colder, and it sent an icy shiver down Vila's spine. It held an underlying deviousness that she didn't like. There was no way out of this, and she felt caught.

"You haven't and there aren't any others that I want with me. I specifically requested you. I've done my research and there are no others that I would bring to my abode."

Research? Vila thought. The thought of what sort of research he could be conducting made her sick. The madame cleared her throat again.

"Lord Maccio has already paid a generous sum to request your presence and has graciously offered more to have you attend with him. It is done." There was a finality in her tone that Vila had only heard a few times growing up and it always meant saying no wasn't an option. She could feel her anger start to boil but held her tongue. There would be more words when Lord Maccio left.

"It's settled then, I guess," Vila said, her face placid.

He smiled regardless, his pearly teeth gleaming with a sickening glow. Vila could sense his elation at the victory, and it made her want to vomit. "Wonderful. I will have an escort pick you up at Drifter's Gate tomorrow evening, seventeenth hour."

"She'll be ready," the madame cut in, her anger and embarrass-ment barely hidden under a thin veil of good-natured smiles and eyelash batting.

"I look forward to it," he said as he placed his over-sized hat on his head with a flourish.

Giving the women one more smile, he exited the room, leaving a silence that hung as heavy as a winter fog. The two generations stared at each other, the unspoken anger shifting and writhing just under the surface. Vila was the first to break the dam.

"You are un-*fucking* believable."

"I could say the same about you." The older women held up a hand, pausing the coming onslaught as she drained the last of her glass.

Vila held her ground as the empty glass flew over her shoulder, the shards crashing around her in a violent cascade. A piece nicked her exposed shoulder, the little trickle of blood giving fuel to the rage building inside of her. Madame Molena moved closer; her breath stunk of the expensive wine.

"You can be as petulant as you want. Be ungrateful and angry. But how DARE you embarrass me like that."

"Embarrass you?! Look at yourself. You don't need any help from me to do—"

The slap jolted her head back before the rest of her words could leave her mouth. She tasted blood, the tinge of metal building up around her tongue. It didn't hurt, she'd been hit harder by bigger opponents. What hurt was who had delivered it. As big a bitch as she could be, Molena had never struck her before.

"You are a Blue Lady, Vila. You are one of the most sought after and expensive women in the Planks and you look like a two-glass whore. I have girls out there that would do anything to be in your shoes and you come in here like this? Bleeding, bruised, filthy. I should rip those beads off your wrist and shove them down your throat because you clearly don't understand the privilege you have!"

That was the final straw.

"Privilege?" Vila said quietly, wiping her hand across her mouth. The cut would heal, but the damage behind it could never be undone. "You trained your own daughter to be a prostitute, mother. Who the fuck does that? Why the hell should I be grateful to you for shackling me to a life on my knees, fucking whoever pays the highest price? I don't want this, I NEVER wanted this. You stole away any chance I had at a decent life!"

"I gave you this life! I gave you the chance to have a life at all, you ungrateful little bitch! The only reason you were allowed to come into this world was because Iltar Del'Sor was a better man than he should have been. You know what we become when one of us bears a child. Baggage, used goods, worthless. But your father made me carry you, begged me to give you a chance at something. It took me years to work my way into the position I have now, and I handed that to you on a platter. You have no idea what kind of life you would have had if I hadn't."

Vila's anger was still hot under her skin, but the mention of Iltar Del'Sor made her heart hurt. She clutched the bracer around her wrist, holding close the only thing she had left of a man that she knew too little of and loved too much. She never wanted the burden of a family legacy, only to know the man who left it for her.

"And what would he say if he knew you raised his daughter in this life, huh? Shackled her with a ringlet and set her loose on the streets?"

Her mother sat down, taking the half-full bottle to her lips.

"He would have hated me, but he was a hypocrite and a fool. Idolize him all you want, but he came down here like all the other men. He just happened to have a larger heart than most and it cost him his life."

She took a deep breath, rubbing her temples.

"I promised him I would raise you, protect you and I did it the only way I knew how. I need you to do your job. I need you to stop battering your body, it's the only asset that lets me keep you here."

She crossed her legs as she held the bottle tighter. "And you have to stop seeing that priest."

That caught Vila off guard, even though she knew deep down that it shouldn't have. Her mother survived off her good looks, her status, and the fact that she knew everything that happened above and below, especially when it came to who was fucking who.

Vila tried to open her mouth to speak, but her mother got there first. "Don't be coy and try to lie to me. I know all about your little tryst and it needs to stop for more than one reason."

"That's not an option."

"You are going to get both of you killed. For one thing, you wear that damned piece of leather everywhere despite how much you say you hate the legacy behind it. The Del'Sors may be mostly forgotten to the common folk, but what do you think would happen if someone with real power and money knew who you really were? If you really hated the name so much, you'd burn that thing."

"I'm not leaving Temson. And I'm not getting rid of this." Even as she said it, she knew her mother was right; a thought that made her sick. Taragin had recognized her because of it and there would be others. But she couldn't bring herself to take it off and discard the one remaining connection she had to him—the one connection that she actually cared about. Vila's mother sighed, leaning her head back against the pillows as she stared up into the ceiling planks.

"You *will* be ready," she finally said. "Lanya will come get you tomorrow and help you get prepared. Please, *please* behave yourself. Not because I ask you, but because you must. If you want to keep the life you seem to enjoy, then for Fathus' sake follow the rules and do your job."

Vila seethed inside as she gave in. She didn't have much choice at this point. They had had this argument many times. The sad reality was that her mother was right. Despite being forced into it against her will, she was still a Blue Lady. Though she was protected against harm, as much as one could be, by Upper Planks law, there was no escaping this life now that she was in it. She could never walk around free of the burdens that came with the life.

She needed to hit something, and hard.

Leaving the room, she found Lanya skulking outside, and the young girl gave a her a sad smile. Vila wasn't sure what all she had heard, but the gesture was appreciated, if not annoying at the same time. She ignored the girl's sympathetic glances and stalked out of the brothel, tears filling her eyes as she recounted the painful words, hating herself for focusing on them.

21

"I heard anyone who is anyone is going to be at the gala, and I for one don't plan on missing it."

~A rich person~

The stench of death hung in the room like a heavy blanket, smothering everything in its grip. Vila was no stranger to death or the unpleasantness that often surrounded it; she had caused plenty of it herself. But seeing Rance's lifeless body on the bed nearly brought her to her knees. There was nothing peaceful about the sight, no sense of a calm passing that so many talked about. The old man was contorted on his side as if he had been in extreme pain during his final moments. His eyes were completely crusted over with black shards and the bed was stained with blackened blood from the countless protrusions of razor-sharp crystals all over his body. His hand grasped the bed sheet like an iron vice, and his knees were tucked into his chest.

Vila knew she had screamed, but her own voice was deadened by the thumping of her heart and the rush of anger and despair that washed over her as she laid eyes on her friend. She didn't care about the hundreds of tiny cuts she recieved as she rushed to his bedside and cradled his frail, lifeless body in her arms.

Blood and tears mingled together in a flood of anguish as she rocked her friend in her arms, wishing she had been there. All the regretful thoughts that come with death raced through her brain, even though she knew there wasn't anything she could have done differently to stop it. No number of hot meals would have changed the outcome; arriving a few hours earlier wouldn't have miraculously caused the corruption to slow or given him relief. There was no cure, nothing to be done, and now he was gone.

She might have been holding him for hours—she didn't care. Nothing could have ripped her from that spot on the bed. Nothing except the disgusting presence of Agustan Tempé standing in the doorway.

"Looks like I don't have anything to clean up anymore."

Vila slowly let Rance's body fall onto the bed, her movements deliberate. She could feel the press of her sea glass knife at her back, her muscles tensing as she readied herself to strike down the imposing Warden. She didn't bother wiping the tears from her eyes. She wanted the White Warden to see. Agustan was unreadable as his eyes passed over the gruesome sight, his face showing no sign of remorse or sympathy. Instead, he casually picked at his fingernails with a wicked looking blade of carved bone as he spoke.

"Taragin was always too sympathetic to be a Warden. Stubborn, but sympathetic. Took quite the beating to find out about this one." He pointed the knife at Rance.

"If you killed him..."

"You'll what? Cut me to ribbons? Use my innards as a noose? Please."

He was suddenly upon her, his broad-shouldered frame looming over her before she could rise from the bed or pull the weapon from the strap on her back.

"You can't kill me, and you know it," he snarled at her. "You might be a killer, little girl, but I'm a monster. And monsters can only be slayed by their own kind." He knelt close to her face and Vila's body tensed from the imminent danger. "Are you a monster, Vila?"

"Why don't we find out?" she whispered, willing as much threat into her voice as she could. Her hand snapped to her backside, but his were faster as he restrained her arm behind her. His breath stank and he kept his mouth uncomfortably close to her ear as he held her there.

"In due time," he smiled, his teeth flashing in a wicked grin that spoke of horrors Vila couldn't put words to. Every fiber in her body told her to attack, to wrench herself from his grip and slash his throat—watch him bleed out on the floor. It took all her strength to reign in her impulses and take the verbal beating. Agustan was a monster, that much was true; but it didn't just take monsters to kill monsters. It took observation, learning, and the right moment. This wasn't it.

"What do you want?"

"I came to make sure he was dead. Like I said, it's not time for anyone to know what is happening. Finding you here in a puddle of sobs and pity was just a plus. Take care, Vila."

Tempé released her arm and took a long stride backwards, his eyes never leaving hers.

"I heard we are going to the same party tomorrow. Maybe you'll get your chance there. Who knows?"

With that, Agustan Tempé tipped his hood and slipped out of the shack, the warm air in the room returning as he left. Vila sat for a long time, her body shaking with restrained emotion. Agustan had violated her private moment of mourning with his presence and now the room only stank of his filth.

She had learned one important thing from their horrid interaction: for whatever reason, he was going to be at Lord Maccio's gala, and she felt a rising sense of pleasure at the thought of murdering him in front of all those people.

She gently rolled Rance over on the bed and began to pick the shards off his body, not caring about getting cut or the fruitlessness of the endeavor. One by one, late into the night, Vila pulled at the shards until the gentle, kind face of her friend was visible once more, marred as it was. A mortician would have done the same, but she couldn't bear the thought of them examining him and cutting into his body to find the source of the infection. Rance deserved a peaceful rest, undisturbed by prying eyes and hands. The man had so little in life, it was the best she could offer him in death. She wrapped him up in a sheet and carried him out the door and down to the docks.

Vila watched as Rance's body slowly descended into the dark waters until it was no longer visible. He would have wanted it this way, to return to the ocean that had both scorned and provided for him his entire life. If the Church's teachings were right, then his soul would find its way to Fathus' temple, the sea glass stone she'd put in his hand guiding the way. She ignored the onlookers as she turned her back on the water and stalked away. None of them knew the man who was sinking to the deepest parts of the Swell, his body set to become part of the lifecycle of the deep. No one knew the pain he had suffered in those final moments, or the hard and unrecognized life he had lived.

Another thread in the fabric of her comfort had snapped when she dropped his body into the water, and it threw her off balance in a way she couldn't describe. She only had a few lines left to grasp onto, and she was desperate to hold onto the last fading shreds of control that she had left. Tonight, she would bloody her hands with another unknown victim in the arena, taking pleasure as she crushed the life out of them.

Then she would go to see Temson.

"What did you find out?" Narrio paced around their room at the inn, running fingers through his greasy hair. Renalia had left early that morning to take the eel-thing to SULHAP and Narrio hadn't left the room at all. The sun was casting its rays over the ocean and flooding the city in a bright, orange glow. But even the brightest light and hottest heat couldn't burn the anxiety from his body as he thought about the previous night's encounter.

"You need to relax."

"You're right, I do. But I can't. You didn't hear them out there; something is going to happen and it's happening tomorrow when the full moon rises. There were weapons and rocks and Del'Sors—"

"Narrio!" Renalia grabbed him by the arm, stopping his frantic pacing. "You can't do anything, and we don't know anything! You heard something; I understand. But you have to get that stone. That's the only thing you need to be focused on right now!"

"I need to find that woman."

"Then go do that!"

"Did you find out anything about the eel?"

Renalia gave an exasperated sigh. "No, not yet. I'll let you know as soon as I hear something." She sat him down and shoved a mug of tea into his hands in effort to calm him down. "Now what is your plan?"

"I guess I'll go down to the Lower Planks again and look for Blue Ladies with red hair."

"Good, do that then."

"What are you going to do?"

"I'll look at your eel for you." She rolled her eye at Narrio's snicker. "And then I have to help my brother. I'll be in touch."

"Okay."

She leaned down and gave him a kiss on his forehead. He soaked up the soft touch of her lips and the sweet smell of her perfume before she left the room. Narrio leaned his head back, trying to make sense of everything. There were Wardens stalking the city and one of them seemed to be in league with someone powerful. The rich man was mad about losing weapons and his rocks. The eel creature had rocks coming out of it.

Connection.

The secret door to the church was locked by a key in the shape of a secret symbol. Hinaldo Del'Sor most likely built and used the secret door to satiate his sexual appetites. That red-haired woman was most likely using the door as well and had to have the key. She had to be a Del'Sor.

Connection

The mystery man was gathering a bunch of people together at the behest of the White Warden. The Warden made it very clear the Del'Sor was to be there. If the red-haired woman was a Del'Sor, then the Warden wanted her for something. Something big. Something involving the full moon. The rocks on the eel looked like moon shards. Could you make weapons out of moon shards?

Narrio's head hurt.

He pressed his fingers deep into his eyes, working to push the rushing thoughts from his brain. He knew that the only thing he needed to focus on was getting that key, retrieving the stone, and getting out of here, but Narrio had learned to trust his instincts when they screamed at him and right now, they were a cacophonous roar. The figure on the boat had said events were going to happen that would alter life or change something. Was any of this related?

Something told him there was a deadline approaching on the mission that he hadn't anticipated, and that he must have things in place quickly or forfeit his life.

He couldn't waste time running around the city looking for this mysterious woman, so he downed his tea, laced up his boots and headed out to buy some nicer clothes before he made his way down to the brothels. People were always more willing to talk to you if you looked rich.

22

"Dear Vila, I doubt your mother will ever give you this, but I'm writing it anyways. I know that I won't be there to watch you grow, but I've made her promise to raise you, to see you become an incredible force of nature. You won't understand why I can't be there, I know, and I am so sorry. I would have loved to meet you, talk with you. Maybe in another life, but I won't be long for this one. Don't hate her; I'm sure she'll do the best she can. You're a Del'Sor, which means you survive. It's what we do, and I know that you'll live up to that legacy. Stay strong. I love you."
~An opened letter from Iltar Del'Sor~

Vila hung on the metal rungs that were embedded deep into the ancient rock. Above her, the door to the church lay like a heavy burden above her head, below her the long narrow passage that led down to the hidden tunnel inside one of the Pillars of the World. She clung to the rungs, unsure of what to expect when she came through the door and into the sanctum. Conflicted feelings coursed through her as she thought about Temson. Their relationship was fraught with complications from the very beginning;

sexual dissonance, burdens of livelihood, and differing opinions on her family legacy and its importance.

His words, both spoken and unspoken, had left a deep wound that she wasn't sure would ever heal. She knew what he really thought about her life as a Blue Lady, even if he didn't; she had never told him the truth about her past though. How she was born to a whore mother who forced her into the sexual slavery, or the father whose mysterious life and death had left a hole in her life that couldn't be filled. She didn't think it would make a difference. It might garner her some sympathy, but she told herself Temson was going to judge her regardless. He couldn't help it; it was in his nature.

They were unevenly matched in most regards, yet she felt a deep longing for him when she wasn't there. She felt that way now as she hung in the dark and it ate at her that she desired him—that she didn't want to imagine a world without him. Neither of them had anyone else and it scared her even more with Rance's passing. Her attachments were stretched thin and losing the last thread of connection to Temson would thrust her headfirst into a hole of seclusion and loneliness. She wasn't ready to return to that yet.

With a breath she removed the bracer and placed the cast inside the relief, slowly turned the lock, hearing the click reverberate down the shaft. A faint glow of warm oil lantern light crept through the crack as the door began to lift. She took a few more deep breaths and carefully pulled herself into the inner sanctum, wincing at the pain of the fresh wounds from the evening's matches.

Temson was sitting at his desk, empty bottles of kelp wine littered the floor and tables. He looked like he hadn't slept in days, but she could see a light glisten in his blue eyes as he looked up at her. He rose, his hands clutching the table as he cautiously moved around the desk. Vila closed the door behind her and faced him, her expression guarded and her body tense. He paused, a silent understanding happening.

"You can't take it back Tem, I just wanted to make sure you knew that."

"I know..."

"You knew this about me when we met. I never hid it from you, never pretended to be anything different. What I do, what I *have to do* sometimes, has nothing to do with us. When I'm here, you're the only one. But we aren't simple people; we both belong to others and that's how it is and will be. Do you think I like coming up here in secret, swimming through filth because I can't come in the front door? Don't you think that just once, I'd like to walk through the streets with you, enjoying the sun and rain and not worry about who sees?"

Temson's eyes were glistening, and she could see his hand shaking as he steadied himself against the desk. "I'm so sorry I hurt you."

"You did hurt me. You pulled a scab off a deep wound, Temson. But I never told you the wound was there. I want to tell you now."

"You don't have to."

She moved a little closer but kept the distance between them as she spoke. "Yes, I do. If we want to move on from this, you have to hear it."

She watched Tem's face contort and cringe as she relinquished her life's story to him, starting with the birth of an unwanted child to an unwed prostitute from the lower planks. Of a father who she never knew, and who no one would tell her anything about other than he was a great man who was murdered before his time. Of a mother who forced her daughter into sexual slavery to save her from a fruitless or short life. She bore it all to him, all the dark deep resentments and anger that had plagued her. There was only one thing left.

"Fighting in the pits isn't just for money or fun, Temson. It's the only thing that I have that no one else owns. I kill because I want to, because I like it; it arouses me, Temson, in ways you can't understand. You may think the darkest part of me is the Blue Lady, but could you still love me if you knew how much pleasure I get from the feeling of a life leaving its body?"

He studied her, his question forming carefully before it left his lips.

"Why?"

There was no judgement there, no sense of apprehension or disgust. Just a curiosity as he tried to understand her, the woman he had been so intimate with, yet never really knew.

"All those men in the pits can be anyone I want them to be. Nameless, faceless people that represent all the times I've spent on my back or my knees without an ounce of control or freedom. They enter that arena, expecting another weak and vulnerable victim that they can have their way with; but that is the one place where I don't have to be submissive. That is something I won't change or give up; not for you or anyone. Do you understand?"

The blood of the men she had killed that night was still caked under fingernails as she spoke, and she could see Temson's gaze drift towards it, studying the dried gore. He didn't speak as he let go of the desk and took her hand. She didn't pull away, giving him silent acceptance and forgiveness.

"Did you kill tonight?" he asked, his breath hot against her ear.

"Yes. Multiple times." She closed her eyes as his lips traced the bulging veins in her neck. Her blood pumped hard, her heart beating faster as he gripped her waist. She gasped as he lifted her up and placed her on the desk, knocking bottles and scrolls away as he did. He ripped the belt from her waist as Vila began unwrapping her seal skin skirt and spread her legs wide across the smooth wood of her perch. She took pleasure from his eyes darkening as he stared longingly at the wetness between her thighs.

"Tell me what you want to do," she commanded.

"I want to taste you. I want you to cum."

"Good boy."

Taking his beautiful auburn hair in a tight grip, she lowered his head down until she could feel his hot breath against her. His beard brushed her thighs and she started to pulsate in anticipation. Vila closed her eyes and felt a shudder of pleasure roll down her body as his lips pressed against her clit, slowly moving in gentle presses. His tongue slipped between her folds, and a slow moan escaped her, her pleasure only heightened as she imagined him expanding under the folds of his garments. She could hear his heavy breathing as he licked her up and down, tasting her and wanting more. She gripped his head in both hands and pressed him deep, feeling him shake with excitement as his tongue started to move in and out.

He reached up and grasped her thighs hard, plunging in as deep as he could, causing her to gasp sharply, letting her moaning motivate him. His breathing stopped altogether as he pressed harder and moved his tongue in circles around her clit.

Vila's legs trembled and she threw her head back. She could feel his body tensing, sweat starting to glisten on the back of his neck, but still held him for a few more seconds before she released him. He pulled his head back, sucking in air, all the while looking up into her eyes, a sheen of wetness on his lips and dripping down his chin. She reached forward and wiped her finger across his skin and pressed them into his mouth, his lips closing and sucking around her with fervor. She felt his tongue roll across her finger as he swallowed her taste, never breaking eye contact.

She grabbed his head again, pressing him back between her legs and guiding his mouth upwards as she ground herself against his face. While massaging his scalp, she kept him moving up until she felt the faint brush of his teeth against her clit. She moaned louder as he moved in circles, starting gently with intermittent flicks of his tongue that sent shudders of excitement through her. He pulled his head back and looked up at her. She saw his hand move down between his legs wanting desperately to enter her.

"No," she commanded.

He pulled his hand back up, placing two fingers in his mouth before pressing them inside her. He pushed deeper, turning his hand until she felt the full width of both fingers. Slowly, he worked them back and forth as he brought his mouth back down, mapping the outline of her lips with his tongue. She moaned again as he began to pump faster, his tongue continuing to trace her bundle of nerves.

Vila gripped the edge of the table, her cheeks flushing as he moved faster, never letting up on the pressure from his tongue. She could hear him moaning too, his pleasure a sensation that she could feel as she slid her legs over his shoulders and squeezed him in a tight embrace. Without warning, he pushed as deep as he could go and held, the tip of his tongue flying across her clit until she found release in a rush of uncontrollable energy.

With her body still racked with pleasure, she let out a deep groan of delight and dug her fingernails into his back, pressing him closer as the waves of ecstasy continued. Her legs tensed as the convulsions ran their course, each orgasmic pulse sending a shockwave of pleasure through her.

"Oh, god..."

She could feel her cum flow out as he removed his fingers and pushed his tongue back in, rubbing her clit until he'd wrung every drop of pleasure from her, and she leaned back in a satisfied exhaustion. She slowly released her grip on his hair and Temson stood up, his mouth dripping and his cheeks reddened.

He grabbed her by the back of the head and crashed his mouth against hers, his beard still dripping. She could taste herself and couldn't help but groan as she felt his hardness pressing against her tender flesh from inside his garments. Not wanting to let the moment end, she slipped off the table as he released his belt. His erection springing free and throbbing with anticipation as she wrapped her lips around it and let him thrust into her mouth.

She was still in control, and she reached around and grabbed him by the back side, forcing him deep into her throat. She felt his hands in her hair as she moved back and forth, feeling his tip hit the back of her throat again and again. She squeezed his cheeks and forced him to thrust harder, giving him permission to speed up his movements. Her tongue curled up against his shaft, tightening around him as he grabbed the back of her head.

Temson let out a feral growl, twitching in her mouth, and she squeezed his ass to the point of pain. He thrust faster and she hollowed her cheeks, sucking with all her might. A deep shudder ran through him, and an almost pained groan escaped him as he convulsed in her mouth and she felt his hot seed hit the back of her throat. She moaned as he continued to pulse between her lips, the warm liquid filling her throat and dripping down. His erection softened but she continued the pressure, massaging him with her tongue as the muscles contracted one last time.

When there was no more, she slowly pulled her head back, letting her tongue run along the length of his shaft. She licked the last bit of milky white liquid from the tip and stared up into his eyes as he still gripped her hair.

"You ruin me..." he gasped, his cheeks red and knees shaking.

Vila smiled as she rose to her feet and kissed him deeply. "I know."

He moved his hands down her back as he placed gentle kisses on her neck, uncaring of the blood and sweat that stained and scented her skin.

"I would end all this for you. Nothing in this life matters if I can't have you or be with you outside of these walls. You don't deserve to be secreted away in the dark, and I would have you untethered and free."

"You'd leave your charge? Leave this city?"

"Gladly."

She pressed him to her mouth again, the taste of her still hot on his lips. She wished it to be true, desperate to hold him to the promise. The thought of seeing the Planks far behind them as they sailed away into an unknown future excited her, and she steeled herself to bring that future to reality.

"When?"

"When you say you're ready."

She grew quiet, her face serious as she thought of the coming gala, her coerced and unknown part in it.

"Tomorrow night. I have one more duty, one last obligation." She held up a finger to his lips as he began to protest. "This one is for me. I have to do this."

He nodded, relenting as he kissed her again. She tingled with the thought of shedding the filth of this city and being truly free; not the forced and false feeling of self-rule she had accepted, but true and unbridled freedom.

There was only one thing to do before they left and that was kill Agustan Tempé. She knew there would be people there who had bought her and used their money and power to hold sway over her and doing it in front of them would make it all the sweeter. The thought of the Warden bleeding out on the floor, his skull crushed in front of all those men gave her almost as much pleasure as Temson's tongue.

23

*"Madame Molena runs her establishment with a brutal effi-
ciency that would rival the Church of Parity. And with just
as much salacious activity."*

~Unknown~

The second journey down to the bustling epicenter of the
Lower Planks wasn't quite as grueling or time consuming as
the first, but Narrio still found himself on edge as he made his
way through the maze of shipwrecks, sailcloth, and scaffolds. His
encounter with the eel in the water had shaken him, and he found
himself stepping gingerly; even when he was nowhere near the
bottom. It didn't help that his leg wound throbbed painfully at
every step.

The low humming of the ocean outside still set his pulse racing
and he couldn't fathom living out his days here. Now that he knew
that everyone who lived down here never left, he couldn't help
but look at it with pity. The patrons of the Upper Planks kept an
iron fist tightly gripped on the Lower Planks and its denizens, but
it didn't make it right. He supposed having no choice probably
helped create a sense of resolve and fortitude, but he didn't want

to stick around long enough to find out. Best to get the job done as quickly as possible.

Despite the anxiety that being ten fathoms under the ocean gave him, he did have to admit there was a charming energy to the Lower Planks, especially in the central hub. The entire center was bustling with activity and dirty, ragged people who couldn't give a shit about their appearance. The occasional well-dressed Upper could be seen enjoying all the pleasures and wares that the Lower Planks had to offer. Everything from strange and exotic looking foods to brothels and sexual extravagances, anything one wanted that the Upper Planks didn't offer could be found down here. Despite the impulse to find the mysterious Del'Sor woman and leave, Narrio let himself relax, albeit warily, grab a pint of drift beer, and wander over to the fighting pits that seemed to be drawing quite the crowd.

Narrio wouldn't necessarily classify himself as a violent person, although he'd been in a scrape or two in his time. He didn't consider himself a pacifist by any means, he just didn't have any particular need to bash a head in or watch a gruesome death unnecessarily. However, he found himself falling into the growing crowd nestled around the lowered arena to watch the violent engagements.

As he pushed through the thick press of people, he heard the barker proclaim that someone named Vila Geran had just won her third fight of the evening. He wished he could have gotten a glimpse at whatever woman was holding her own down there for a single match, let alone three. He imagined her as a giantess of a woman, straight out of old lore. Maybe made of rocks with big stone tits and a gaze that could shatter glass.

Whoever she was, she was no longer in the arena, clearly done smashing heads in and off collecting her winnings. Narrio pushed towards the front and watched in morbid curiosity as a few young boys rushed in and started cleaning up the mess that was left. His stomach turned a bit at the site of the mangled corpse being unceremoniously dragged out, brain matter smearing across the sand. He thought he saw a head still attached, but the whole person was such a bloody, gushy mess that it was hard to tell

Narrio sipped his drink in wide eyed wonder as two more combatants entered the arena and began to beat each other into bloody pulps that barely passed as human beings. The violent exchange was a flurry of muscled arms and large-knuckled fists as the two massive men slammed their meaty appendages into each other with enough force to take down a ship's mast. He found himself wincing every time a punch landed in a rib or jaw with the hollow thud of meat on meat. The fresh sand that had been poured after the last fight was already covered in a veritable swamp of thick, red liquid that soaked in and created a clumpy mess that stuck to the combatants as they continued their struggle. The wild cheers of the onlookers were deafening, but Narrio didn't find himself participating. Instead, he was a little revolted by the whole affair and ready to move on as one big man finally got a hold of the other big man's head and proceeded to pop his eyeballs like a pair of sea grapes; all to the wild cries of the bloody thirsty crowd. The winner didn't look much better, their face a jumble of softened flesh, cracked teeth, and oozing eye sockets. The man raised a gore covered fist in the air regardless and howled in wild exultation as blood poured from where his lips used to be as he was led out of the arena; it would be a miracle if he could ever see again, or chew for that matter. Narrio had seen enough.

As he backed out of the press of sweaty bodies, he realized he had no idea which brothel he needed to be searching for or even where to find any of them.

Fuck. I used to be better at this, right?

After a few annoyed conversations and more than a few clutches at his full purse and fancy buttons, Narrio finally identified Madame Molena's as having premium offerings and the mostly likely place to find the Blue Lady of his dreams. Downing the last of his warm beer, he pulled his collar up against the ever-present chill of the Lower Planks and wandered off through the maze of stalls and dimly lit alleys of wreckage to find the brothel.

In a past life, Narrio might have found himself quite at home in the den of iniquity he found himself wandering through. There wasn't a single brothel to be found in Anthema, but his time in Drift-burg had led him through a few houses of pleasure, though none could hold a candle to the magnificent Madame Molena's. Gilded seashells decorated the beams and ornate sculptures of coral and driftwood did much to create an atmosphere of enjoyment and high-class entertainment. The rotted wood and moldy structures that made up the rest of the planks were hidden behind sea-silk curtains and old muslin dyed brilliant shades of purple and blue. The strong scent of incense burned his nostrils, just barely mask-ing the scent of sex and bodily fluids. The patron mother had done wonders to make this establishment a place of invite and rapport, filling every corner with expensive materials and beautiful, naked girls.

As he stood in the main room, however, Narrio felt a hollowness inside that he'd never experienced before as he watched the girls slide by him with seductive eyes. Men entered and left rooms and young girls in various stages of undress waited until they were picked for duty. He couldn't quite put a finger on it, but he found himself growing a little sick at the sight. Any other time he would have gladly taken some time away from the job to participate in some carnal pleasure; but as he watched the far too young women, he couldn't help but see fear and distance in each eye where moments before had been seduction. They no longer looked like busty young women, ready to spring into bed with a man with the deepest pockets, but more like scared, young girls forced into service.

His thoughts wandered to Renalia and her perfume, imagining the intoxicating scent instead of the wretched mix that currently filled his nostrils. He thought about the glowing green of her eye and her naked skin in the moonlight. All those thoughts coalesced together into a feeling of shame as he stood in the room, and he found the entire sensation utterly confounding. There was no pleasure to be had here for him and he desperately wanted to be out as quickly as possible.

He must have been standing there a while, because a topless young girl approached him with a tentative smile. He averted his eyes from her form, his cheeks reddening from embarrassment as she spoke. Even the slightest glance at her perky nipples threatened to send him into a state of guilt-ridden flight.

"Can I help you, good sir? Perhaps find you someone suitable to your particular tastes?"

He couldn't help noticing the bruising around her eyes, masked by the dark blue makeup caking her eyelids. He smiled back, a deep sense of sadness sifting around in his stomach.

"I'm actually here to hire the services of a Blue Lady. I heard Madame Molena's had the finest offerings of high-class merchandise." The words made him sick even as they rolled off his tongue.

"Of course, let me take you to the madame."

The girl snapped a finger at one of her mates who dashed off through a curtain. She took him by the hand and out of the main room through long, winding hallways lined with curtained rooms. He ignored the sounds he heard, noting the slight tremble in the girl's fingers as she led him on. They stopped at a pair of ornate wooden doors, and she gestured for him to enter as she smiled nervously.

He paused for a moment, his cheeks continuing to redden as he fumbled with his coin purse. He placed a handful of ten glass coin in her hand, his eyes still avoiding her bare chest.

"Here," he said as he gently closed her fingers around the coin. "Thank you for your help."

Her eyes widened as she clutched the money, a look of fear passing over her face. "I can't accept this. I haven't done anything for you…"

He held up his hand, smiling more genuinely and compassionately than before. "It's alright, please, take it. I'm not asking for anything. Save it up, maybe you'll find a good use for it."

With that, he turned his back to her and entered the chambers of Madame Molena.

The most stunning older woman he had ever seen lounged gracefully on a plush couch made of soft, red-dyed fibers as he walked through the doors. She smiled at him, her shockingly white hair pulled back into an immaculate bun that accentuated her sharp features. She pressed a crystal goblet to her full lips, the slightly wrinkled skin of her cheeks flexing has she sipped and swallowed deeply, never letting up eye contact with him. Narrio swallowed as well, his mind retreating to the room in the inn where Renalia lay in the dream bed and stroked his dream hair.

"The girls tell me that you are a man of exquisite taste. You made the right choice, as my ladies are of the highest caliber and breed. A Blue Lady can barely deign to hold her title if she doesn't come from Madame Molena's."

Her eyes traveled up and down his body, sizing him up. He had the fleeting thought she might be mentally undressing him, but he quickly realized she was taking in his appearance and calculating the worth of his outfit to see if he could afford what he was asking for. He felt gladdened he had bought the fresh blue overcoat that hung crisply over his ironed trousers and thigh-high leather boots.

"My ladies range in price, but one does not hire her services if they cannot pay in full upon purchase. And they aren't cheap; you're getting the cream of the crop, the best the Planks has to offer in terms of companionship, entertainment, and pleasure."

Narrio could see the evidence of her pricing and quality control all around him. Madame Molena had clearly done quite well for herself in this grimy underworld. He realized he hadn't come up with a new character for this particular ruse and quickly ran names and occupations through his head until he felt one click into place.

"Of course, Madame," he said as he bowed deeply from the waist, his hands flourishing out at his side as he removed the tricorn from his head. "My name is Lord De'Fraughd, and might I first say that your establishment is quite extraordinary, as are your *girls.*" He put a little more emphasis on the last word than he meant to, feeling oddly gallant despite his history with brothels. He reminded himself of what Renalia had said, about the reality of their lives.

She didn't seem to notice his shift in tone. "You're too kind. Now, let me show you what I have."

The madame set her glass down and clapped her hands. Three gorgeous women entered the room and Narrio was very grateful to find them all fully clothed in sumptuous robes of multi-hued sea silk. Each one had azure blue tattoos swirling around their arms and up onto their chests, the patterns dynamic and evocative. A ringlet of blue pearls with a small lock was bound around each of their wrists, one of the signs of their status and servitude he guessed.

Madame Molena introduced each one and he made a show of examining them like he would fish at the market; Denatia, in green silk and large earrings of patinated metal. Lonalai, wearing a purple dress that flowed past her ankles, with eyes to match her outfit. And Yana, her crimson tunic barely containing what lay beneath as she gazed at him with large eyes. The women exchanged pleasantries with him, patiently waiting for him to make his choice. When he'd finished, he turned to the older woman and gave her his best smile. "They are wonderful, truly amazing. However..."

The madame pursed her lips, her fingers tightening around her glass. "Yes?"

"Well, they really are wonderful, truly. Mistresses, please take no offense. I was however hoping to meet...the other one? Your fire-haired beauty?"

A scoff from Yana caused Narrio to twist around to face her, surprised at the reaction.

"Mistress Del'Sor came highly recommended..." he said, the name slipping out in confusion.

The madame stared at him, bewildered glances passing between the Blue Ladies, and Narrio felt equally as befuddled.

"You must be mistaken. The Del'Sors are no more," the madame replied, her face placid.

Narrio wondered if he'd made the wrong hunch but decided to double down. He was in it now; no place to go but down. "No, I'm pretty sure that's what they—"

"What acquaintance?" The madame's eyes narrowed, her brow crinkled as she studied the man.

"Just an acquaintance—"

"There is no one here by that name." The woman carefully set her glass down, her eyes never leaving his. The ladies shrank backwards and Narrio could have cut the tension with his gaff, suddenly feeling very small under her gaze.

"It's time for you to go."

"But—"

"Now."

The finality in her tone left no room for argument and Narrio found himself backing towards the door, hat in hand. He let himself out and closed the door behind him, his heart racing and frustration rising. He was out of ideas, and he wasn't sure where he'd gone wrong. Did he make the wrong guess?

A whisper from behind one of the lush curtains caught him off guard and he looked up, surprised to see the young girl from before gesturing from behind the curtain.

I can help you, she mouthed, her eyes darting about nervously.

He glanced around and quickly slipped behind the curtain, finding himself inside a hidden alcove of decaying wood. Her perfume filled the space as their bodies pressed against each other in the tight room. He tried to leave a little space between them, but her bare upper body left none.

"You're looking for Vila?" she whispered, her eyes studying his face for answers to questions he didn't know.

"The red-haired Blue Lady?"

"Yes. How did you know she was a Del'Sor?"

"...I have reliable sources. Your madame said there were none left tho—"

"She lied. I overheard them talking. Vila is a Del'Sor, but no one else knows. I think."

"Huh. What's she doing down here?"

"That's not important. Why do you want her?" There was an air of protectiveness in her question and Narrio's thoughts spun wildly between truth and fiction. He finally landed on half-truth, which had worked well for him before.

"I'm not here to hire her services," he said as gently as he could, noticing her shoulders relax a bit. "She is part of something bigger, something more important and I need to find her soon. I think she is in danger. I can't tell you what it is happening, I'm not even sure I know myself—but you can trust me that I mean her no harm."

The young girl leaned against the wall, continuing to watch him as if discerning whether she could really believe him.

"I don't know where she is right now. But I know where she will be. She was hired to go to some gala tomorrow night with a lord. Maccio, I think it was. He hired *her* specifically. She didn't want to go, but the madame made her."

Narrio's gut tightened, confirming his suspicions about her heritage, and engraining a deep sense of fear for this woman he had never met. Whatever was waiting for her at that event was nothing good. "Lord Maccio..." That had to be the mystery figure he had heard the night before. He tried to keep his mind on the task of the stone but found it hard to focus as things developed around him.

"That's all I know. I won't take you to where she lives, it would be too dangerous for all of us. But if you need to talk to her, you could try to get into the gala. You're less likely to get caught by the madame there. She won't be happy you're looking for her."

"Thank you," he smiled sympathetically and turned to exit but stopped himself. "Why are you helping me? It sounds like you're afraid of the madame, so why tell me this?"

The girl hung her head low, and he thought he saw a tear slide down her cheek. "You didn't look at me, at my body. You were the first man who didn't make me feel like something they could have just because they paid for it."

A pang of guilt went through his chest, accompanied by a sense of sadness as he thought about what she was saying. He hated what was happening to him and desperately wanted to make a joke. Instead, he said something that surprised even him.

"I can get you out of here."

Her eyes widened in disbelief. "Please don't lie to me."

"I'm not, I promise."

"How?" she asked warily.

"There's a secret way out of here. I want nothing from you, but I can help you escape. Be here tomorrow night. After my business at the gala, I'll come for you. We may have to play the ruse of patron and product, but I know a secret way out of the Lower Planks."

She went quiet, her arms crossing over her chest as she thought of whether she could trust him or not.

"I have a companion, a woman. You'll like her. She can help us, help you." Renalia was going to hate him.

The girl finally relented. "Thank you," she said through watering eyes. "I'm Lanya." Her sincerity tore through his heart.

"You'll be okay, Lanya." He smiled at her again and slipped back through the curtain.

Narrio quickly made his way out of the brothel and slipped his hat back on his head as he ran through the streets towards the long path back up to the Crusted Whale. He pushed Lanya from his mind and tried his best to refocus on his mission. The pieces were there, now he had to move them where he wanted. This was the part that he hated the most; planning, plotting, and hoping it all came together. But it usually led to a chaotic finale fueled by his uncanny ability to wiggle in and out of tight spots and deadly interactions. His excitement only grew as he pictured the end.

24

"I spied two lovers above and below.

One said stop and the other said go.

One went up as the other came down,

And they both went laughing all over the town."
                                      ~A children's play song~

Vintar Maccio III's sprawling estate stretched out in all directions, eating up as much of the meager space available in the floating city as it could. Tall, coralcrete walls lined the perimeter while filigreed iron studs decorated the top and provided some extra deterrence against trespassers. Narrio could see the intricate shapes of sculptures and fountains rising above the walls as he sat on a bench, munching on some mussels soaked in a suspicious brown sauce. A large, domed tower rose above the estate, its gilded roof and mosaic tile work standing out against the dull grays and browns of the surrounding structures.

Renalia's leg tapped in an offbeat rhythm as they sat in silence, waiting for him to finish his meal. He'd spent the previous afternoon and evening scoping out the premises and learning what he could about the upcoming gala. The general populace had no knowledge or no interest in the event reserved only for the richest and most influential people in the city, but he was able to line the pockets of a few lower high class folk and snag some helpful bits of information.

He and Renalia basked in the rare sunlight, watching carts and servants move in and out of the heavy gates set into the rear of the estate. Narrio set his bowl aside and licked his fingers, feeling much more like his original self and ready to get into the final steps.

"Are you going to tell me what you've found out now?" she asked, unable to mask the annoyance in her voice.

Narrio wiped his mouth on his sleeve and gave a satisfied sigh as he picked up his mug of drift beer. "Yes, I'm ready now."

"Thank the gods."

"The gala is being paraded as a celestial celebration to honor the second full moon of the month and potentially catch more sightings of meteors. I guess our Lord Maccio fancies himself an amateur astronomer and is possibly using the event to raise funds for the astronomical society, though if you asked me, he could probably fund the whole thing himself. He's quite the affluent fellow."

"So, how are you getting in?"

"I'll get there. We also know that this mystery woman, whose name I found out is Vila, is Maccio's personal guest. I've confirmed that she is in fact a Del'Sor and that Agustan Tempé wants her there for some reason; I'm sure it's nothing good. Tempé said some big event was happening tonight and that it would give Maccio a lot of power. I don't think he was referencing the gala. So, and I'm only guessing here, that tells me that we are under a time limit and should be getting out of this city with the stone as quick as we can."

"We?"

The simple question took Narrio by surprise and he realized how many assumptions and made-up realities had been floating around in his head about the coming events. It also gave him a brief insight into his growing feelings for Renalia. He was acutely aware that he may have grown a little more attachment to her than he should have; and more than maybe she was reciprocating.

"I guess I just assumed you'd be coming too. You know, to see the stone to safety." He shoved his face into his mug to cover his reddening cheeks. She gave him a distant look before turning her head away and he wished he could read whatever thoughts were running around in there. There was a touch of sadness to her tone.

"Narrio, I told you, I can't leave. I have family here, people that need me. Once you get the stone, my job is done. I was hired to help you, but that help ends once you leave the Planks."

Normally, Narrio would have flashed a grin and made a joke about how much he enjoyed her help, both for and unrelated to the mission, but he couldn't hide the growing burden of sincerity and the feelings that had pummeled him over the last few days.

"I really think you should reconsider. Something is happening *tonight*, and I don't think it would be a good idea to stay and find out exactly what. You could all come, your brother, his children. I have money and they are paying me quite a bit more. We could...you could start a new life somewhere else."

"Narrio, this is my home. We've weathered bad storms like Vintar Maccio before. It's not so simple for me; I'm not free to roam like you are. And besides, you don't know anything. Whatever you think you heard? There is nothing that tells us exactly what is going to happen tonight if anything. And I can't take a risk that big based on your eavesdropping."

"You did tell me to question everything."

"Well, I clearly regret that now." She laid a hand on his knee. "I appreciate you thinking of me."

He flashed a grin, masking the previously unknown sting that only comes with dashed hopes one didn't know they had.

"I understand. Would you at least check on my boat for me and make sure it's ready? I have a feeling that things are going to move pretty quickly tonight. And the offer still stands if you change your mind. There's enough room for the six of us."

She cocked an eyebrow. "Six? I thought your math was better than that."

"I...may be helping a young girl escape one of the brothels."

"Oh. So, you had a good time down there?"

"Hardly. I seem to have developed what you would call a conscience in the last twenty-four hours. She helped me find out about the gala; she also looked very sad, and I couldn't leave her down there once I saw what...well, anyways. She's coming."

"You continue to surprise me, Narrio." He thought he saw the hint of a smile puckering at the corner of her mouth. "I'll have your boat ready and coordinates for you. Now are you going to answer the original question?"

"Ah yes, how to get into a gala I'm not invited to. Well, in a few hours, our handsome cleric will be getting his evening meal delivered to him; a scrumptious feast of red gill soup, toasted crab cakes and a heaping side of sleepy-time juice. He should be out long enough to attend the gala, have a few drinks, get the key, and make off with the stone."

"How are you getting in?" she repeated, her cheeks flushing as they did when she was annoyed.

"Apparently tonight's entertainment is a series of brutal and exciting matchups between some of the Lower Planks' most ruthless fighters. Rich people love to see the poor folk batter themselves into an early grave, it seems. They're bringing up a small group of them before the gala kicks off."

"Narrio—"

He cut her off, the widest grin he'd ever worn plastered to his face as he imagined escaping death in the most dramatic way possible. "Right, how am I getting in? Simple: I'm going to be a fighter."

Vila sat on the wooden stool in one of the madame's readying rooms, her reflection staring back at her with deadened eyes as she was prepared for the gala like a fresh fish in the market; caught, still breathing, the best parts being divided up for the highest bidder. Step by step, she transformed into someone she barely recognized.

One of the madame's many girls applied blue powder from Inaché Coral under Vila's eyes to bring out her natural blues and cover the bruising.

Lipstick made from the pulp of red kelp was applied to her lips. The stinging toxins from the plant puffed her lips to a full size and helped to hide the lesions.

Her dingy red hair was washed and cleaned, the matted pieces and grime painfully pulled or cut away. Whale oil was rubbed in to bring out the natural luster and sheen. The girl pulled it back above Vila's head, folding it around and around itself into the preferred style of the upper class and clasped it tight with an ornate iron pendant decorated with purple wing shells.

Vila let herself be prepared, her anger seething like a hot spring beneath the ocean's surface. The night might end with an opportunity to put a knife between Tempé's ribs, but she was still being forced into someone else's schemes; again. Her mother could profess how she didn't have a choice about her upbringing and that her daughter should be grateful that she was made a Blue Lady earlier than any other. It didn't change the fact that Vila had been forced to sell her body, emotions, and time from the moment she was deemed a woman by the laws of the Planks. Nor could it ever erase the terrible memories of acts and disgusting men she had had to witness as a child.

Vila's seal skin trousers and cloak were removed and thrown into the refuse along with the kelp wrap that covered her arms and legs and kept her breasts in place. The girl averted her eyes as Vila rolled her own. Many of the girls here still held on to some prudish sense of shame at the sight of nakedness, even amongst their peers.

"You should look," she said, turning her body towards the girl. "You need to look. If you're going to survive and thrive, then you have to be comfortable with this, or at least pretend to be."

The doe-eyed girl lifted her eyes and took in Vila's fully naked form. Being shy was a sure way to get yourself killed or worse in this life and the only way to break the habit was to force oneself to be confident when the clothes came off. The best place to practice that was in the safety of rooms like these with the only friends you had. Sometimes those bonds went deeper than just friendship and Vila carried many fond memories of safe, intimate moments with the only people she felt she could truly trust; before she met Temson. Those physical connections were a point of solace in an otherwise scarring and disturbing environment, and she truly hoped that this girl and others could find the same sense of connection. But right now, the girl was a fish, a helpless fish in a city of sharks and monsters. She needed to know what cowering would cost her and Vila was in an angry mood.

"If you show fear or timidity when your tits are out or someone pulls out their cock and starts shoving it in your face, then you might as well jump into the Swell and drown yourself, because that's what's going to happen to you anyways."

She stepped forward and grabbed the girl by the arm. The child's eyes went wide at the sudden movement, and Vila could feel her tense as she tried to move away. She squeezed harder, even as tears began to fill the younger girl's eyes.

"They can force you to do whatever they want. The madame, the patrons; they can batter your body, but only if you let them. And you will let them if you don't grow some fucking nerve and stop acting like a spineless jelly. My body is a tool because I let it be, and I control how it's used. Do you understand that?"

She wished there was truth in what she was saying, but she knew the words sounded hollow and bitter as they came out. Whatever little bit of control she thought she had had, was slowly being stripped away and it was eating her from the inside like poison. The girl looked back up at her, her fingers grasping at Vila's hold on her arm, desperately trying to loosen the iron grip. She was openly weeping now.

"I'm not like you...I'm not a fighter!"

Vila relented, pulling her hand back as the girl cowered before her. Purple bruises appeared where her fingers had dug in. Vila stared at her hands, feeling her blood pumping and her heart rate rise. There was a moment of contrition as she watched the girl nurse her wounds and shattered sense of confidence. No one had taught Vila those lessons. She'd had to figure it out for herself and the best thing anyone could do for these girls was to make them angry, make them be the fighters they didn't think they were.

"That's why I'm a Blue Lady. Not because the madame made me one, but because I commanded it. I never sway. I am the holder of power. Always."

The girl stared at her in terror and Vila realized she wasn't sure who exactly she was sending her message to anymore. She stepped forward, taking the girl's arm again even as she tried to recoil. The touch was softer this time as Vila gently rubbed the areas where her hands had left their mark. She closed her eyes and tried to be as soothing as she could, letting the girl feel some tenderness that she had probably never experienced before.

"Let's finish up," she said, sitting back down on the stool and handing her outfit to the trembling child.

The girl kept her head down in a subdued stance but continued with the preparations. Vila slipped the sharkskin corset over herself, releasing air as the strings tightened behind her spine.

She felt her breasts rise and her waist constrict, and there was a brief moment when she thought the girl might take revenge for the tirade she had just been the victim of. But then the grip was released, and the final elements of her costume were put together.

Vila looked in the mirror, taking in the gaudy sight. The dress was beautiful, no doubt and it must have cost Maccio a fortune. Genuine sea silk, dyed to a gorgeous blue and lined with sea glass rivulets of violet and deep viridian. Ornate lacework hemmed the wide top that left her shoulders bare and her breasts pushed to a pleasing height, exposing her cleavage for all to see. Her back was exposed, and she could feel the chilly air of the Lower Planks trace its way up her spine. The base was layered upon itself, creating a sense of depth and movement in the deep blue fabric; like water that spilled from her waists and splashed down just below her knees.

She hated it.

They could dress her up like an animal, parade her around to be seen, but Vila wasn't a beast of the land; those were all extinct. She was a shark and a killer. A creature of water and thirsty for blood; untamed, and unmatched.

Dominant and deadly.

25

"Salvage has always been at the industrial forefront of the Planks. Driftburg has its deepwood harvested from the rare wateroak tree that has made a life for itself on the ocean floor; Anthema reaps its bounties from the great Tangle, exporting the enlarged kelp leaves across the waters; Tideland mines sea glass from the seemingly never-ending supply of the Harnathian Ruins. Each one of the great cities found its spot in the ocean and benefit from the natural resources that reside below them. Not so for the Planks, always adrift and searching for something new. Maybe someday a resource will appear, and the Planks can find its spot in the Swell and lay a permanent anchor."
~From Yania Torino's "The Planks: A History"~

Not a single piece of rotted driftwood, rusty metal, or coral-crete could be seen once Vila's rickshaw passed beyond the walls and entered the courtyard of the massive estate. The doors to the mansion were made from thick boards of deepwood joined together and stained to a brilliant turquoise. Deepwood cultivation was expensive and could only be imported from Driftburg. Obviously, the Lord Maccio was a rich man if he was bringing in such quantities of the rare ocean wood that could make even the arch vicar blush. The number of estates like this one were few in the Planks. With no solid manufacturing or mining operations to its name, the Planks relied on fishing and salvage as its major exports, while the internal economy ran on sin. Vila had been in one or two of the more affluent mansions over the years. Most other members of the wealthy class were rich enough to afford a Blue Lady, but poor enough to settle for painted driftwood doors.

Vintar Maccio III was waiting at the at the top of the large blue stone steps when she arrived, looking gentlemanly and gaudy in a spotted seal fur coat trimmed with gold lace and purple buttons. He smiled as she walked up the steps to the landing and he offered her his hand. She took it, tapping into a reserve of inner resolve to stay pleasant and play her part. Maccio's intentions at inviting her here were unclear, but she could bide her time and be the Blue Lady she was raised to be.

"Mistress Geran, you look absolutely ravishing. Not that you weren't stunning before, but I must say the dress fits you exquisitely."

"It was most generous of you to provide it for me."

"Think nothing of it. And you are to keep it after tonight's gathering. No, no, I insist. I'm not going to wear it myself!" He guffawed as he kissed her hand and put his arm through hers.

"I'm just happy I could treat you to something extravagant. If nothing else, I want you to enjoy yourself tonight. My home is your home. Eat, drink, and relax. You'll have to endure some celestial banter and boring theories about coming events, but I hope it's a small price to pay for a good time. You won't find a better menu and I don't skimp on the liquor."

As if on cue, a porter bustled over with a silver tray holding two glasses of shimmering blue sea glass. Lord Maccio took one and handed the other to her, the contents almost glowing and a delicious odor wafted up from the amber liquid.

"Ambergris port," he said as Vila eyed the drink. "Very rare and very expensive."

He threw his back in one gulp and gave a satisfied smack. She did the same and was pleasantly surprised at how much it burned, even though the taste was delectable.

"Now that is the way to start the evening!" the merchant boomed, his voice echoing down the marbled halls. Vila couldn't help but agree, her nerves loosening as the liquor went to work. They passed through the entry hall and up a grand staircase made of gilded coral. At the top of the stairs, two servants opened another set of deepwood doors and Vila marveled at the sight of the lift made of lacquered iron.

"Have you ever been in one of these before?"

"No. It's quite marvelous."

"Just wait till it starts moving." He winked.

He led her into the small cage and the porters closed the open-faced doors as the carriage slowly began to ascend. For a few moments she could only see the marbled walls of the shaft as they climbed higher. When they gave way to crystal clear glass, Vila's breath rushed out at what she saw.

Laid out before her was the entire port side of the Planks, the mishmash architecture of the city sprawling in all directions. The great wheels that directed the city were visible above the rooftops. Tiny lanterns twinkled across the maze-like streets that were swallowed up by the towering buildings made from wreckage. Ropes crisscrossed the vista in a web of hemp and kelp, all building up to the portside beacon that stood at the outermost edge of the city. The giant beacon burned bright, waiting for the sun to say its final goodbyes and disappear for the night.

"It's beautiful, isn't it?" Maccio asked, breaking the awed silence.

"Yes. It really is."

"I've been around the waters, and I truly think there is not a place on the Swell as incredible as the Planks. For all its flaws, our city is the most inventive, vivacious, and resilient structure floating in this god-forsaken world. As are its citizens."

Vila could almost feel his gaze on her. She ignored it, continuing to look out the window in amazement as their ascent slowed.

"Especially the common folk," she said, finally turning to meet his gaze as the doors opened. The Lord's mouth twitched into a smile, and he held out his hand, gesturing for her to step out into the observatory.

Compared to most cramped buildings in the Planks, the room was huge. Marbled columns of blue stone bordered the perimeter in a circle and climbed twenty spans before careening out over the space in fluted patterns. Between the supports were sections of crystal-clear glass that showed the first colors of the evening light.

But the real statement piece was the large, gold telescope that demanded the attention of the room from its place at the furthermost edge. Sea glass rivulets decorated the seams, and every inch was polished to an impossible gleam. The body stretched an impressive ten spans as the end disappeared through a large opening lined with shutters. Maccio led her over to the impressive instrument and she ran her hands along the small eyepiece, marveling at the construction.

"Do you like it?" Lord Maccio asked, smiling at her impressed expression.

"I've never seen anything like it."

"Few have. I had all the parts shipped here from Anthema. There is only one other like it in all the known world and this one is the biggest. The grand scope at the observatory in Anthema boasts a lens of fourteen sections. I demanded that mine be more and went through countless debates and arguments about the physical limitations of the glass. I finally won and am the proud owner of a fifteen-section scope. Then I hired the man who forged the glass to stay on my staff and keep his secrets here. There will never be another like it."

Vila was unimpressed by the boast and scope measuring contest, but she had to admit that the device itself was impressive.

"May I look through it?"

"Of course! But I must leave you to it for now. We unfortunately are no longer alone, and I must play host. Have another drink, grab some food, and most importantly, enjoy yourself. The night's entertainment will begin soon and I'm quite excited to see what you think."

With a wink and a tilt of his head, he turned towards the open door with arms stretched wide as an influx of guests began to shuffle in from more lifts. Vila's stomach tightened at all the people she was expected to flatter, and grabbed another drink as it passed by. She wondered at his end game in bringing her here; surely it wasn't just to hang on his arm and look pretty. His original offer had been to sponsor her in the fights and now he was parading her about his fancy party; something wasn't adding up. She downed her glass, the contents burning a little less now, and stared at the darkening sky through the scope.

Narrio lounged against the barnacle encrusted beam, watching the gathering fighters as they pushed their way into the pit. They were some of the biggest, ugliest men he'd ever seen, and he hoped he didn't look too out of place. The selections announcement would be happening soon, and he smiled to himself as he waited for his name to be called.

Getting his name on the list had been a simple matter of some greased palms, a quick pick pocket as the list travelled down from Upper to Lower Planks, a couple of pen marks to change *Yaran Trasp* into *Marans Drasper*, and slipping the list back in pocket of the unaware messenger. There were two other names on the list, names Narrio did not know. Four fighters, three matches—the fourth fighter being a special guest from the Upper Planks. All Narrio had to do was get close to the Blue Lady and get the key before it was his turn to fight. That part would have to be planned once he was inside and had a sense of his surroundings.

"Are you sure about this?" Renalia asked, leaning her chin on his shoulder as she came up behind him. He felt the heat of her breath on his neck and closed his eyes for a moment as he basked in the seductive feeling of her.

"I'm never sure about anything until I'm doing it."

"Be careful. I'll meet you at the boat before you leave."

"Remember what I said." He turned his head and gave her a quick kiss above her eye. She turned his head and pressed her mouth hard to his.

"Go on." She gave a small smile. "They're about to call names. Don't get yourself killed."

He gave her hand a squeeze and headed into the press of bodies as the first name was called. Narrio pushed himself closer to the front as the next man gave a roar and ambled up the dais, elated at the opportunity to garner some fame and glory, and hopefully riches.

"Marans Drasper!" The final name was yelled out and Narrio squeezed himself out of the group of sweaty bodies, ignoring the murmurs and deadly glares. He was a good head shorter than the other two men and of a much slimmer build; he was made for running, not brawling, and he could see those same thoughts on the faces of the angry crowd. He gave a shrug and followed his companions down the ramp and into a darkened alley lined with dripping metal rain pipes from the surface. He looked back towards the arena, hoping to catch one last glimpse of Renalia, but the press of bodies was too thick and sailcloth curtains quickly obscured his vision. He sighed and turned his attention back to the walk.

The grim group navigated the passageways in silence, the floor shifting and the walls creaking in their wake. No one spoke, each focused on the coming blood bath and Narrio hoped he hadn't made a terrible mistake. There were probably other and better ways into the estate or even to get the key, but he was running out of time; or at least he had convinced himself he was running out of time. Renalia had told him to always question, but there was nothing he could question about the interaction he had witnessed outside the bar window. To him, it was clear: something big was happening tonight and it could have a direct impact on his quarry.

The group finally stopped in a small cavern of dripping boards and rotted cloth. The portly man who led them now turned to face the group of killers before him.

"Alright, listen up. Tonight's fight is big, and Lord Maccio has promised a large reward to the winner. Couldn't cause a ruckus up there, but the money ain't half of what you get if you make it out alive tonight. You all know what's at stake; ain't four of you coming back. But him who does? He ain't never gotta come back down if he doesn't want."

The men glanced at each other, murmuring inquisitively.

The man smiled a gap-toothed grin. "Tha's right. Permanent freedom. You be the last one standing tonight? You get a ticket to the Upper Planks and a new life if you want it. Worth killing for?"

Narrio gulped at the wicked grins that spread across the faces of his companions and he tried to match their menacing snarls. He had to get out of the group and fast.

"Tha's good. Cause you ain't fightin each other. Bag em."

The last command was given to whoever thrust a foul-smelling bag over Narrio's head as his arms were pulled sharply behind his back. He felt the cold touch of metal as heavy manacles were clasped about his wrists and he was shoved roughly along with the other fighters. Narrio cursed himself for his stupidity as his companions' protests could be heard through the headwear. Maccio must have his own way in and out of the planks; a way that he clearly didn't want advertised.

Panic set in as the group was pushed and shoved through endless openings and tunnels, the noise of the ocean droning in his ears even through the bag. He took deep breaths of the vile air, trying to calm his nerves and steady his senses. There was nothing he could do but try to pay attention; changes in sound, the number of steps he took, familiar smells (that one would be the most difficult considering the disgusting fabric over his nose.)

Things were off to a bad start, and he had a feeling it was only going to get worse.

Vila watched the sun's last rays disappearing over the horizon from the tall bay windows of Lord Maccio's observatory tower. The sounds of the guests mingling and laughing dulled to a low roar in her ears as she gazed out at the brilliant and fading colors. From this height, she could see over the ramshackle roofs of the hodgepodge structures and to the vast ocean surface glowing like fire in the last light of Solan's burning kingdom. She had waved off advance after advance from nobles and merchants looking to regale her with pleasantries and offers until she couldn't take it anymore and retreated to the solitary corner bay.

Her thoughts drifted down over the rooftops, over the rotted planks and into the deep waters where Rance's body was now being devoured and stripped by the denizens of the deep, his corpse giving back to the life cycle in a sad display of symbiosis. Opening and clenching her fist, she stared at the scars that lined her palm, wondering why there was no trace of the corruption that had taken her friend's life. Even the deep wound from the shard blade had not shown any sign of crystalline infection and she felt both relieved and guilty. Why him and not her? Why not Taragin? What other innocent, gentle lives were being claimed by unknown forces, while those who thrived on violence and blood went free of harm?

There was no sign of Agustan Tempé and she started to wonder what he was scheming. The overall pleasantness of the evening's affairs was disturbing, and she could feel the tension pulling at her spine and up the base of her neck. Her nerves were on edge as she waited.

A sharp tapping on the blue, marbled floors rang out as Lord Maccio brought his cane down in successive clicks. Reluctantly, she left her post and joined the flow of patrons as they gathered around to hear his announcement. She noticed movement at the edges of the room, catching brief glances of large men in heavy armor moving slowly and deliberately to create a perimeter around the bustling hall. Her nerves tensed further as Vintar began his speech.

"My friends! Tonight is a night of celebration as we honor the second blooming of Lunus and Celenia's divine kingdom this month. The powers of moon and sea are intertwined, and we should count ourselves lucky at being the recipients of their blessings. A blue moon! What an occasion! To many of you, it is nothing more than another mundane and uninteresting celestial event, but I truly believe by the end of the night your opinion on the matter will be changed."

He paused to smile but Vila thought it looked a bit more like a sneer.

"Past, present, future. We live in a city built on the past, thriving in the present, and building towards the future. At one with the sea and striving for perfection. That is what you will see tonight."

Maccio clapped his hands together and a group of porters rushed in pulling carts covered in brilliant purple cloth, the clinking of glass coming from underneath. The porters pulled the carts to the center of the room as the guests stepped back and Maccio stepped in, his cane waving in flourishment as he spoke.

"My family has always been at the forefront of innovative industry in this city. From the first sea glass alteration facility to the multitude of salvage yards you see along our docks, a Maccio has always been there, guiding the future of both Upper and Lower Planks. And tonight, is no different. A new power is on the horizon, and you will be witness to its rise."

Maccio whisked off one of the purple shrouds as the porters did the same to the others and Vila nearly threw up at the sight. The carts were lined with weapons of all styles, glittering in the lantern light, and looking just as deadly as she remembered them; crystal weapons, cut and forged from the energized moon rocks that lay far below the surface of the city. She finally had a face to put to the evil that had killed her friend and he was standing right in front of her, mocking her with the very objects that had taken Rance from her.

"You see before you the future: weapons crafted from the sky and her bounties. Deadly instruments given from Lunus and Celenia themselves. Tonight, is an auction and demonstration so that you may see first-hand the changing tides. But for the demonstration, I have a very special guest..."

No.

"...someone with the legacy of a great past..."

No.

"...to give us a peek into the future..."

Fuck. No.

"Vila, would you please step forward?"

Vila didn't budge as the perimeter of guards began closing in, carefully pushing bodies this way and that until she found herself alone near the center of the room, all eyes on her. Her fists tightened again, knuckles whitening as she glared at the grinning host with a vitriol that she reserved for only a certain few. She was about to find out her true purpose here.

"I present to you the last of the Del'Sors!"

Vila felt strong hands grab her arms before she could react and she heard the harsh rip of fabric as her dress was torn from her body in shreds, revealing the tight shark-skin corset and leather trousers underneath. She wanted to scream as the rough hands dragged her to the center, turning her so she was in full view of the shocked onlookers.

"Hiding in the depths of this city, parading about your homes as a Blue Lady, Vila has been here, a Del'Sor among us. The great line of heroes, ever protecting and leading us until recently. Tonight, you will get to see the past meet the future; heroes of old navigating the new. I can think of no one I'd rather see show off the divine weaponry on display here for you. Shall we begin?"

Vila's heart raced faster than it ever had before as the large doors at the end of the hall opened and three bound figures were shoved into the room, their heads covered by bags and their feet shackled together. The mask of the first man was pulled off and his chains removed as he blinked rapidly, trying to adjust to the bright light of his new environment.

Vila recognized this man, though she couldn't place his name. He was a well-known fighter, a brutal artist in the pits with many a bloody canvas to his name. He seemed to know why he was here, and a wide smile spread across his face, dripping with evil delight as he laid eyes on her.

Vintar Maccio had used his power and influence to strip away her agency, her control, in one quick moment and reduce her once more to a pawn in a grand scheme. He had watched her, studied her, learned what made her tick and what she valued most; and now he'd taken that from her and made it his. She would be forced to kill, not because she wanted to, but because she had to; he had taken her choice away through sheer force of will and the thought nearly made her vomit.

"I won't do it," she snarled through gritted teeth as the guards released her arms and backed away. The crowd was lined around the room, the armed guards posted at regular intervals to block all possibilities of escape. Her opponent cracked his knuckles as he plucked a wicked looking axe of green shard from the rack and began stalking towards her, his eyes gleaming in the light of a hundred candles. Someone strapped a blue crystal gauntlet sword to her arm as Lord Maccio laughed, his voice booming through the silent hall.

"Of course, you will. You don't have a choice. And we wouldn't want to disappoint all my honored guests, now, would we? Let's show off my merchandise and let them see what their heroes are made of."

The burly man in front of her was now running and Vila had no choice but to brace herself for the attack and deliver on the promised violence.

26

"The invention of pressure hardening has been as much a key to our success as the introduction and harnessing of sea glass. Bone is more common than steel these days, and the ability to strengthen it into weapons and tools has been invaluable in both military and engineering efforts. Combined with unaltered sea glass, the possibilities are endless. I strain to think of what new substance could match the efficiency and durability that we have managed to pull out of the ocean's resources."
~Ulutan Rorsh, Lead Engineer of Rorsh Manufacturing~

N arrio listened in abject horror to the brutal murder that was happening just in front of him, unable to witness it with the bag on his head. *I really am an idiot,* he thought to himself as he connected the name *Vila* to the savage sight he'd witnessed at the pits. *That Vila,* he realized. He cursed himself for not recognizing it sooner and now here he was, about to have his skull crushed in by the very woman he'd come here to find. And based on the gruesome noises that battered his ears, he'd be lucky if that was the worst of it.

He listened through gritted teeth to the screech of weapons clashing, the sickening crunch of bone and the muffled screams of a man until a nauseating crack sounded and then silence permeated the room. There were no cheers in the hall, although he could tell the room was packed with people. The host said something grandiose as he announced Vila Del'Sor as the winner of the first bout. Narrio was pushed forward a little and heard the manacles click off another pair of hands. He thanked whatever gods were listening that they weren't his yet; he needed time to think, to plan. He ran scenarios through his head, hoping he could come up with something in time before he was called to the slaughter. The next fight began and Narrio did his best to block out the sounds of flesh and blood being spilled, as he tried to think and hold back from pissing himself.

The first man went down easily enough, his eagerness and blood lust getting the better of him. Her opponent had been used to using his fists rather than the unwieldy axe and it caused his downfall. The gauntlet sword in her hand was now streaked with red gore, the crimson contrasting against the glowing blue blade. Though she was uninjured, she was tired already, her still mending wounds taking their toll.

Her body begged for another drop of the mystical blood tincture to soothe her aches and give her strength as her head pounded. She tried to block out the crowd's staring, some horrified and some rapt in grotesque wonder. She had never felt more naked in her life and battled against the feeling of objectification more than her opponents. She had no issues with fighting or killing, but she did it on her terms and those terms had been written for her tonight.

A guard approached her and took the sword gauntlet from her hand, replacing it with a spear that hosted a head of red shards. The light emanating from the blade seemed to be alive and growing stronger with every moment. Money exchanged hands and the gauntlet was given to one of the patrons, the axe to another owner. She'd walked into a weapons auction, and she was the advertisement.

Vila looked at the body as it was dragged away, and she could see the beginnings of crystalline growths in the wounds on his torso. The gaping hole in his head where she had landed the final blow was also starting to sprout shards and she silently resolved herself not to get cut in the next fight. The crystal's potency was growing, most likely with the rising of the moon. That was the importance of this gala, to show off the new and growing deadly power of these weapons. Maccio was setting himself up to be the leader of a new arms race and she was his proof of concept. She examined the scars on her hand but still couldn't find a trace of the moon rock's corruption; the absence still bothered her, and it became more problematic by the speed at which her previous opponent was being consumed.

Her next opponent was unchained and held a flail and sword made from the same fiery colored crystals. The man watched his predecessor's body be dragged away and turned back towards Vila as he tested the weight of his weapons. From his stance alone and the confidence with which he swung the sword and flail, she could tell he knew how to use them; this would be a much tougher fight.

Narrio could feel his knees shaking now. Whatever terror he had experienced in the trench with the eel paled in comparison to the impending doom that settled on him like a diving bell, crushing all hope and squishing his spirits. Thoughts of the mission were pushed aside as he ran through options in his head. Getting the stone didn't matter if he never made it out of the estate. He thought about Lanya, the poor girl waiting for him to return and make good on his promise.

He hoped she was down there, that she trusted what he'd said and would be willing to take a risk on it. His heart ached for her, and he used the compassion to fuel him. He had to make it out of here, if not just for himself but for that poor girl as well. He also desperately wanted to be in Renalia's arms again and he hoped she was waiting for him at the sailboat.

The thought of Lanya sparked a crazy idea in his head, and he began to formulate a path forward. It was risky and probably wouldn't work, but it was the only thing that might. He had to live—he had to get that key.

Narrio's brain sped through possible sequences, playing out scenarios and outcomes in his head. When it came down to it, the outcome would be decided by his ability to recognize the opportunity and seize it before he got his head cut off.

Crystals sung and vibrated as Vila batted away attacks from the deadly flail and sweeping strikes of her opponent's backsword. Sweat gleamed off bare shoulders and muscled arms as both man and woman danced around each other, warding off attacks and looking for the right opportunity. The man was a vicious fury of unrelenting blows and Vila was struggling to pinpoint an exploitable weakness. Several times she was pushed into a retreat, the ball of shards creating wide arcs of red light as it flashed too close.

On one such pass, she lost track of his other hand and was met with a searing pain in her right thigh as the crimson blade found purchase and severed flesh. She cried out in alarm and barely managed to roll out of the way as the flail came smashing down where her head had been. Shards of tile exploded outwards, sending little bits of the material into her exposed back and shoulders. The crystal head of the flail was un-damaged, and the man quickly pulled back to continue his onslaught. He had her on the run now, his swing and strike method proving effective as he deftly kept the direction of his sword strikes secret until it was upon her, and more searing cuts tore across her body. She smelled burnt leather and dared a look down when she gained some distance.

Where warm, flowing blood should have been on her legs and sides, she instead saw the ugly puckered flesh that resembled burns. Her sharkskin corset was singed where the last strike had landed as if a red-hot iron had struck her. She brought her own weapon to her face and could feel the heat rising off it; the shards *were* red hot, each one producing an extraordinary amount of heat.

She was forced back into the present as the flail came at her again, the sword striking soon after. The pattern was recognizable, but she still missed a cut and another bout of blinding pain bloomed in her right shoulder. She struggled to hold onto her sword through the screams of protest from her body and rolled yet again as the flail crashed into tile, coming closer with each strike. The man didn't seem to be tiring, but she was falling prey to exhaustion as she fled each brutal hit. His strategy was working, wearing her down with every blow and producing new wounds that drained her energy further. He saw no reason to change his tactic and that was the advantage Vila needed.

The flail always came from his left and she would duck or move back, giving him an opening to strike with the sword. She had to anticipate and change her movements to throw him off. On cue the flail swung towards her, but this time she rolled into the attack and under the swing, his sword stabbing into the blank space where she would have been. Propelling herself forward, she swung her spear out to her left, feeling the satisfying impact as the sharpened crystal blade sliced through boot and tendon. The man screamed and went down on one knee, desperately trying to turn around in time as she rose behind him. She brought the tip of her short spear down into his left arm, splitting his hand at the wrist and cauterizing the wound instantly. His final scream of agony was cut short as she shoved the tip of the five-length spear through his neck and out his mouth, his tongue frying from the heat. All sound choked out as flesh melted and charred on the blade.

She withdrew the spear as the corpse fell heavily to the ground, the foul stench of burned flesh becoming overwhelming as it filled the hall. She cast the spear aside as the guards began their clean up. Vintar Maccio watched the whole affair with a childlike wonder and giddiness, his weapons showing their worth in the hands of a skilled fighter. A fighter that he could never have for himself. She had one more to kill and then she would wreak havoc on her benefactor, unless Tempé showed his face first. Vila spat at Maccio's feet as more money was exchanged for the discarded weapons and the final opponent was brought forward.

It was Narrio's turn at last, and no words could describe the dread that now sat in his stomach like a rock sinking into the black abyss of the Swell. He felt the manacles release and shielded his eyes as the bag was removed, his sight blinded by the brilliant glow of the candles in the room. He was in some sort of observatory and night had fallen, but the full moon had not yet reached its apex in the sky. Stars twinkled far above, and he tried to focus on the beauty of the evening, anything to calm himself as weapons were shoved into his hands.

Across from him stood an angel of death, her presence made all the more terrifying by the red hair pulled back sharply above her head and the oozing wounds that marred her body. There was no emotion in her face as she eyed him, her arms flexing as she tested the weight of the black crystal knuckle-dusters encasing her fingers. She was beautiful and petrifying all at once, her visage one of death and seduction mashed together into a mortal frame that exuded a violent lust. She could kill him, there was absolutely no doubt in his mind about that. His life meant nothing to her, and he prayed he could last long enough and get close enough to enact his plan.

The host was saying something about moon weapons and a new era as Narrio looked down to examine the pair of obsidian daggers in his hands; the blades looked wickedly sharp, but killing this woman was not part of the plan. He didn't want to either; a strange magnetism drew him to her even in her terrifying state of blood rage. The last Del'Sor, standing before him, a gruesome resurrection of heroes long past—with a key upon her wrist.

Narrio tested the weight of the blades himself and stepped forward to meet the red-haired reaper that was rushing towards him at an astonishing pace.

27

*"As long as there are Deep Wardens to protect our waters, we
have nothing to fear."*

~A father to his son~

T he man was fast and agile, but that was all the compliment
Vila could give him. Whatever he did to get his name on the
list of fighters for this event was obviously a lie as evidenced by his
frantic dashing and absolute lack of control. He flailed like a fish
on the dock, his knives swinging wildly as he tried to keep her at
bay. In short, he was an idiot. An idiot who she couldn't get close
to and had razor sharp knives of black crystal.

She recognized the shards as the same type that had killed
Rance, and she was cautious about letting them near her even
though she hadn't shown any signs of the corruption. She didn't
want to take any risks, especially given that she was only equipped
with a pair of knuckle dusters. Maccio clearly wanted to test her
abilities in this final match and present a brutal finale as the
evening's entertainment. Vila was exhausted after the first two
fights and the frenzied movements of her opponent were making
her head spin. She repeatedly lunged at him, her fists swinging
with practiced purpose, but came up short each time. The wild

and scrappy man couldn't be pinned down and it was making red bloom up her neck as her frustration grew.

She was going to kill this man, if only because he was irritating her to no end.

Narrio was growing tired as he continued to dodge and roll erratically, the black bashers on her knuckles had come dangerously close to crushing his bones on several occasions. Vila was clearly a skilled fighter, and it was all Narrio could do to stay out of her reach. He lashed out with his knives, hoping to drive her back without inflicting any real harm. He really didn't want to kill her, even if the feeling wasn't reciprocated. The flash in her eyes told him that he was a dead man if she got her hands on him and the thief's mind raced as he tried to figure out his next steps—a task that was becoming more difficult with every mad dash and frenetic movement just to stay alive.

He could see the cast on her bracer, the four stones gleaming in the lantern light. Narrio knew he would need to get dangerously close to her to get it off and he tried to steady his ragged breathing as he prepared himself for the inevitable.

His only skills of note were unpredictability and harnessing the chaotic powers of the universe to his will. Those skills were about to be pushed to their limits as he lunged.

Vila stumbled backwards as the man thrust himself at her, his knives swinging in wide arcs. The sudden forward movement caught her off guard and she found herself stuck in a tangle of limbs as he threw himself upon her. She heard the ripping of leather as his arms swung above her and she crashed, the hard marble cracking against her skull. The world went white, and she struggled to regain control as she desperately tried to block his attacks. Her saving grace was that he was so frenetic that none of his blows landed with any real purpose. Vila struck at his sides and tried to wrench him off her. The tangled fighters rolled over again and again, until he was back on top hitting her with bare hands. His knives had clattered off to the side and he was now completely defenseless. Vila saw her opportunity and smashed her knuckledusters into his temple, sending the man reeling off her with blood gushing from his head.

Narrio thought he was dead, the blinding and excruciating pain in his head caused him to convulse as he tried to regain his senses. He threw a blind punch and found his arm caught in an iron grip. There was a sickening crunch and a searing pain shot through his arm as his left hand broke at the wrist, his fingers crushed. His scream was cut short by the crystal duster that buried itself in his stomach. He vomited as another hit cracked his ribs and the woman leapt on top of him.

He was going to die; the thought repeated itself in his head even as he fought back. His knives here gone, and his only defense was to punch wildly in front of him with his good hand. He made contact and saw the woman's head snap sharply to her right as his fist busted her nose. He swallowed his remorse and took his chance. This was it, the moment of truth.

"I'm...going to save Lanya," he choked out, blood and bile pouring from his mouth.

A hand wrapped around his neck, which wasn't very titillating in the present moment. He tried again, his throat and voice under extreme duress.

"Lanya! I'm going to rescue Lanya!" he whispered as loud as he could, letting his arms fall to his sides in a hopeful gesture of placation. The pressure on his neck let up, if only a fraction.

Vila struggled to control herself through the bloody haze that clouded her mind and eyes. She paused in her battery, leaning in close to his face. Her nose burned and she wanted to crush his eyes in through the back of his head, but she stopped.

"Say that again," she whispered, the statement a threat as much as anything.

Blood poured from her nose onto his face, but she dared not loosen her grip. The man spat more blood to the side and looked into her eyes, blinking away the drips that landed on his cheeks. She saw real sincerity as he ceased his struggling.

"I'm not here to kill you," he whispered quickly, his breathing coming in sharp rasps. "I came to warn you; you're in great danger. If you let me live, I'm leaving the Planks and taking Lanya with me. She will be safe. Something is happening tonight, and you need to leave too."

Vila stared into his face, searching for lies. He wasn't telling the whole truth, but she couldn't find any evidence that what he said was false—and he knew Lanya's name which gave her pause. The room was deathly silent as she straddled him. Until someone shouted out that she should bash his fucking brains in and quit the foreplay. She ignored the calls for bloodshed and remained in place. Grabbing him by his shirt collar, she pulled him close.

"What is going to happen?"

"I don't know, but it is something with the moon rocks. Something about a Warden wanting you here."

"Tempé." She snarled the name, disgust roiling through her gut. What did this man know about Agustan Tempé? "Why? What is going on?"

"I don't know, but I swear to you I'm going to help that girl. If you let me live."

Vila wanted to smash his head into the tile and be done with the whole frustrating affair, but she couldn't get over the sensation that he was telling the truth. She let his shirt go and pulled herself up, breathing heavy as her heart pumped blood through her body at an astounding rate. The crowd looked on in shocked silence, unsure of what had occurred. Maccio just eyed her curiously as his hands twiddled about on his cane.

"You're not going to kill him?" he asked, his voice betraying no emotion.

"I'm done with this!" Vila yelled for all to hear. "Where is Agustan Tempé? I know you invited him, and I know he wanted me here, so let's be done with this charade and get to the real finale."

Murmurs rustled through the onlookers at the mention of the White Warden. Maccio smiled as a slow clap echoed through the room and Agustan Tempé strode out from behind the telescope to stand at the merchant's side with a sneer on his face.

Narrio wasn't exactly sure why he'd warned Vila of the night's coming danger, but he felt extremely proud of himself for surviving. He was forgotten as the menacing Warden revealed himself, all of

Vila's and the crowd's attention turned to him. Narrio scuttled off to the side and slipped one of the knives into his jacket, his head still throbbing as he clutched his broken wrist, his ribs screaming in excruciating pain.

The key was heavy in his sleeve as he quietly weaved through the crowd towards the back exit. The knife had severed the bonds holding his prize neatly, his experienced hands slipping it up his sleeve before his wrist had been crushed and brutalized. None of that mattered now, as he stole through the exit, desperate to find a way out of here and back down to the Lower Planks. He had a promise to fulfill and a job to complete, no matter how much his body and nerves protested.

He wanted to scream in triumph, but he knew the night was far from over as he dashed through the dark halls of Maccio's estate, trying in vain to recount his steps.

The White Warden, protector of the deep and captain of *Hardor's Gaze;* Vila's own personal vendetta in the flesh. Maccio may have found the moon rock causing the spread of the crystalline corruption that killed her friend, but Tempé let it happen; willed it into being. The Warden wanted her here, he wanted this moment to happen and Rance was just another unfortunate byproduct of scheming beyond the common folk's control. The man didn't look quite right as he stretched the muscles in his neck and stared at his prey. There was a glassy film that seemed to move over his eyes and the veins in his neck pulsed with an unnatural rhythm, seemingly glowing from within.

He showed no rush to engage with her, his stance was relaxed other than the tenseness in his muscles that spoke of oncoming violence. At a gesture, the crowd pulled apart and the bound figures of his three Warden companions were brought into the room, their hands pulled tightly behind their backs, their faces bloody. The guards pushed them to their knees and surrounded them, four to a Warden with their own weapons at their necks. Taragin looked at Vila with a defeated gaze, the betrayal clearly causing him deep pain. She was surprised to see the other two bound. Whatever blind devotion they had showed Agustan Tempé ended tonight it seemed.

"A new era is about to begin," Tempé proclaimed as he left his place by Maccio's side. "The age of water is coming to an end and old crimes will be paid for in the blood of the Del'Sor."

He pointed a finger at her, his eyes no longer glassy but shining with an eerie blue light. The moon was finally at its full height in the sky, casting its bright light through the observatory glass and onto the morbid scene. Tempé was in the center of the room now as he removed his hood and murmurs of shock and fear rippled through the crowd. A large, blue crystal of celestial origin protruded from the back of his skull, the flesh and bone becoming one with the moon rock that seemed to have replaced his brain. The inherent light within the structure glowed as the moon beams met it with their full power.

"What have you done?" Taragin's eyes were as wide as the rest of the crowd, clearly in shock at what they saw. Tempé just grinned viciously as he shed his cloak to reveal finely toned arms of pure muscle. He held out his hand and caught his bone saber as it was tossed to him, putting the full magnitude of his corruption and betrayal on display. On one arm lay the four blessed glass stones that gave him his strength and mastery of the water's elements, fused into his skin in a permanent bond. On the other lay the corrupted mirror of those same stones; four moon shards that throbbed in their full power.

Vila could only watch in sick fascination as Tempé ran the blade across his arm, severing the bonds of the blessed glass and letting them clatter to the tile in a pool of blood. Even Lord Maccio seemed horrified, this new revelation an unknown to him. With a sneer, the corrupted Warden crushed the stones under his boot and there was a palpable blast as the magical energy in the glass was snuffed out. The wave of energy stripped the flames from the candles, leaving the room lit only by the moon's bright glow and the pulsing light from the discarded weapons. Vila watched as the flesh of his arm restitched itself in crystalline tendrils of synthetic fiber that emanated with the same celestial magic.

Screams resounded throughout the room as the moon rocks in the pendants of Parity all glowed with the same magical power, the transformative energies of the moon coursing through the unsuspecting victims that filled the hall. Flesh began to tear, crystals emerged, and chaos befell the room as Tempé lengthened his trick weapon to its full extent, the saber becoming a glaive. He lunged at Vila in a maddened rage.

"Loamia shall be avenged!" His scream resounded through the hall as chaos ensued. Vila gritted her teeth and braced for the coming bloodshed.

28

"You shall know your brethren by the pendant at their heart, the Four laid tight against their breast. Trust not the one who strays from the faith, casting aside the morals of the Church. The inner thoughts of their heart cannot be known, but by their outward expression may we see true the followers of the faith."
~A Sermon from Arch Vicar Tortenano~

N arrio crashed through the back halls of Lord Maccio's sprawling estate, twisting, and turning through endless corridors of marbled stone and gilded coral. He clutched his ruined hand as he ran, the pain jolting up his arm with every heavy step towards the kitchen. A frightened porter stupidly directed him to the pantry where he could find Maccio's private entrance to the Lower Planks; he thanked his manic nature and terrifying appearance for delivering swift information and preventing him from having to wander around for much longer. He recalled a brief memory of delicious smells on his way up, confirming the hunch that their secret way in was through the kitchen.

It seemed that most of the guards were either in the observatory or busy dealing with the growing screams that echoed through the halls. Whatever Narrio had feared was going to happen was happening now and he willed himself to run faster, hoping that Renalia had that boat ready. He also prayed that Lanya was waiting for him and ready to go.

Rounding the corner to the kitchen, he skidded to an ungraceful halt and bounced against counters as he tried to stop himself. There were two mangled bodies on the floor and a terrified cook holding back his two attackers with a carving knife. His blood ran cold as he took in the sight of the crystal-encrusted marauders who were hacking at the screaming man with various kitchen utensils.

Green shards had sprouted from the pendants the attackers wore on their necks and had fused themselves to the chests of the cooks, throbbing in a violent glow. More crystals had sprouted from various parts of their bodies, the veins seemingly spreading the infection until it burst through the skin in jagged points. Upon further inspection the kitchen knives and spatulas were not only in their hands but were their hands as the strange crystals ripped and fused flesh and metal together in a twisted transformation.

As he watched, one of the former human's mouths wrenched open and more shards burst through, creating a maw of green light and crystal as his jaw flopped around by a thin strand of muscle. Narrio had never been more thankful that he wasn't religious as the source of the corruption seemed to be the pendants. The uncorrupted man was summarily hacked to bits and Narrio forced himself to crawl through the kitchen, mortified at the sight and deeply pained that he could not help. He wasn't sure what he would be able to do in his current condition and he'd already proved his prowess in the arena.

Nestling his cowardice and his ruined hand close, he shambled on until the gruesome noises ceased and he slowly closed the door to the pantry. Careful not to make too much noise, he pushed the heavy crates covering the trapdoor away and began the long climb down with only one good hand.

The Lower Planks were less chaotic than he would have thought as he ducked under rotted beams and dashed through sail cloth. He heard some far-off screams but couldn't find much other evidence of the crystal corruption that was happening upstairs. People were more or less going about their business of surviving down here in the dark. It was disturbing to think of the massacre that was happening upstairs having no effect down here. Somehow the gulf between the two worlds was wider than he thought.

Sweat poured down his back even in the chill as he came upon Madame Molena's. He didn't have time to change his appearance and hoped Lanya would be waiting for him. His plan was to get her into a room and find a back exit they could use to get to the secret tunnel. He wasn't sure how feasible it was, but he was never sure of anything until it happened. And somehow, he'd made it out of the observatory, so he was sure that he could find a way.

His hopes were dashed when a large hand grabbed him by the back of his neck as he approached the door and thrust him inside the brothel with violent force. His knees slammed into the floorboards, and holding his broken wrist against his chest, he caught himself with his face.

Those same strong hands pulled him up and he was staring at the intimidating figure of Madame Molena, a goblet in one hand and Lanya's hair in the other. He could see some of the other girls hiding behind curtains, sneaking glances at the affair but unwilling to come out. His handler was a massive side of meat with beefy hands that held Narrio's neck and shoulders like an iron vice. The thief's arms were wrenched behind him and held in place as he inwardly screamed at the pain in his wrist.

Both Lanya and the madame wore pendant's of Parity around their neck. He waited for the crystals to come alive and bury themselves in the women's chests and was confused when nothing happened. Theories began to run through his mind, but he pushed them aside as the madame spoke.

"I knew you were up to no good," she said, her lips pursed tightly as she glowered at him.

"Good's all relative I guess."

"Thought you could sneak her out? Have yourself your own private little whore when I wouldn't let you have Vila?"

Narrio was done with jokes and answered as honestly as he could. "No. I offered her a way out of here with no strings; something I don't think you would know anything about. As for Vila, my business with her is done. And we all need to get out of here. Something is changing people into—"

His thoughts were cut off as the madame cast down her cup and slammed the prostitute's face into the table, crushing her nose and forcing pained screams from the girl. Narrio yelled in protest, struggling against the muscled fingers holding him down.

"She has a life here," the madame said calmly as she pulled the girl up by her hair and slapped her across the face. "A better life than she could ever have hoped for. But she is still my property and now you get to watch what happens when you try to take what's not yours."

She struck the girl across the face again, her rings slicing the crying girl's cheeks to ribbons as curtains closed around the room and the other girls hid from the sight. A rising surge of anger and hatred flowed in him, no longer able to stand the brutal circum-stances. The thug behind him kept Narrio's hands clasped roughly behind his back, but Narrio could feel enough wiggle room for his damaged hand if he was willing to put up with some pain. The cost/benefit analysis was brief as the madame struck the girl a third and fourth time; Narrio screamed as he wrenched his damaged hand free, fumbled the black crystal dagger out of his pocket and slammed it into the thug's boot.

The man let go of Narrio with a yell of pain and the thief dashed forward to the startled madame, crashing into her as she released her grip on Lanya. Holding the older woman down, he looked back to see the man writhing on the ground. Narrio and the two women watched in horror as his blood turned black in his veins and jagged bits of rock began to protrude out of his pores. The man struggled and gurgled until his life was cut short and two final crystals burst forth where his eyes used to be, blood and black gore dripping from the shards.

Narrio slowly turned to the madame, her eyes wide with fright, terrified from the calm and emotionless demeanor that now covered the thief's face. He looked up at Lanya, her battered face gushing blood as she clutched her naked body. Turning back to the madame, he let a gruesome sneer tug at the corners of his mouth and slid the blade across her neck. A small cut, nothing life threatening; but he could already see the black crystals forming and seeping into her veins as her eyes went horrendously wide. Her voice choked on a scream as Narrio discarded the knife, threw his cloak over Lanya, and grabbed her by the hand. The girl stared at her former employer in fright as he dragged her from the room. The crunching sound of crystals forming through flesh disappeared, but the thrilling and sick feeling in Narrio's gut did not. That woman had died, almost instantly and a strange dichotomy of emotions coursed through him at the thought.

The two ran through the maze that was the Lower Planks and Narrio was starting to see the effects of the corruption take hold as they entered the center square. He saw several crystalline monstrosities wreaking havoc in the crowds, each one of them wearing the more tailored and expensive garbs of the Uppers. No Lower Plankers were affected until someone got caught by a crystal monster and was cut to shreds. Then, and only then, did the infection start to spread. Narrio grabbed the girl and the two broke into a sprint towards the secret tunnel up to the church.

"Is that a moon crystal in your pendant?" he yelled as they pushed through the frantic crowd.

Bewildered, the girl answered in the affirmative. "It's not real though!"

"What?!" Narrio dashed under rusty iron plates and through jagged openings. Lanya struggled to keep in step with him, aware of the danger that was happening around them even if she didn't know the source.

"It's a fake. Couldn't afford a real one."

That was the key, he realized. "Everyone down here have fake moon shards?"

"Most do, I think. The real one's are too expensive. What is happening? Is that what killed the madame and that man?"

"Yes, and a whole lot more people up there. Anyone who has a real moon shard around their neck. I'll explain more when we get out of here, but if you still trust me then we need to leave now."

"I'm not staying here," she said through a quavering voice.

"Good. We're almost there."

Narrio wished he could eat his words as the floor in front of him exploded upward from the force of the giant head that burst through.

29

"Oh, can you see the moon,

The light of night upon us soon.

It makes my heart sweep and swoon,

To see the light of the bright blue moon."
~A sailor's song~

The world was a haze of dark energy, blood, and the screeching sound of celestial materials scraping together as almost anyone with a pendant went from human to rock-crusted monstrosities in the blink of an eye—and Vila was no longer standing stalwart against the coming storm.

Her knees had buckled, and she was crashing down into the tile as Agustan Tempé's massive form descended upon her. She willed her body to move, but it wasn't listening. A film started to cover her eyes and drown out the room as she felt the tiny pinprick of shards piercing through her hand and side; the wounds had finally come alive, and she was slowly consumed by the interstellar magic. Vila Del'Sor was dying.

She gasped for breath as the slow creep of death marched on until it came to a sudden halt and her vision returned in a sharp snap. Her limbs obeyed her command once again and the cacophony of sights and sounds filled her eyes and ears. Tempé was upon her, his lengthened glaive swiping towards her head as he howled with madness.

The pressure-hardened bone went flying as Taragin Echilar's flail smashed it aside, his body pressing close to Vila's and holding her steady. The blessed glass on his arm glowed with power and she felt the warming energies of the divine glass touch her skin and seep inside. The crystals receded from her form as she watched him ward off his captain. All around her, the chaotic battle ensued as crystal covered aggressors of varying colors released a hellish assault on the uninfected. Whenever the razor-sharp crystals pierced skin, the infection would spread. Vila didn't have time to think about which crystals were causing what mutation—that was a mystery for another time. The broad shoulders of Shaila O'Caan came into view as she battled the White Warden, giving Vila and Taragin a moment to breathe amidst the chaos.

"Here!" he shouted to her as he thrust her father's falchion into her hand. The blade felt good, the air stone in the hilt making the blade feel light and deadly in her grip.

"It's the blessed glass!" she yelled back.

"What?"

"The blessed glass tempers the crystals' powers!"

Taragin harrumphed as he smashed the crystal skull of an oncoming attacker.

"You'll have to stay close then. We need to take out Tempé."

Vila backed away, testing the radius of the blessed glass' divine powers. When she was less than a span away, she felt the cold creep of the crystal crawl back and she rushed to Taragin's side once more, as he bloodied his way through towards his former captain. She battled against the panic that set in as she held herself as tight to Taragin as she could. She was dependent on him now, her body fighting against her every time she strayed too far. The reliance was almost crippling, forcing her into a state of dependency that she was unaccustomed to. She swallowed the sick feeling that caught in her throat and focused on the battle. There were things to kill, and she had to stay focused.

O'Caan was wavering in her fight with Agustan who was steadily gaining the upper hand through his speed, skill, and the celestial energy coursing through his body. The shards on his arms crackled with divine magic as he parried and dodged his combatant's comparatively slow attacks. Shaila's screams pierced Vila's ears as Tempé's glaive came swiftly down on her arm, severing the appendage from her body in a ghastly display of strength and speed. She fell back clutching her bleeding stump as Taragin rushed in, his flail catching the White Warden in the chest and throwing him across the room.

Vila pulled herself into the radius of the protective energies from the stones in Shaila's arm, and began ripping pieces of the woman's seal leather tunic to bind the wound. Around her, Taragin continued to clear the area of rock people while Quinlan kept the path to the exit free for the lucky few who had not succumbed to whatever mad infection was running rampant in the observatory. Vila shuddered to think what chaos was happening out in the streets and possibly to Temson.

It was time to end this.

She finished binding the Warden's arm and grabbed the other one laying on the ground. "I'm going to need to borrow this," she said as she tied the arm to her back, feeling the warmth of the blessed glass and dripping blood against her bare skin. Vila tightened her grip on her father's falchion and turned to face Agustan Tempé who was back on his feet and looking none the worse for wear.

"Del'Sor. This has been a long time coming. Are you ready to pay your penance?"

"I'm ready to cut your fucking head off," she snarled, ignoring his strange way of speaking.

"Insolent mortal."

Tempé lunged at her, his fully extended glaive slicing the air in wide arcs as he leapt. Vila ducked and rolled to her left, the sword passing over her head as she sliced through his thick boot and into the flesh. Tempé howled and swatted at her, catching her head with a shard covered hand. Vila felt the crystals bite into her skin and wondered if there was any cure for the moon sickness as she flew through the air. Her body crashed against a column, head cracking against the marble. She slumped to the ground, feeling blood rush down her back from the gash as her vision went hazy again. The former man was insanely strong and normal wounds seemed to have hardly any effect. She barely had time to fall out of the way as his glaive stabbed into the marbled column, splintering the hardened plaster where her head had been.

She brought her sword down on his outstretched arm, feeling the satisfying bite as bone met flesh, only to be cast aside again as he jerked his arm free. Her sword clattered away as she stumbled away from the monster. Vila watched in horror as the wound on his arm stitched itself back together yet again.

She backed away until she felt the cool touch of glass behind her back as she reached the edge of the observatory, trapped. Tempé took his time approaching her, retracting his glaive before sheathing it back against his side. He sneered at her, his mouth glowing with energy and his eyes crackling as he wrapped his arms around the giant telescope. With unheard of strength, he wrenched the metal equipment free, glass and debris cascading to the ground around her. He raised the device high above his head, preparing to crush her as she pressed herself against the glass and waited for the inevitable.

The inevitable never came.

Vila barely had time to cover her head as Shaila O'Caan's full force crashed into Tempé and took both Wardens and telescope through the observatory glass, bodies, and instrument crashing against the rooftops far below. The sounds of their impact disappeared, giving way to the sounds of chaos in the observatory. The two remaining Wardens and a few uncorrupted guards battled hard to keep the monsters at bay.

Vila shuddered and closed her eyes, working to control the adrenaline rushing through her veins. She knew he wasn't dead, and she would have to face him again; maybe even before the night was over. Whatever vendetta she had against him paled in comparison to the mad ravings that came from his mouth. There were questions that she didn't have answers to yet, but she had to survive the night first. Focusing her energy, she rushed back to her sword and jumped back in the fight as Taragin battled against the last remaining creatures.

Together, the two worked back-to-back, slicing through crystalized flesh, and severing limbs from bodies. They made sure no heads stayed attached in case any showed the same regenerative abilities as Tempé. Vila ignored the guilt that creeped up inside of her as she thought of the people that had stood in the place of these monstrosities mere moments ago. She knew this was happening everywhere and she was saddened at the thought of all the innocents down there who were being corrupted by uncontrollable forces; she also felt extremely grateful that Rance was already dead, and she wouldn't have to deliver the same fate to her friend.

Sharp fingers grabbed her from behind and she whirled around to see a woman clawing at her, the head completely encased in green shards as her emerald fingers scratched and dug at Vila's skin. As the woman lunged closer, there was a flicker in the crystalline skull and Vila caught a brief glimpse of the woman's terri-

fied face amidst the shards; the proximity to the blessed glass was
tempering the effects of the moon powers, if ever so slightly. She
didn't have a chance to see how far she could force the magical
reversal before Taragin's flail crashed down into the cluster and
crushed the shards into a thousand pieces. The magical energy
drained from her head and the body eventually stopped twitching
as Vila stared in horror. Taragin dispatched the last of the monsters
as Vila knelt beside the woman's corpse.

"She was almost human again," she said barely above a whisper.

"Maybe," Taragin grunted. "But we can't stop to find out right
now. This city is going to be overrun and fast. We have to get out
of here."

"We have to help them."

"Can't help them if we're dead. We need to get to the *Gaze*. Here."
He handed her a vial of Deep One's Blood, and she chugged the
contents, ecstasy following the wicked sting as her wounds began
to heal. As she lowered the vial, she took note of the bracer on her
arm and her brain struggled to recognize what was missing. The
pieces suddenly fit together, and she threw the glass vial across the
room as she screamed.

"Fuck!"

"What is it?" Taragin's question was laced with concern at the
outburst.

"That man, the last fighter. He took the key."

"The symbol on your bracer?"

"Yes! It's a key to the chapel." She had no reason to keep secrets
tonight. The stakes were too high.

"How do you know he took it?"

"I just do. He begged me to keep him alive, said he was going to
save Lanya. I'll bet anything he was after that key. We have to get
to the church, now."

What she didn't say was the deep concern she had for Temson;
not only was she worried about the corruption, but if that man was

after the key, then there was a good chance that someone knew about the two of them and was going to harm him to get to her.

"Yes, we do."

She turned towards the aging Warden, surprise on her face. "I expected more of a fight."

"That symbol is more than just a key. Those stones? Those are blessed glass, Vila. That's why you hadn't been corrupted yet."

Vila staggered. "Blessed glass? How?"

Screams echoed up from the streets as the city began to come alive from the ensuing madness.

"No time right now. We need to get that glass and get back to the *Gaze*. It's the only way we are going to be able to stop this."

Vila paused, the weight of her father's sword heavy in her hands and on her heart. She had so many questions, but she knew they would have to wait.

"Fine, but we are taking whoever we can fit onboard with us."

"That's not—"

"It is going to happen," her eyes flashed as she pushed her entire will into the command. "You swore to protect the oceans; that includes the people in it. Quinlan?" The younger Warden jumped at his name. "Get to the *Gaze* and get it ready. Gather anyone you can find on the way and get them safely aboard. We'll join you soon."

"Yes ma'am." The spry Warden dashed through the door and disappeared down the hall.

Vila looked about the room as Taragin headed towards the door. "Wait. Where's Maccio?"

"He must have escaped in the chaos."

Vila cursed. "We can't let him get out of the city with more weapons."

"We may not have a choice. Maccio will have to wait."

"Fine. Let's go," she said as she turned her back on the carnage of the room. Taragin followed behind her, and she could feel his gaze on her back. She didn't care what he thought about the survivors.

She knew she was right, had to be right. But she also knew there would be so few they could save, and it tore at her heart. There was also one fewer than there had been in their group.

"And Taragin?" She didn't turn her head towards him, but she could feel him stop behind her. "I'm sorry about Shaila."

There was a moment of silence before the older Warden responded, a heaviness in his voice. "We need to keep moving."

30

"*Ever had plank eel before? It's good shit, mah friend. Grubby little things live right under the floorboards. Fat, juicy, greasy little bastards. Some like theirs raw and wriggling, but ah like mine dipped in coral flakes and fried in whale fat. Fuck, makin meh hungry jas thinkin about it.*"

~Unknown~

N arrio had never seen an eel that big before; in fact, he had never seen any monster of the deep that big. It was his life's goal to stay as far away from the larger predators of the Swell and he'd done a pretty good job at it so far. Now he watched the monstrosity of flesh and shard slam out of the floorboards, thrashing wildly and smashing into beams, the surrounding structures shaking in a terrifying display. From what was visible the creature had to be over ten lengths, it's body writhing as it gnashed blindly at everything around it. Green crystals covered its body as they jutted through the slimy flesh, and the whole room was cast in its eerie glow.

Narrio and Lanya crashed to the side as the monster flailed towards them, smashing into the ceiling, and causing numerous debris to come toppling down on their heads. Water gushed into the room and Narrio's panic hit him like a hard punch to the gut. There was no way to tell, but if he was a betting man, he'd say the substructure of the Planks had been punctured.

"Run!"

He grabbed Lanya's hand and half dragged her out of the way as the head came crashing down where they had been, slime and wood fragments spraying in all directions. It was then that Narrio realized he wasn't looking at just one creature, but a horrid conglomeration of writhing eels all coalescing into a single whole; a slimy, crystal fused, monstrous whole. What he thought was a single head with a gaping maw was an abundance of the slimy things all fused together, their crystal ridden bodies split and stitched back into a gruesome new being. Multiple heads of gnashing teeth joined as one to create a new head hellbent on shredding and devouring. Crystal shards protruded from every angle, and he could see tiny eyes floating inside the shards.

Disgusted and terrified, he kept running with the girl close behind him as the creature followed their movements and smashed through the small openings to close the gap. They were running through ankle deep water now that continued to rise quickly and would soon be up to their knees.

The two ran up a landing that gave them some height over the rising waters but did little to ward off the creature. Narrio could feel the wooden planks and supports shaking and snapping as they ran, the monster swimming behind and underneath them as the waters continued to rise. They rounded a corner, ducking underneath a low opening as more of the structures around them began to shake in protest. He found his stash where it was nestled under an old sailcloth with the fading letters N.H.S barely visible. They were back in the water now as they made the final sprint towards the secret entrance.

Narrio heard a scream behind him and turned around to see Lanya struggling with the cloak on her back, the edge having caught on a rusted piece of iron. She fumbled with the material, unable to free herself as the monstrous predator approached. Eel parts opened wide, and the slimy, toothy maw threatened to come down on her head as Narrio extended his gaff and thrust the steel into the gruesome mess.

A thousand shrieks pieced the air and the creature fell back into the water, disappearing in the murk. Narrio retracted the weapon and waded to the girl, using the blade to cut her free.

"We're here, can you swim?"

She stared at him with frightened eyes and shook her head. His gut sank.

"Okay, hold onto me. Don't let go, no matter what and hold this up." He handed her the sight stone lantern and pulled her towards the beam. The water was up to their chests as he tightened his pack and prepared to dive. Movement in the water about thirty spans away signaled that the creature was back and still hungry. Narrio gave Lanya's hand a squeeze and the two submerged themselves in the inky water as he searched for the opening.

Instinct pushed him on and having a second person to hold the lantern helped, but it was still a long swim, and that thing was coming fast. Working to calm himself, Narrio found the original opening and pulled himself through, Lanya's hand gripping tight on his ankle. The tunnel felt even tighter now that he was dragging another body through the jagged openings and small crevices. He moved fast, uncaring of the cuts and lesions he caused along the way. Lanya's hand still gripped him as he pulled them along, his lungs already screaming for air.

They were nearly halfway there when he heard muffled crunching and felt the pieces of shipwreck shifting around him. He risked a glance back and could see the eerie green glow through the water as the eel worked to squeeze into the small underpass. Bubbles leaked out of his mouth in a silent scream, and he willed himself faster as the thing crushed through the driftwood and rotted boards in a desperate attempt to catch up to its prey.

Reaching behind him, he pulled Lanya forward and shoved her through openings as he grasped and clawed his way through. The light grew stronger behind him, washing the environment in a sickly glow and illuminating the filth that swirled around him.

With his eyes burning, he saw Lanya move upwards, her feet disappearing above his head. Narrio pulled himself through the final opening and pushed up as the muted sounds of crushing wreckage grew closer behind him. His head finally breached the surface, and he felt the girl's hand grab his collar to help him up onto the ladder. The water churned around him as it rose, and the celestial light grew stronger as the eel's head appeared below in the opening.

"Climb! Fucking climb!"

Lanya obeyed and started up the ladder as fast as she could. Narrio hobbled his way higher, his ruined hand making the climb more difficult. He wasn't going to make it up fast enough and he hooked his bad arm around the rung, as the monster's head lunged out of the depths below. Narrio extended his gaff again, the force of the spring-loaded contraption meeting the upward momentum of the hulking mutation in a violent clash.

The eels screamed in unison as all six sections of steel and two lengths of shaft went straight through one of the crystalline eyes with a sickening scrape and pop. Bright green liquid burst out of the crystal, mixing with the red and black filth that leaked out of the creature's body as it writhed. Still alive, the beast finally gave up and pulled itself downward in a violent retreat, wrenching the gaff from Narrio's hand.

He let the weapon go with a brief sense of sadness at the loss and let himself breathe a sigh of relief as the light from the eel disappeared. The water tickled at his feet, and he turned back to the long journey up, one rung at a time with his good hand while Lanya clambered up far ahead. He just had to move faster than the water.

At this point, Narrio didn't have any care for silence or stealth as he jabbed the key into its slot and shoved the door to the chapel open. The whole city was quaking as water flooded into the Lower Planks and he could feel a slight tilt as he clambered out of the hole.

"Where are we?" Lanya asked as she pulled his cloak tightly around her still naked form.

"Last stop before we can get out of here." Narrio started searching around for the stone amongst the various relics in the room. The sleeping form of the priest was huddled under thick blankets on his cot in the corner. He made no movement as Narrio searched and the thief sighed in relief at having gotten the dosage correct in his draught. Lanya watched the thief as he frantically searched through objects on shelves, cubbies, and the desk. The water-stained drawing in his hand was blurred, but he couldn't find anything that looked remotely like the rock in the sketch.

"You're a thief," the girl finally said, her voice wary as she backed towards the door to the sanctuary.

Narrio didn't turn as he continued his frustrated search. "Yes, I'm a thief. That's why I'm here. If that bothers you, you don't have to stay with me; but I do have a boat and I meant what I said about getting you out. I'm a thief, not a degenerate." He tilted his head and corrected himself with a grin. "Complete degenerate."

A violent shift in the floor structure caused them both to stumble and relics to come crashing off the shelves. Muffled screams could be heard from outside, punctuating the quake and sending more cold sweat down Narrio's spine.

"Are you with me?"

Lanya bundled herself tightly and nodded.

"Good. This is what I'm looking for," he said, holding up the drawing. "We need to find it fast and get out of here."

"What is it?" she asked as she joined in the search, toppling items over and opening drawers.

Narrio didn't answer as he continued looking, cursing to himself. There had to be another room or vault or something. He changed tactics and began ripping tapestries off the wall. He approached the large artistic depiction of the five gods that hung behind the desk and ripped the expensive fabric from its hooks. Before him was a square outline of stone, similar to the door they had come up through—the same symbol that matched the key in his hand lay engraved in a small metal circle, barely perceptible.

"Thank the gods," he whispered as he inserted the key. This had to be it. "See if you can get the keys off his wrist. We're going out the front door. Knock him out if he stirs." He paused. "I'll try to carry him with us."

The excitement building, he placed the key in the lock and gave a twist. Tiny clicks indicated a functioning mechanism and the door slowly opened to the scent of something Narrio had only ever read about before; grass and green earth.

His eyes widened as he looked inside the small vault in wonder. On a small dais of stone sat the object, but it wasn't the innocuous piece of rock he had been led to believe. The markings were the same, but instead of a dull piece of stone, he beheld something that felt alive with raw power.

Life sprang forth from the smooth stone, a cornucopia of abundance and fertility. The pulsating waves of life-giving energy gave birth to an ecosystem that he had never witnessed, and it brought tears to his eyes in a confusing bout of raw emotion. Moss and grasses lined the floor of the small box and grew up the sides as small blossoms of white, purple, and yellow flowers budded around the green stone. The air in the room suddenly grew fresh and Narrio didn't have words to describe the green and living beauty that lay before him. He cautiously reached his hand inside and could feel warmth on his fingertips that sent another wave of ecstasy through him. This was no weapon; this was life.

"Narrio!"

Lanya's voice woke him from his reverie, and he grabbed the stone. A strange feeling of importance washed over him, and he weighed things in his mind that he would never have comprehended before. Choices and risks, greater causes, and selfish desires. As he removed the stone, the life left the box and the previously green and fertile environment shriveled and died before his eyes. He gasped at the quick and sudden death before him as he stared at the life-giving stone that throbbed in his hand.

"Narrio! Come here!"

Lanya screamed at him again and he carefully shut the vault door before joining her by the cot. Lanya had pulled back the covers on the priest to reveal a body covered in black shards, the intrusive crystals piercing through his flesh and choking out his life. His eyes were closed and covered in a thin layer of rock that fused his lids shut and cracked the skin.

Narrio jumped back, pulling Lanya with him.

"Don't touch it!"

"Is...is he dead?"

The thief examined the cleric in front of him, searching for any signs of movement or breath. He found none, all life consumed by the creeping black crystals.

"Yes."

There was a heaviness in his heart at the sight of the poor man, but there was nothing he could do. If they didn't get out of this cursed city, they would all end up like him.

"We need to go."

"Did you find your rock?"

Before Narrio could answer, there was an explosion of stone that blew them off their feet. Stone shards battered his cheeks and crashed around him as a Deep Warden burst into the room, followed by the furious form of Vila Del'Sor. She set her violent gaze on him, and the cold feeling in his gut returned as she looked from him to the body of her lover. The most gut-wrenching wail Narrio had ever heard pierced the room and drowned out all the outside chaos.

31

"The Whistling City; The First City; The Wayward City;
The Drifting City—the Planks has had many names over the
years, all of them accurate but for one vital part. Cities are
not made of wood or stone or coral; they are made of people.
Should the unthinkable happen, the city will endure as long
as the people of the Planks carry on."
~ From Yania Torino's "The Planks: A History"~

Vila clutched Temson's ruined body to her chest, her cries echoing in the stone room as she held him tight. The shards that pierced his skin now pierced hers, but she paid them no mind; they were nothing compared to the chasm she felt inside. Taragin was yelling something from the shattered doorway, his voice lost in the emotional ruin that was her mind. She'd lost everything that had kept her anchored and she was already drifting away. The last thin thread of human connection had been severed and Vila felt the empty pit fill as rage bubbled inside. She turned towards the thief.

"You."

The words were not spoken so much as growled, but he didn't cower before her this time.

"I'm so sorry," he muttered softly.

Taragin left his post at the door and roughly grabbed the man by his arms. The intruder winced as the Warden tied his arms behind him and stripped the thief of the black dagger in his coat. She looked from the instrument to the shard crusted corpse of her love, feeling the rage about to burst.

"What did you do? Why?"

The man hung his head in silence as Lanya stepped forward. Vila had barely registered her presence. Whatever had happened here, he had told some form of the truth in their fight.

"He didn't do it, Mistress! He..." she gestured at Temson, unwilling to look at the sight. "He was already like that when we arrived."

Vila didn't want to believe it. She needed to have someone to blame, someone she could kill. She knelt close to Temson and saw the origin of the corruption; it wasn't the pendant of parity which lay on his desk or one of the man's daggers.

Lying at the end of the bed was a small, black shard pulled from a fish and sitting atop a worn history of the moon. A small cut in the priest's fingers revealed the source of the spiraling shards that consumed him.

"Oh, Temson..." she sobbed. She felt Taragin's gentle hand on her shoulder and let herself be pulled away. Vila threw herself around the older man, holding him close as tears flowed.

By the thief's side lay the missing key, the stones glowing with divine energy at her feet. Gingerly, Vila pulled herself away, kneeling to retrieve the symbol. She picked up the item and held it close, feeling the warmth of the blessed glass in her hands. Pocketing it away, Vila willed all her fury into the man before her as she stared at him.

"Why are you here?"

He didn't answer, but a quick glance between him and Lanya told her things she didn't understand. She repeated the question with more force as Taragin gripped the man's arms and pulled hard.

"Answer her," he growled.

The man stayed quiet, and it was Lanya who spoke. "He's a thief. He said we could sell some of the artifacts here and be free."

The girl was lying but Vila couldn't figure out why.

"That's it? All this for money?"

He gave a sad smile. "That's what I do."

There was a scream from outside, shifting everyone's attention back to survival.

"We need to go!" Lanya was at the door, her face terrified as the noises grew louder.

Vila couldn't move, her mind racing with questions and grief. The girl grabbed her by the hand as Taragin wrenched the thief from the ground and pushed him towards the door.

"You're not getting out of this," he snarled at the man who didn't protest as he was led away at a run. Vila pulled herself into the present and threw one last glance at the body of Temson. He wouldn't get a proper burial, and few would mourn him. Another victim in her life that she couldn't save. Another hole left gaping. She didn't even know who to tell about his passing. Carefully, she pulled the blanket back over his body and ran from the room, dragging Lanya with her as they dashed out into the sanctuary.

There was another great rumble and the city shifted again. Large stones came crashing down into the sanctuary as they made their desperate run. Taragin led the way, the thief keeping pace with his arms still behind his back. The crystal covered bodies of the provosts at the door lay where they had fallen upon Vila and Taragin's swift entrance. The moon was burning in the sky, its blue hued light casting about and soaking the world in whatever divine magic was taking over her world. There was a groaning of stone as the statue of Trillian Del'Sor crashed into the courtyard and the world shifted as the whole city began to lean.

"The city is sinking!" Vila yelled to no one in particular.

"It was a creature!" Lanya said as the group made the long run up the switchbacks to the city center. "It came after us on our way up here, burst through the bottom!"

The Planks had survived flooding before, but Vila had the sinking suspicion that tonight was the last night for the First City. The whistling seemed to be at an all-time high as the wind whipped through the ropes, a death cry shrieking as everything began to crumble. Timbers cracked and buildings began to topple as the city ate itself from the inside. Another violent wretch nearly sent Vila tumbling over the side as she held onto Lanya for support.

"Can't have been the only one! This whole structure is going down!"

They came to the top of the switchback and into the chaos that was rampaging through the city. Citizens and city guards ran in all directions, chasing or being chased by their crystal covered peers as the moon's sickness took hold. Vila took the head off a creature as it grabbed at her, the corpse spraying red blood and shards out of its neck. Lanya was screaming as more people around them were taken down by the growing number of corrupted. There were bodies mangled together in monstrous mutations of flesh and crystal where two or three had become one. Fires raged, blood covered the streets, and the ground continued to tilt at an unnatural angle.

Their retreat continued down the streets as panicked citizens from above and below flooded to the docks in a desperate attempt at safety. There was no care for one's fellow man as people were trampled and crushed in the surge of fear that drove them towards the water's edge. Taragin's flail cleared the way as they pushed through more attackers. The thief in front of Vila made no show of trying to escape, clearly grateful to be taken away from the terror that had taken over. She kept Lanya close, holding off the lunging forms of crystalline intruders until the ocean appeared in front of them and Vila could see the black sails of *Hardor's Gaze* against the dark purple skies.

Quinlan was on the deck as the ship prepared to launch. Vessels were crowded with refugees, the boats pushing off the docks as fast as they could to escape the chaos while others were overrun with monsters. Panic was the predominant feeling as citizens clambered aboard ships or leapt directly into the Swell below—anything to escape a horrific death. The *Gaze* was already teeming with people and Quinlan waved at the four to keep them moving as the ship prepared to set sail. The double bows were beginning to grind back into place as Quinlan raced towards the helm. Taragin and the thief ran up the ship steps onto the deck, pushing through the crowds that clambered aboard. Vila let Lanya go ahead as she ushered more on board.

Everywhere there were more crystallized people appearing from the dark shadows on unsuspecting victims and there were fewer and fewer armed fighters to hold them at bay.

"We have to pull anchor!" Taragin shouted down at her as the ship steps started to retract, leaving a terrified crowd stranded and screaming. Vila ran along the length of the dock, preparing to leap across the water to the waiting rope Lanya had hanging over the side. There was no more time, her mind an empty pit as she thought of all the people who wouldn't make it out. Before she could leap, a deep and resonating voice called out across the docks as a hard rain began to fall.

"Del'Sor!"

The refugees scattered to the sides, desperately looking for another way off the city as the docks began to pitch and crack. Vila turned around to see the monstrous form of Agustan Tempé once again, his glaive extended and the shards on his body crackling with light and energy. His shredded cloak flapped around him in the wind, the rock in his skull radiating. Behind him, more buildings toppled with resounding crashes as the city started to breathe its last.

Tempé leapt at her, propelling himself across ten spans of shifting docks to come down with a crash behind her, his glaive sweeping the air as she ducked and rolled. The violent movement of wood bounced her away and she struggled to regain her footing as she held her father's blade tight. The polished bone of Tempe's glaive flashed in the moonlight, its scrimshawed face looking to add another tale of victory written in Vila's blood. She parried the attack and leapt backwards as a moon crusted fist reached out for her. Her blade swung back, knocking his hand away as the boards below her feet gave way and she plunged into the swirling water below.

Vila barely had a moment to take in a breath as she was swallowed by the sea. Lightning crackled above her, and she was tossed against the shattered carcass of the Planks as the city continued to crack in its final death throes. She wore no diving mask and the blessed glass on her person gave her no help, unfused as they were.

Unfused.

Vila was pulled further down, her lungs screaming as the Swell took her. Far above, she saw the shining form of Agustan Tempé diving towards her with glaive held ready to rend her head from her body. There was no other choice.

Vila pulled the key from her pocket and struggled at the four pieces of blessed glass held tight in their metal divots. Her iron boots took her further down as her vision started to go black and her ears popped in rapid succession.

Tempé was almost upon her as she made one last desperate move.

Taking the back of the key, she slammed the face onto her chest above her heart. The glass felt warm to her skin and quickly turned to a raging fire as the stones came alive and began the painful process of fusing to their new host.

No one could hear her scream down here but scream she did as the pain worked through her body.

Power rushed through her blood in hot torrents of divine magic as the bonding process came to its conclusion and Vila felt the full power of Fathus' blessing course through her. The metal carapace shrieked as the glass expelled it away and the stones glowed with their full power above her breasts.

She opened her eyes and the world turned red as new sight took hold. She could see everything from the ruined shape of the sinking city to the terrible, tentacled monstrosity that was rising from the depths as it felt the violent struggles of a new prey.

The air swept through her lungs, and her skin and blood hardened against the cold and pressure.

She was free now.

Truly free and terrible.

There was no time to revel in the shocked and angered face of Agustan Tempé as she propelled herself upward through the depths, their bodies colliding as they sped towards the surface.

The corrupted White Warden and the newly blessed arbiter of the ocean blasted out of the water, swords slicing at each other as fists pummeled with resounding strength. They arced through the air until their forms crashed onto the docks in a spray of debris. Vila felt Tempé's grasp release as she bounced across the heaving deck. Both parties leapt to their feet, weapons brandished and fury flowing. Vila ran at her enemy, preparing to sever his crystalized head from his body when the Planks gave one last heave and the world tilted again as the city turned on its side and crumbled underneath her feet.

She clambered up the docks as they turned vertical, the screaming form of the White Warden careening past her as she climbed. He landed thirty spans below on a ruined building as the structures crumbled and cracked. Even amidst the cacophony, the rending sound of the port-side beacon breaking free of its restraints could be heard and the massive beam with its fiery head came crashing down behind her. She dared one last look as the blazing pillar of light smashed into the warden, silencing his screams, and hastening the descent of the sinking city in an explosion of flame. Beacon, warden, and fire were swallowed up as the Swell continued its ravenous consumption of the First City.

Vila clambered up her vertical and quickly sinking ladder, the boards slick in the pouring rain until she stood at the top, the city groaning and crumbling behind and below her. She looked down as the black shape of the monster she'd seen in the depths opened its arms to accept its meal. Tentacles burst through the fragile structures of coralcrete and crushed the brittle beams in their grasp. Moon crystals protruded out of the tendrils, the energy from the moon's rays coursing through the creature as it pulled the oldest city in the world into its deadly embrace.

Vila leapt from her perch, leaving the chaos and destruction behind her as she propelled herself towards the *Gaze*. The echoing sounds of the dying city flooded her ears as she swam away. She felt its death as the water pulled against her, the beast and its prize sinking back down to the depths to begin some horrid new journey as the moon's power began to transform the only world she had ever known.

Her new strength propelled her on and she felt an energy in her body that she'd never felt before. She was the force in the water now, not the other way around; powerful and flowing, master of the waves.

She leapt out of the water and landed on the deck of *Hardor's Gaze* with a stunning and captivating impact that sent shocked cries through the onlookers. The wild woman that stood before them raised herself up from her knees, the blessed glass in her chest glowing with unbridled power.

Loud whispers passed over the onlookers as they gazed at her, the new Del'Sor, Warden of the deep and defender of the Planks.

But Vila had no room for the awe, wonder, or even worship that she felt blossoming from the wide-eyed crowd around her as she stood. They would look to her for leadership now, but she had none to give. She could only stare out over the water at the blank space in the ocean where the Planks had floated mere moments ago. The cries of thousands of dead called to her from the deep and she let herself feel each and every one of them.

A small part of her hoped that Agustan Tempé was down there, alive and searching for her. She needed to kill him, needed the sweet release of vengeance and blood to quell the despair and grief that threatened to consume her.

The *Gaze* sailed away as the storm grew in the skies, forcing the refugees into the hold as Vila watched the lightning shatter across the night. The moon stared back at her, its glowing visage a looming presence that seemed to taunt her from its place in the sky. She stood alone, the stones heating her blood as she gripped the rail in a futile attempt to regain control.

32

"Fathus will save us as he has before. We must trust him now
and put all our faith in his plan and his Wardens."
~A mother to her children~

Vila watched Taragin lead the thief across the gangplank and onto the small floating platform where a group of guards played Scuttlers at a table in their shack, unaware of the sinking of the Planks or the deadly scourge that was working its way through the waters. She almost envied their ignorance as she replayed the previous night's horrors in her mind.

The thief, whose name she now knew as Narrio Olitarth, looked back at her, an expression of sadness and fear on his face as Taragin led him to his fate. She felt no pity for the man, a small part of her unable to keep from blaming him for Temson's death. If he hadn't been there, hadn't drugged Temson then maybe the cleric would still be here. Maybe he could have found help. Maybe anything could have happened rather than the horrible fate that did.

Deep down, though, Vila knew nothing would have changed. Temson died because of her and because he wanted to help her. Being asleep at least meant that maybe he didn't suffer as much.

Lanya insisted that Narrio was good and true to his word, but Vila couldn't help feeling anger towards him. Regardless of whether Temson's death was his fault or not, she'd almost lost her father's blessed glass because of him. He deserved whatever fate befell him down there now and she felt a small bit of satisfaction as the guards took the quivering man down the hatch to the diving bell that waited for them.

"I wish you didn't have to do that. He saved me."

Lanya stood at her side as Narrio's head disappeared from view.

"He's a criminal, Lanya. That's where criminals go."

"He's a thief, that's all. He don't deserve it. You know we'd be criminals too if we lived somewhere else."

"Not anymore. You don't have to have that life again. And it's no thanks to him."

Vila cringed as she thought of all the lives lost and many more at sea, directionless and scared. She had no idea how many escaped the Lower Planks before the city was sucked to its doom, but she had no more tears to shed.

"I wish I knew what life I could have now," Lanya said. "Things are never going to be the same, are they? Do you think anyone else is even out there? What about the other cities?"

Vila didn't have an answer for her. The fact was that both she and Taragin had discussed the same thing and come to the same conclusion; they had no idea what was going to happen next or what fate had befallen the rest of the Swell.

"Madame Molena is dead," Lanya said, breaking Vila's thought.

Vila scoffed. "Unlikely. That old crust will have figured a way out of there. She's a survivor. That's what she does. She'll come back to exploit someone else."

Lanya's hand lightly touched her own and Vila looked into the girl's eyes. There was a confusing mix of emotion swirling in there that Vila couldn't identify.

"No, she won't. I watched her die. He killed her." She tilted her head in the direction of the small trap door that the thief had exited through. "I watched him slice her throat with that black dagger and the shards cover her body. She's not coming back."

Vila's breath caught in her throat as a tangle of feelings battled for dominance. The madame was dead, crystalized in perpetuity and never to come back. Her mother, the woman she reviled and wished to love, the reason for her life and all its misery.

She felt like she should shed a tear, mourn the wretch, but none would come. Vila felt relief and sadness all at once and her mixed emotions extended to the man who had wielded the blade, Narrio Olitarth. The mysterious thief and hero who had killed her mother. She felt gratitude, remorse, and anger all at once; thankful she was gone, guilt that she felt glad, and anger that Narrio had once again wrenched a life away from her. Her mother's life was not his to take and she burned at the thought of another thread snipped beyond her control.

"All for the best," Vila whispered. "Forget that man, Lanya. He's unimportant and forgotten now."

Taragin stepped back onto the ship, his graying hair glowing in the early morning rays of the warm sun. The moon may have shown its true strength, but in the daylight, it was almost easy to set it aside and revel in the strength and heat of Solan's shining kingdom. Vila could feel a new energy in her and not just from the glass that continued to charge her body with their magic. She felt alive and free, if not a bit trepidatious about the future.

"Any word from the other Wardens?" she asked as Taragin came beside her.

"I received a bottle early this morning. Crissa and Arturian are all that's left of the *Wayward Voyager*'s crew. No word from Anthema, but I'm doubtful it made it through the night, what with the Great Rock sitting in the cathedral courtyard. We'll keep sending word out to the other cities and townships, see what we can find out. Quinlan saw one of Maccio's vessels escape the harbor, and if he was on it then he'll be up to something to recoup his losses. I doubt last night's events will do anything to change his mind about using moon rock as weapons."

"It probably just gave him new ideas. We should go to Anthema. We can't let Maccio or anyone else get their hands on that rock or others."

"In due time. We need to get these people somewhere safe and then we will reconvene with the other Wardens at our hub."

"I don't think there's anywhere safe, Taragin."

He let out a deep sigh. "You might be right, but we can't keep them here. As far as we know, there's only five Wardens now, including yourself and this is just the beginning. I don't know what Tempé's ultimate game was, but I don't think we've seen the end of it."

"I'm not a Warden."

"You've got blessed glass thumping against your chest and we're down in numbers, so until this is over? You're a Warden."

Vila placed her hands on her chest, taking in the warmth through her fingertips. "My father was a Warden, wasn't he? That's why the glass was on his bracer."

Taragin leaned over the rail as the *Gaze* pulled away from the small dock. "Yes. For a while. He changed his name when he joined, didn't want to be saddled to his history; something the two of you have in common I think."

"I didn't know you could stop being a Warden."

"You can't."

They went silent for a few moments as the waves lapped gently against the hulls. Quinlan began flipping levers behind them and the ship sprang into automated motion. The previous night's events could almost be forgotten as the wind blew through Vila's hair and filled her nose with the scent of salt and sea.

"My mother said he was killed; that being a good person got him killed."

Taragin sighed. "She's right, in a way. Your father had his mistakes, like we all do. But once you were born, something changed in him. He wanted to be a good person, a good father. But one does not simply abandon the Deep Wardens. The punishment is death and your father had to be punished."

"He tried to quit for me?"

"Yes."

"Who killed him?"

"A dead man."

Vila's throat tightened and she fought back the tears. Just another thing taken from her. She was done having things taken from her.

"I'll fight with you and see this to the end, but I'm not a Warden. And I'm not just my family name."

"You may think that, but to them?" he gestured to the refugees around the boat, "Word is getting around that the lost heir to the Del'Sor legacy has been found, the only daughter to a line of sons. And that she's a hero."

Some of the refugees watched her with smiles or awe, some averting their eyes in embarrassed admiration as they met hers. Vila felt for them, felt their sadness and fear. But she couldn't help them, couldn't be the savior or hero they needed. Heroes could be controlled, used, directed. Vila wasn't interested in that; she would fight because she wanted to, needed to.

"Don't say that again," she warned, placing as much emphasis on each word as she could.

Taragin gave his usual harumph and sauntered off to assist Quinlan while Vila stayed at the prow, her father's falchion at her side and his glass on her chest. Taragin's words echoed in her mind, and she held onto them. Her father loved her, had loved her enough to risk death.

It was enough to give her the strength to continue and keep fighting. Whatever else had been stripped from her, that knowledge could never be taken from her now and it spurred her on as she watched over the vast ocean in front of her.

Narrio wished he was back in the Lower Planks, swimming through the wreckage as the eel monster threatened to devour him. Not that he wanted to drown or be eaten alive, but at least it was better than sitting in the tiny diving bell with the guard and two other prisoners that were stealing the stale air around him. His knee wouldn't stop shaking and he'd given up trying to make it stop about a hundred fathoms down. That was an hour ago, at least.

There were no windows in the small bell and the only light came from the large survival stones that lined the perimeter. If he looked through them, he could probably see some of the ocean world around him in hued brilliance. He didn't want to do that.

He instead focused on things that he didn't have the answers to, because it was more comforting than thinking about where he was going. His biggest concern was whether Renalia had gotten off the Planks before that squid thing had sucked the whole structure down to the depths. Everything was so chaotic in the moment, people screaming and dying. He knew there were ships that had managed to get away, but he hadn't had a chance to see if his little sailboat was one of them; what with all the dying and all.

He was wary about sending up a prayer now, but he silently willed her to be alive, hoping some benevolent cosmic force in the universe would listen and take pity. He hadn't known her long, but there was a tiny sting inside at the thought of never seeing her again. The sting stung greater at the thought of her escaping but her family perishing. He sent another thought out to the cosmic force for them and changed topics in his head.

That cult was still out there somewhere and now that he'd seen the rock he was meant to retrieve, he was certain they wouldn't stop until they found it. It was most certainly not a part of any axe and he chuckled to himself; they really must have thought him an idiot. He liked money, sure, but seeing the life-giving power of that stone gave him chills and he'd surprised even himself by not giving it up.

He could feel its warmth inside his leg, the stone tucked neatly into the missing flesh where the first eel had tried to burrow in. He hoped it didn't give him an infection or worse. The low, thrumming energies from the stone burned his wound, but he gritted his teeth and tried to ignore it, grateful that no one had cared enough to try to change his bandage.

It was the one comforting thought about heading down to the prison colony; there was a chance, however small, that the Shepherds of the Earth wouldn't be able to reach him there. They were going to come after it and Narrio had no intention of giving it to them. He didn't know what he was going to do with it, but he liked the thought of having a little greenery in his cell. Once he got out, he'd find someone smarter and braver to help him figure out what to do.

One of Narrio's fellow criminals decided it was time to get chatty and kill the time with some light conversation.

"Whatcha in for?" he asked.

"Being too pretty."

The man guffawed. "Me too," he said as he smiled through a mouth half full of yellowed teeth.

"Shut up!" The guard gave a kick to the man and the conversation stopped as the diving bell continued its slow descent. The steady clicking of the chains as the lengths of metal travelled through the double purchase pulley system could be heard resonating in their little metal container. The sound was maddening, but it helped drown out the deep, low hum of the ocean depths right outside. All the survival stones on the bell pulsed stronger the further down they went, each one working hard against the elements that threatened to devour the group of men that sat huddled inside.

After an eternity, the bell jolted and Narrio heard the hiss of pressure and air stones working to clear the shaft below of water. A series of loud clicks and then the floor opened below them, revealing a dark hole lit only by a few sight stone lanterns. Narrio was shoved in and tried to calm his breathing as the guards inside patted him down for the second time. He winced as they knocked his shattered hand and slapped the bite on his leg.

"Well boys," one of the new guards said through a grim smile, "Ye're home."

He opened the door and Narrio felt the contents of his stomach rise as he stared down the long shaft that led into the main hall of the prison. Thick windows of clear sea glass lined the passage and the quickly moving bodies of bioluminescent creatures could be seen darting outside in the Swell. He thought he saw something big and dark move past—he quickly switched his gaze from the windows.

Survival stones lined every inch of the hall, dousing it in a rainbow of color that ran in dissonance to the otherwise oppressive atmosphere. The noise of the deep was a drone that didn't stop and the whole passage seemed to shift back and forth as the waters moved around it. This was the scariest place on earth to normal people and to Narrio it was a special kind of hell. The prison colony was known for being an inescapable fortress at the bottom of the ocean and Narrio was now shaking with fear at the thought of never seeing the light of day again. The stone in his leg no longer provided him any comfort and he almost wished the Shepherds would find him and put him out of his misery.

"Step lightly and don't try anything funny; that glass cracks and we all go down." The guard continued to smile, a sight that didn't help Narrio's nerves at all.

The men were ushered down the passage and he tried to ignore the darkness just outside the windows. Every step echoed; every piece of the tunnel creaked as the Swell pressed against it. They stopped at the end and the guard opened the door into the prison beyond, flooding the passage with an eerie red light from the sight stones in the great room.

"Welcome to Grim-Mire Hold."

EPILOGUE

There was no escape for the white-shark now that its hunter had it in their sight. The great predator of the ocean had become prey. Unaware as it was, it moved gracefully through the black waters of the deep, muscles rippling under its ivory skin as the great hunter searched for the scent of blood that had called to it. The mighty fish was hungry, its nostrils flared as it followed the tangy smell in the water. It followed the trail through the knotted leaves of giant kelp, weaving fluidly through the Tangle with ease. The light of the full moon could not pierce the web of seaweed that made up the giant kelp forest, but the white-shark didn't need the light to hunt; and neither did Bal De Bao.

Six lengths of violet sea glass shot out from behind a monstrous leaf, the delicately curved blade of the litania sending ripples through the water as it cleaved the caudal fin from the rest of the white-shark. The water warmed as the creature's lifeblood poured from the fatal wound, the body of the shark careening to the bottom of the forest in a silent death. Bal De Bao sped towards their prey, slicing through kelp tangles as they dove in pursuit, their long tail working to speed the young Oceanid's descent. This was Bal's third kill this week, and they allowed themselves a grin as their bulbous eyes followed the gout of blood through the forest.

The white-shark's body would be sold to provide leather, bone, and meat; for Bal, it provided legitimacy.

Bal's Sieving would be coming soon, and they knew that their chances of becoming either a Hunter or Soldier were dependent on the kills they made; the ones already achieved and those yet to come. As many as the newly mature Oceanid could manage would be needed before the time came to be placed in a Craft if they wanted to ensure a place of honor for themselves and their name. They would make their begetters proud and make either the name of De or Bao a great name.

Bal gave a great flap of their tail fins and stiffened their body, speeding their descent upon the carcass of the white-shark. Their vision was clouded with blood now, and they instinctively drew their nictitating membrane across their eyes for protection. The body came into view as Bal burst through a flowing cloud of red and pulled their sling-grab from the belt around their scaled waist, holstering the litania against their back. The weighted end of the grapple shot forth, wrapping across the body of the shark in a tight embrace of sinew rope and tonsil stones. Bal's long fingers worked along the rope, pulling and coiling, their scaled and muscular arms straining against the weight of the beast. Its momentum ceased and the Oceanid wrapped the sinew rope in a crisscross pattern across their chest and back, preparing for the swim out of the forest.

Thick tangles of kelp strands and flowing leaves grasped at the carcass as Bal made their way through the forest with their prize. Malar was waiting for them at the edge of the Tangle, keeping a watchful eye out for danger. Bal was not afraid of ocean predators, as they counted themself amongst that group. Humans, however, were the most dangerous threat to Bal's kind, the rift between sea dweller and floater still large and gaping. Being so close to the kelp farming operations of Anthema put Bal and Malar in precarious waters, and Bal could see their companion's anxious twitching as they emerged from the thick growth and into the open water.

"You amaze me, Bal, you truly do," Malar Muin Ralama said as they swam forward to help their friend. "Three this week. There won't be any white-sharks left in the Swell if you make it into the Hunter's Craft!"

Bal laughed, bubbles escaping their lips. "Perhaps you should become a Breeder, then we can ensure the population is maintained."

"If only that could be. I would like that, but it will be Artisan for me. Always has been for the Muins and the Ralamas. I admire your drive for another craft, but do you really think it will work?"

Bal cinched the ropes tighter around the carcass and threw a line over to Malar. "I won't know if I don't try. Farming is honorable and important, but I just don't think I have it in me. Others have put themselves into crafts of their choosing before. I can only try."

"You're doing a good job at it. I hope it pays off, I really do. And I'm here for you until it does." Malar smiled at Bal as they pulled up the white-shark's body and left the Tangle behind them, preparing for the long swim back to Boola's Reach. The full moon's light was now visible through the dancing waters, the blue-white light piercing deep into the Swell.

An intense and pained howl echoed through the currents, causing Bal and Malar to turn their attention back towards the Tangle. Bal's scales stiffened at the sound, their tail fins rigid.

"What was that?" Malar's voice quivered, their eyes darting back and forth. The low groan continued, changing pitch, and resonating in the waters.

"I don't know," Bal responded. "It sounds like an animal. A large animal."

The pained howling continued as a strange glow brought Bal and Malar's attention upwards, their eyes resting on the small silhouette of the floating city far above them. The city of Anthema seemed to be radiating, an unearthly green light emanating from somewhere within its limits. Kelp leaves fluttered as the waters pushed against the pair of Oceanids, the terrifying noise getting louder. Combined with the specter of the city, the whole aura of the evening changed into one of unsettledness and fear. Bal pulled on the ropes, ushering them along quickly.

"We need to get out of here."

Malar did not object, and the two young Oceanids pulled their quarry along as fast as their tail fins could go.

Boola's Reach appeared over the ridge, the medium sized city filled with Farmers, Artisans, and Merchants. Coral guard towers lined the perimeter of the city and floating sacks filled with biolu-minescent sea life lit the streets. Large nets spanned the distance between the curved and organically shaped towers, keeping larger predators out and forcing Bal and Malar to enter through the western portcullis.

Bal and their family operated a large anemone farm outside the city limits, but they were no stranger to the Reach. Bal and Malar showed their passes made of engraved sea glass and gilded coral, each of them throwing a wary glance over their shoulders. They were miles away from the Tangle, but Bal could still feel the terror in their scales that the ghastly howling had elicited in them. They could see the same signs in Malar, neither of them saying much during the long swim. Only when they were safely inside the city gates and flowing along through the teeming streets did Bal allow themself to relax.

They pulled the white-shark carcass along, making their way to Doolin Gal's, a family friend and butcher who always gave Bal the best price for their catch. Bal took note of the awed glances that came their way from other un-sieved young they passed on the streets. Scales turned from indigo to violet as the other youth watched the aspiring hunter's lithe form, their perfectly formed gills puffing in egotism and flirtation. Bal's lover, Rulina Narra Moor, would have words if they saw the lustful glances and Bal's display, but Bal was a newly mature Oceanid specimen and had developed an inability to ignore their own attractiveness. Bal gave a great flap of their long tail, smiling widely as they moved past the group and nearly crashed into Malar.

"Malar–" Bal was cut short by Malar's spindled fingers gripping their shoulder, eyes glued to the crowd in front of them. A Stentor was floating high above the crowd, a coral tablet in their hands as they read.

"...indeed. But with the passing of Custodian Omoona, their honored position must be filled. A Falal Fi will be held, and the council will begin taking applications immediately. All aspirants should submit a tablet of their accomplishments to the local prefect, who will submit worthy applications to the council."

An eruption of sound and activity exploded through the square.

"A Falal Fi!" Malar practically screamed. "There hasn't been a Falal Fi in almost a hundred years! Can you believe it Bal?"

Bal was barely paying attention to their friend, the news, and its meaning for them, growing like a tumor in their gut. They wanted to ignore it, tell themselves that it was inconceivable.

A new Custodian, the chosen Oceanid who would directly serve and protect Fathus, an honored life in the immediate presence of the sea god. With an average Oceanid lifespan being one hundred years, the opportunity to join one of the highest ranks in their society was rare if the chosen was in good health and little threat was directed at their patron. The last death duel for the honor occurred after Doena Leel was eaten alive by Melhor the Aggressor, one of the Deep Ones and a long-time antagonistic force to Bal's race. Doena's successor, Yoomel Omoona was a middle-aged Oceanid when they won their Falal Fi. The revered Custodian had then exceeded the average lifespan by fifty years. Now they were dead.

Bal didn't hear how they died, and they didn't care in the present moment.

There was only one thing on the ambitious young Oceanid's mind; how many white-sharks they would need to kill to earn a spot in the most honored competition in all of Lensia.

ACKNOWLEDGEMENTS

There are so many people to thank for helping me get this off the ground and into your hands, so buckle up as I list them all!

Thank you to my mom and dad who encouraged my strange imagination from an early age. I'm sorry I wasn't better at chemistry, but this is more fun. Thank you to my grandparents who gave me my first copy of *The Lord of the Rings*. You had no idea the obsession you were about to create. Thank you to my wife for pushing me to do this. I could not have done this without your support, truly. Apart from marrying you and raising our kids, this is the most fulfilling thing I've ever done. Thank you to my brother, one of my biggest fans, for reading this and promoting it. I hope chapters twelve and twenty-two weren't too awkward. Thank you to my amazing cover artist, Alex. It's everything I hoped for and I can't wait to see what you do with the rest of the series! Thank you to my editor, Savannah, for helping me fine tune and polish this weird book. I hope the coming twists continue to surprise! Thank you to all of my ARC readers and launch team. Your support and interest in this book means so much and I'm so grateful that you wanted to be a part of this. Thank you to me, for believing in myself and putting in the hard work. I've loved every minute of writing this book and can't wait to read my own physical copy. And finally, thank you to you. Yes, you, the reader. A book is just a stack of paper until it's in your hands. Stories are meant to be shared, and I'm so thankful you took the time to read mine. I hope you enjoyed it as much I enjoyed creating it, and I look forward to sharing many more with you.

SNEAK PEAK

TAINTED SEAS: ELDRITCH DEPTHS BOOK 2

Spring 2024

I

The ocean was eerily calm as the black frigate traversed the surface of the Swell, its double bows cutting through the dark water with ease. The full moon was beginning to wain from its peak power and there had been very little sign of the crystalline corruption that had taken over the former floating city of the Planks—up until tonight.

The creature that now grasped at the sides of *Hardor's Gaze* looked to at one time have been a white-shark of immense size, its ivory skin rippling with muscles as it thrashed at the boat. It also looked to at one time have been a squid of immense size, its sucker-laced tentacles ripping at the hull with a rabid ferocity. In truth it was both creatures smashed together in a horrible monstrosity of teeth and tendrils fused and riveted together by green shards of moon rock that pulsed with celestial power–if not more faintly than nights previous.

Vila hacked at the creature with her falchion, careful to avoid the razor-sharp shards that laced the long tentacles swinging wildly around the deck. The green shards protruded from the suckers and jutted out of the skin of the transformed beast. Even with the sea glass fused to her chest, she was cautious of getting sliced by the moon rocks; not just for the immediate injury but also the corrupting power when they touched human flesh. The theory was that blessed glass (a well-kept Warden's secret) held the moon sickness at bay but Vila didn't want to test that theory more than she had to. She had been touched and sliced by the celestial rocks enough already—and this creature was a truly awful thing.

Where the gills of the shark should have been there were now dozens of eyes of varying size poking through the slits and growing through the skin. Beneath the bulbous, moving mass of oculi was a much larger eyeball the size of a human head, swiveling and writhing as it searched out prey. The maw of the shark was stretched to unnatural proportions, flesh rent and pulled to breaking as muscles and tendons broke free from the skin. The teeth were made from the same shards as the suckers on the tentacles—those had blasted their way out of the back of the shark, replacing the dorsal fin and spine with a mass of snake-like tendrils that Vila continued to dismember.

Every member that she sliced at seemed to reattach in a fibrous web of crystalline growth if she didn't get a clean cut all the way through. The appendages that she managed to completely remove were slowly growing back, the skin now an iridescent green and mottled with glassy rivulets. Vila roared in frustration as the refugees panicked around her, with only a brave few taking up arms against the vile abomination.

"Get back!" she screamed at them, not wanting to risk an outbreak of the moon rock and its altering powers. There was no room for ordinary folk to become heroes here, even though the outbreak seemed to have slowed since the night of the full moon when the corrupting powers were at their strongest. She didn't want to chance it, and the gaff wielders shrunk back at her command. A few days ago, Vila would have counted herself among them, but everything had changed since then: the energy from the blessed glass pumping through her veins being a significant indicator.

Vila felt a screaming pain rip through her calf as she was dragged across the deck. The sneaky tentacle had a strong grip on her leg, and pulled her towards the gaping maw. The creature had managed to pull itself halfway up on the deck of the *Gaze* and Vila tried not to panic as she was dragged towards the beast. More tentacles sprang from the monster's mouth, licking and slapping the planks as it hungrily awaited its meal...

ABOUT THE AUTHOR

Seth Campbell is an independent author of dark fantasy and generally weird stories. Your standard, functioning nerd, Seth is a lover of all things strange and obsessive. *Bloodborne* is his favorite video game, and he's seen *Jurassic Park* at least thirty times.

Seth left a thirteen year career in technical theatre, and now works in the construction industry, which has given him more time with his wife and two young children. When he's not writing, he enjoys playing video games, painting models, carving fairy houses, and making board games.

Printed in the USA
CPSIA information can be obtained
at www.ICGtesting.com
CBHW031837061223
2443CB00008B/45

9 798218 293420